Also by *Karla Brandenburg*

The Epitaph Series

Epitaph

The Twins

The Mirror

The Northwest Suburbs Series

Cookie Therapy

Return to Hoffman Grove

Living Canvas

Touched by the Sun

The Mist Trilogy

Mist on the Meadow

Gathering Mist

Rising Mist

Other Novels

Intimate Distance

Heart for Rent, with an Option

Epitaph 4: The Architect

Karla Brandenburg

Epitaph 4: The Architect

Karla Brandenburg

Copyright 2018 © Karla Lang

ISBN 978-0-9991213-4-4

This is a work of fiction. Names, characters, places and incidents are the product of the author's imagination or are used fictitiously, and any resemblance to actual persons, living or dead, business establishments, events or locations is entirely coincidental.

This is a work of fiction.

For questions and comments about the quality of this book, please contact Karla@KarlaBrandenburg.com

Cover art by The Killion Group

Acknowledgements: As always, thanks to Terry Odell and Steve Pemberton as my other sets of eyes who help point out what I miss throughout the writing process, and my editor, Kelly Lynne. Special thanks to Sarah Dring for taking on a new friend, and for educating me on all things architectural (any inconsistencies or misrepresentations are completely my fault).

Chapter 1

The ladder of success is best climbed by stepping on the rungs of opportunity. —Ayn Rand

Kathleen McCormick rode the elevator, wringing her hands. She was going to work on Aria Walton's house—Aria Walton, the movie star.

As excited as she was to be assigned to the New Orleans restoration, her new project manager, Sebastian Brooks, had a reputation for throwing his associates under the bus, one of many rumored personality defects.

She was a damn fine architect, which she'd proven not only during her apprenticeship but also on her subsequent projects. This was the chance of a lifetime, her ticket to the promotion fast track and one step closer to buying a house of her own. She'd dealt with her share of arrogant men, starting with her father, and more recently with her male competitors in the architectural program in college. She could hold her own against a patronizing senior project manager.

Sebastian Brooks. Even his name was pretentious.

The elevator stopped on the 24th floor. As the door opened, she slipped the scrunchy from her wrist and gathered her wayward curls into a ponytail. She raised her chin and headed for the offices along the periphery inside the Chicago skyscraper in search of Sebastian Brooks' nameplate.

When she found his office, she straightened her sweater, smoothed her skirt, and took a step forward. He stood with his back to the door, on the phone, staring out windows that overlooked Lake Michigan. He didn't look so intimidating. Average height, short dark hair, dark dress pants, a white dress shirt. He had a picture on his desk—him and a woman, both of them dressed in formal wear—that looked like a page from a celebrity magazine. When he turned around, Kathleen ducked out of the way so he wouldn't think she was eavesdropping.

She'd seen him in passing, but thanks to water cooler talk, she hadn't taken the time to introduce herself. He had a tendency to be self-absorbed in the elevators, or dismissive in passing. People generally thought of him as reasonably attractive, but his chilly personality overshadowed his looks. At least that's what the gossips said.

Not that she listened to gossips.

He'd never spoken to Kathleen.

"Then I'll pick you up around seven?" she overheard him say. "Great. See you then."

Sounded like the end of the conversation. Kathleen took a deep breath and stepped forward. Sebastian had one elbow on his desk, his hand covering his mouth, staring at the photo she'd noticed.

"Excuse me, I'm Kathleen McCormick. The head of my design group told me I've been assigned to you and that you wanted to meet me."

Sebastian straightened and Kathleen took her first real look at the man. He had bronze skin and striking hazel eyes. His hair was cut one razor setting above military short. He rose from behind his desk and crossed to shake her hand. "Nice to meet you, Kathy. Welcome to the firm."

She cleared her throat. "Actually, it's Kathleen, and I've been here three years if you include my internship."

"Right." He motioned her to a chair, settled behind his desk. "I'm told you did excellent work on the Frank Lloyd Wright restoration in Highland Park. You've been highly recommended."

Kathleen fought the urge to squirm under his scrutiny.

"To give you some background," he said, "I did a renovation for a high-profile client in Lake Forest who recently purchased a home in New Orleans, Aria Walton. She's asked us to restore the new home to its original grandeur. The last owner subdivided the place into apartments."

Kathleen nodded.

"I'll need you to check into the building codes and track down materials, color samples and millwork profiles. Accents and brackets in Eastlake, Queen Anne, Neoclassical," he paused while she wrote down what he recited, "and check into hurricane shutter manufacturers. The client hasn't given us much time to work with, hence the short notice. Are you at all familiar with New Orleans architecture? The house is in the Garden District."

"I've been doing research…"

"Good. You'll need to block out the next two weeks, although we should finish sooner. I'll need you to book us on the same flight. We can go over my plans on the way out. I realize it's the middle of the week, but can you leave tomorrow?"

Book the flight? Kathleen fought to keep her temper in check. If he was going to treat her like an admin…

"Anything wrong, Kathy—Kathleen? I understood your schedule had been cleared for this trip."

She forced a smile. He knew how to pick up the phone as well as she did, but he was her boss. "Yes, I'm good to go. Do you have a preference on where to stay?" she asked sweetly.

"The same place we stayed when Barrett and I went to pitch the project. My admin should have a record of that trip."

Barrett. As in Barrett Winslow. The man. The legend. The founder of one of the biggest architectural firms in Chicago.

Eye on the prize. With her student loans paid off, the next goal was a house. A beautiful Craftsman-style house with stained glass accents like she'd seen in the Frank Lloyd Wright house.

The last associate to work with Sebastian Brooks had been fired, blamed for a mistake Sebastian made—if you believed the associate. Kathleen's steadily growing paycheck might be in danger of disappearing altogether.

"You sure you're ready for this?" Sebastian asked.

For the job? Yes. For Sebastian Brooks? As long as she reined in her temper. July in New Orleans. Hot, humid and probably rainy. Not optimal conditions, but she could do this. Kathleen forced a smile. "Yes, sir."

"Send me the itinerary. I'd prefer a flight that doesn't arrive before we can check into our hotel." He pushed a stack of papers to one side of his desk and slid a blueprint to the center, apparently his way of dismissing her.

All right then. Kathleen rose from her chair and walked out.

She punched the button in the elevator and crossed her arms.

"Kathy," she said to herself. And then in an imitation of his royal highness, "I trust you can handle the arrangements." Of course she could, but he'd already been to New Orleans for the pitch meeting. He'd have a better idea what flights he wanted, what hotel to book.

She took a calming breath as the elevator opened on her floor, pulled down the electronic key that hung on the extendible lanyard around her neck and pressed it against the keypad to open the security door. At her desk, she looked up Sebastian's admin—Margot—put on her headset, and made the call.

"This is Kathleen McCormick. Sebastian Brooks and I will be traveling to New Orleans tomorrow. Can you book our flights with the information from his last trip?"

"Give me a second to pull it up," Margot replied. "He booked first class on his trip with Mr. Winslow. Do you want that again?"

Kathleen's heart raced. Would Sebastian think she was blowing the budget if she booked a first class seat with him? He did say he wanted to discuss the plans on the flight. "Whatever's in his travel profile, and please book our seats together."

"And I'm showing the Folies Hotel?"

"Two rooms," Kathleen emphasized.

"Last trip, he had a suite. Two bedrooms and a parlor."

"Is there a cancellation fee if we decide to change it to just the two rooms?" Kathleen asked.

"No, not at the Folies."

"Then the previous accommodations should work." If he thought Kathleen was being extravagant, he could make his own damn arrangements. "Can you send a copy of the confirmation to me and to Mr. Brooks?"

"Will do."

Kathleen's irritation had lessened considerably after talking to a reasonable person, but knowing the head of the firm was involved in the project sent her stomach fluttering. "Thank you," she told his admin. "I appreciate your help."

"Good luck," Margot said cryptically.

Kathleen tugged her ponytail holder out and shook her hair. She had a lot more research to do before they left tomorrow.

<hr />

A vacuum cleaner hummed outside Sebastian's office. He glanced at the clock on his computer, leaned back in his chair and stretched. He was as ready as he could be for the trip tomorrow, provided his new associate could keep up.

Kathleen. She'd looked to be about twenty-five, and he'd detected a temper to match her fiery red hair. Barrett had shown Sebastian the work she'd done for the Frank Lloyd Wright restoration and he had to admit it was impressive, but surely there were other qualified associates with more tenure. After the last disgruntled associate, were they questioning Sebastian's ability to lead? Or were they building a case to pass him by this promotion cycle?

Sebastian had put his time in. He had the projects behind him to push him up the promotion ladder. If Barrett wanted Sebastian to prove he could work with green subordinates, he'd train the best damn associate this firm had ever seen, no matter what they gave him to work with.

Sebastian reserved an Uber, packed up his laptop and gathered his plans.

Chapter 2

Always smile when you pick up the phone; people can hear it in your voice.

After a fitful night, Kathleen had given up on sleep and spent hours doing more research and tracking down material representatives in New Orleans. Her head was spinning with the eclectic architectural styles.

She checked through her notes while she sat at the gate in the airport, waiting for Sebastian to show up.

Kathleen had discovered they could apply for rehab tax credits. Sebastian would have to appreciate she knew what she was doing when she told him about that. Clients always liked when you found ways for them to save money—even rich, movie star clients.

The standby board showed people waiting for seats and it was getting close to boarding time. If Sebastian didn't make the flight, should she go on ahead? She knew he'd gotten the itinerary—he'd been copied on the same email she received. They paged him to the gate. If he didn't get here soon, they'd give his seat away.

He marched past her to the podium carrying a tote bag with rolled plans sticking out, wearing dress slacks and a sport coat over a polo. She checked her own travel attire and was glad she'd opted for the skirt and sweater set rather than the jeans and shirt she'd almost worn.

Sebastian scanned the seating area until he found her. He nodded a greeting as the gate attendant called for passengers needing assistance to board the plane.

Kathleen retrieved her carryon and purse and went to stand beside him.

"You're in first class?" he asked.

She tensed. Was he going to make her give up her seat? "You did say you wanted to discuss your plans on the way."

"I did." He scrolled through his phone.

The gate attendant called for first class passengers and Sebastian moved forward. He passed his phone over the scanner and moved through.

Kathleen gave the flight attendant her printed boarding pass.

As they walked down the jetway to the plane, he tugged his ear. Nervous? He greeted the attendant on the plane, waved to the pilot, and found their seats. Sebastian pointed to her carryon and raised his eyebrows to the overhead bins. She nodded, and he lifted it for her, then he waited for her to slide into the window seat.

When he took his seat, he ordered a Manhattan, neat, from the flight attendant. "Anything for you?" he asked Kathleen.

"Ginger ale," she told the flight attendant.

In her experience, alcohol was rarely a good idea, but she didn't begrudge those people who indulged in a cocktail from time to time. Because her father had been an abusive drunk didn't mean…

If Sebastian Brooks was an alcoholic, that would add one more to her growing list of things to dislike about him. She caught a clean scent coming from him, something similar to cola. He didn't look the type to wear cologne. Aftershave? She checked his short hair.

Evidence of a hair product glistened in the sunlight shining through the airplane window.

The flight attendant brought his drink. Sebastian took a sip, closed his eyes and drew a fortifying breath, then shot the rest of his Manhattan back and ordered another one.

She took a second look at Sebastian. "I read an article recently on how the decreased cabin pressure in an airplane diminishes the body's ability to absorb oxygen and, in some people, it mimics the sensation of being drunk." Kathleen lowered her voice. "When you add alcohol, the effects are compounded."

"When I want your opinion, I'll ask for it."

Kathleen inched toward the window in her seat and watched the ground crew.

"You can tell me what you've put together once we reach cruising altitude," Sebastian said.

She forced a smile.

The parade of passengers ended and one of the flight attendants pulled the door closed. The pilot shut the cockpit door and the flight attendants began their pre-flight instruction. Sebastian shot down his second drink and leaned back, eyes closed, gripping his armrests as the plane backed away from the gate.

He was afraid to fly.

Kathleen straightened in her seat. She so wanted to mess with his head for being such a prick. Did she dare? She knew he flew for business trips often enough to understand planes were perfectly safe, but some people never got over the scary parts. She cleared her throat and schooled her features.

"Mr. Brooks?"

He opened his eyes and gave her an annoyed glare.

"I should probably tell you I'm a little nervous about take-offs and landings. I'll try not to cry, but in case I do… I wanted to let you know. It must be all those stupid airplane disaster movies. You know, the ones where the plane explodes in a ball of fire right after takeoff, or when the landing gear doesn't go down and the plane skids down the runway right before it…" She shuddered.

The flight attendant walked toward the front of the plane and Sebastian stopped her. "Do I have time for a trip to the head before takeoff?"

"A quick one, I think we have five ahead of us on the runway."

He unbuckled and bolted for the lavatory.

Kathleen did her best not to laugh.

When he returned moments later, he didn't look at her, but his voice was low.

"Well played, Miss McCormick. I'll thank you to keep any further comments to yourself until we're in the air."

————————————◆————————————

This associate was most definitely going to test Sebastian's leadership skills. To Kathleen's credit, she had keen powers of observation. Barrett hadn't noticed Sebastian's fear of flying, or he hadn't mentioned it. If Kathleen planned to provoke him at every turn, they would have a long couple of weeks in New Orleans—or her trip would be very short.

No. He was going to prove he could work with difficult people. He could mold her into a decent architect. She had the good grace to be embarrassed, as noted by the way her freckles stood out against her reddened cheeks.

"Don't women usually try to cover up their freckles with makeup?" he asked.

"I *am* wearing foundation," she said, her annoyance evident.

He squinted to look more closely. Criticizing a woman's makeup had to rank right up there with asking an overweight girl if she was pregnant. While he tried not to laugh at the unexpected analogy, her eyes flashed blue lightning at him. She had the temperament of a redhead, for sure. He'd taken a personal jab, most likely due to the two drinks he'd had to settle his nerves. She didn't deserve that, but an apology would make things worse. If he told her the freckles were cute, she'd sue him for harassment.

He needed to shut his mouth before he got himself in any deeper.

The blue in her sweater brought out the color of her eyes, sky blue. She'd tied her hair in a ponytail again, a ponytail that coiled to the bottom of her collar. What would her hair look like hanging free?

What an odd thought. He wasn't in the habit of assessing his associates' appearance.

The plane raced down the runway. Under normal circumstances, he'd be clutching his armrests and clenching his teeth. Instead, he studied Kathleen McCormick, from her observant blue eyes to her slightly upturned nose to her glossed lips.

The wheels came off the ground. He could think of worse things to be looking at in the moments before he died if this was his time to go, if an engine fell off and the plane turned into a fireball.

Man up, boy. There's nothing to be afraid of.

As the plane leveled out, his thoughts turned to the project. Yes, Kathleen had gotten his attention, but he didn't fraternize with employees. Even if he wanted to, Winslow Designs had a strict non-fraternization policy. Sebastian had always made it a point to be the model of professionalism. As he closed in on his thirtieth birthday, he couldn't afford to let anything get in the way of this promotion. Next year would be too late.

Sebastian took his iPad out of his carryon and pulled up his preliminary sketch of the house in the Garden District.

"As I may have mentioned, Aria Walton is a repeat client," he told Kathleen. "I forwarded you photos of her Lake Forest home so you can get a feel for what she likes. We're going in to do the as-built survey in New Orleans. I assume you're familiar with that step? Taking measurements? Plotting windows and outlets and load-bearing walls? I realize you've had very little time to get up to speed on this project, but I'm counting on you to be ready."

"I'm ready," she said curtly.

"Once we arrive, I'll need you to track down information on plans from before the house was subdivided. The client is looking to recreate the original charm of the home." He turned the iPad so Kathleen could see. "This is an approximate floor plan."

Kathleen picked his iPad up and pinched her fingers on the screen to make the drawing larger. Her awkwardness seemed to have disappeared, replaced by something more attractive. Enthusiasm.

"I did some checking, and the renovation should qualify for rehab tax credits," she told him. She placed a finger on the wall that divided the main room into apartments. "These walls are coming down?"

"That's right." And why couldn't he take his eyes off her? Those Manhattans must have been stronger than he thought. She wasn't his type at all. He liked his women cool and sleek and detached. Kathleen was warm and vibrant and… plucky. And a subordinate. Off limits.

He held out a hand for his iPad. "You know," he said, his voice coming from somewhere far away, "on second thought, we should wait until we get there, when we have more room to spread out." When he had a clearer head.

She blinked a couple of times and sat back. "Whatever you think is best."

"You might have been right," he said. "Alcohol and flying aren't always a good combination."

Chapter 3

When dealing with those in a position of authority, be deferential.

Why had Kathleen mocked Sebastian's fear of flying? If he didn't fire her, it would be a miracle. Goodbye, new house.

He'd shown her the preliminary sketch, and put it back before she'd had time to study it. Retribution? Or was it like he said and the second Manhattan put him out of business? He had appeared to sleep for the remainder of the flight, until the pilot called out the plane's descent.

A driver met them in the baggage claim area, another perk of traveling with the senior project manager, or was it because they had an influential client?

Kathleen promised herself she'd rein in her urge to poke Sebastian. Based on his response on the plane, he wasn't amused at her attempt to distract him from his fears. It was a wonder he hadn't fired her already.

In the limo, he scrolled through his phone, answering emails, she assumed. He hadn't spoken since he'd dozed off on the plane, and his expression was dark and forbidding.

She could be deferential. Yes, master. No, master.

Kathleen swallowed hard to restrain the giggle that bubbled up. Sebastian cocked an eyebrow at her and she sobered immediately.

Sebastian's phone rang and he answered it.

"Yes, we arrived safely," he said.

The "safe arrival" call from home? Kathleen pulled out her cell phone to text her sister, Siobhan.

"She's still green, but she seems to know what she's doing," Sebastian went on. "Which reminds me, have you spoken to the client since our last meeting?"

Oh. He was talking to the boss. Kathleen tucked her phone into her purse and clasped her hands.

"So we'll be meeting her agent at the house?" Sebastian continued. "Sounds good. I've arranged to meet with contractors, as well, to make sure we can move ahead once we get the green light. I'll keep you posted."

He disconnected the call and folded his arms. "I trust we won't have any more outbursts like the one on the plane? You're not going to suddenly affect a fear of ghosts at the hotel?"

"Ghosts?" she asked.

"New Orleans is said to be one of the most haunted cities in the world, if you believe in that sort of thing."

Ho-boy. She'd have to remember not to talk about her family. Between her younger sister Mary's ghost materializing to find justice for her murder and her older sister Siobhan marrying a ghost chaser, he'd think the whole family was looney. She managed a nervous laugh. "No, sir. I'm not afraid of ghosts. And I apologize if I was out of line on the airplane."

He narrowed his eyes. "Apology accepted."

Her phone buzzed and Kathleen checked for the text. Siobhan asking which night would be best for dinner. After the years she and Siobhan had been separated, she was excited to have her sister back in her life, until Siobhan had moved again. To Louisiana.

"We'll have a working dinner," Sebastian said. "You can show me what samples you've collected to show to the client."

Kathleen looked up from her phone. "Dinner?" She'd hoped to meet Siobhan tonight, but figured she'd better play it by ear until she knew what the boss expected.

"Unless you have other plans?" he asked sarcastically.

"Of course not."

"But?" He raised an eyebrow.

"I thought I might have time to see my sister while we're here," she began. "Maybe an hour or so over the weekend?"

"Your sister?" he repeated.

"She lives nearby," Kathleen said. "But I'm sure she'll understand if I don't have free time. I am here to work."

"How many siblings do you have?" he asked.

"Three surviving."

"And how many didn't survive?"

"One."

He remained silent for nearly a minute, and then he sighed.

She could appease a workaholic boss for a couple of weeks. "My mistake," she said. "Since we hadn't talked about an agenda, I wasn't sure if I might have an opportunity." She wouldn't be invited to attend meetings with the client or interviews with contractors. Certainly he'd give her one hour to herself in the two weeks they'd be here. Hopefully Siobhan would be available during one of those windows.

"Ask her to join us at the hotel to minimize the interruption."

"Us?" Thoughts of Russ asking to be invited to the Friday night family dinner crowded in, the invitation she never issued, the final breaking point in their relationship. Kathleen had never quite been ready for him to meet the family, and she'd dated Russ since college.

She had no reason to introduce Sebastian to her family, even if it was only her sister.

He faced her and raised his eyebrows. "I'd be interested to see if your impertinence is a family trait, or if it's just you."

"Oh, it's a family trait," she muttered, then forced a smile. "I'm sure you'd be bored, and I don't have to..."

He sat back and folded his arms. If he insisted on dining with her and Siobhan, she'd have to comply as an effort to be deferential, but then she wouldn't be free to talk with Siobhan, and she needed sister time to unload her Russ baggage. Siobhan was the only member of her family who knew she'd been dating a policeman.

"You can see her Friday night, then, while I'm meeting with Aria," he said. "But you should tell your sister you'll be working for the time you're in New Orleans, with little or no free time. That is why you're here."

She resisted the impulse to ask him if she'd have time to go to the bathroom, or to sleep. "Yes, sir."

Sebastian gave her a sarcastic smile. "I like that. At least it's a pretense of respect."

Had she sounded snotty? She couldn't let her smart mouth get the best of her. This project was a rare opportunity and she had to prove she was up to the task. A promotion would mean more money, which would fund her down-payment that much sooner. Kathleen needed to remember he was her boss and give him the respect he deserved, no matter how she felt about him.

Siblings. What was it like to have siblings? Sebastian was saved from too much pondering when the limo came to a stop outside the hotel.

A bellman gathered their luggage while Sebastian paid the driver. By the time he reached the lobby, the check-in clerk was handing Kathleen their room keys.

"I requested the same accommodations you had on your last visit," she told him. "I hope that's acceptable?"

"Yes, thank you."

She showed the keys to the bellman, and he led them to their rooms.

Kathleen wasted no time setting up her computer in the shared parlor between their individual bedrooms once their luggage was dispersed and their room keys were sorted out. Eager to work? Or putting on another show?

"You'd mentioned you didn't have a copy of the agenda," he said.

She glanced at him over her computer.

"We'll be going in tomorrow to do the as-built, to take the dimensions of the rooms. The house is approximately 7,500 square feet. I've scheduled at least two days, although it could take longer." He checked his phone. "Today is Wednesday. I'm meeting Aria for dinner on Friday. She expects to stay in New Orleans for the weekend and will be leaving Monday to begin filming a new movie. She wants designs to approve before she goes. That doesn't give us much time to work with. We aren't expecting any changes to the exterior. You'll need to go to city hall to check on codes and look into permits. Do you know where city hall is?"

"Yes. It's walking distance from here, depending on how much time we have."

Eager to work then. "See if you can find original plans filed at City Hall. Do you have the project's address?"

"Yes, I do. In fact, you'd mentioned original plans yesterday, so I went looking for the address online and I found a place that houses historical documents." She turned her laptop to face him. "This floor plan seems similar in style?"

Resourceful. She'd done her homework. Perhaps he'd underestimated her. "Well done. The City might have designs on file prior to the last renovation. Have you put together samples for Ms. Walton to choose from?"

"I gathered information from the image library before we left," she told him.

He was impressed that Kathleen held his gaze, her expression stoic. She answered his questions as matter-of-factly as if she were in an interview.

"And I've contacted suppliers here for samples in case she wants a closer look," she continued.

Kathleen seemed to know what she was doing. Why hadn't he heard her name before now? Something didn't add up. "How long have you been with Winslow Designs?"

"I started my internship while I was still in school. Officially, I've been with the firm a little more than three years." Kathleen lowered her hands to her lap and tilted her head.

"Odd that I haven't met you in the office before now," he said.

Her nostrils flared, and more blue lightning flashed in her eyes, but she didn't comment. From what he'd learned about her on the airplane, he'd bet she was biting her tongue to keep from making another sarcastic comment. "Out with it."

"Excuse me?" she said, the epitome of proper behavior.

"Now you're worried about offending me? After preying on my fear of flying?"

Her nose turned pink and her freckles stood out. "I was trying to distract you so you wouldn't be thinking about it. I meant no disrespect."

He laughed. "By painting pictures of planes going down in flames?"

Kathleen dropped her gaze.

"I sensed a comment about why I haven't seen you in the office?" he prompted. "I'd like you to feel you can speak freely with me."

"I was only thinking you aren't the type of person to notice…" She pressed her lips together and took a breath. "I've seen you in the elevator. Many times. You're probably more engrossed in preparing for your day than you are in noticing the people around you."

Was he? "You might be right. A hazard of city life. When in a crowd of people, I tend to tune out the world." Except he should have noticed Kathleen, especially with her mane of red hair.

She clicked keys on her computer and closed the top. "We still have time this afternoon. I'd better go to city hall and get things started there," she said.

"Sounds good. I have other business requiring my attention, and then, over dinner, we can address Ms. Walton's requirements, along with other features unique to the Garden District."

As Kathleen rose from her chair, the door to her bedroom opened slowly. She turned to look, her eyebrows furrowing. "I'm sure I closed that."

"Probably one of the hotel's ghosts," Sebastian joked.

Kathleen shot him a look that gave him goosebumps. She hadn't taken him seriously, had she? Surely an architect would recognize when a door wasn't plumb. He glanced at the framing.

Perfectly square.

Chapter 4

Don't let other people dictate your goals.

Despite the high degree of humidity, the walk to City Hall released the pressure in Kathleen's chest. Sebastian Brooks' ego had filled the room, but that wasn't what unsettled her. He had a way of looking at her with those piercing hazel eyes as if he could see her thoughts.

So far, he didn't fit what she thought she knew about him. Oh, she'd seen the sarcasm and the condescension, but there was more. *Well done.* That right there. That's what unsettled her. It was easy to discount his looks when he was being a jerk, but when he said something nice?

She shook her head. The compliment was likely an anomaly. They had a job to do, and she was determined to prove to him she was professional, capable and qualified.

Except she'd broken up with Russ three months ago, and while she didn't miss him, per se, she did miss the benefits of having a boyfriend, which heightened her responses to men, including Sebastian Brooks, in inappropriate ways.

Sebastian wasn't that attractive. Not really. He wasn't ugly, but he wasn't movie star handsome, either.

And why was she so hung up on his appearance?

Sebastian Brooks is a jerk. Sebastian Brooks is a jerk. She repeated the mantra in her head to reinforce her opinion. He was her boss and he would not appreciate her objectifying him as a way to relieve her body's cravings. She had to stop assessing every man she met, wondering how to fill the physical void Russ had left.

Kathleen hadn't slept well and she was travel-weary, which might account for some of her wayward thoughts. Sebastian certainly hadn't done anything to suggest activities beyond a working relationship. He had a girlfriend. Or wife. Someone she'd overheard him making dinner plans with. She'd seen the photo on his desk.

He was a respected architect. She could learn a lot from him, as long as she stopped baiting him and, instead, showed him she knew what she was doing.

Starting with building codes and permits.

She'd arrived at City Hall.

When she found the Planning Commission office, a clerk—an older gentleman named Armand—walked her through the "one stop" process for permits, including a certificate of appropriateness with the Historic District Landmarks Commission, or HDLC. When Armand asked Kathleen which address they would be renovating, he clapped his hands and bounced on his toes.

"We'd heard of Ms. Walton's intentions to restore the house and we are eager to assist in any way possible," Armand told Kathleen. "I happen to know there are photos for that house registered with the Library of Congress if you think that might be of assistance. Photos and a plat of survey."

Armand's excitement was contagious, and armed with the information she needed to proceed, minus the documents they had yet to prepare, she left City Hall an hour later when business hours ended.

The HDLC was an added layer of complexity, but from what she'd learned, the Commission supported the renovation to a single-family home and, according to Armand, New Orleans was called the Big Easy because they liked things to be easy. Kathleen hoped that was true.

As she walked, she shivered and had the uneasy feeling she'd walked through a cloud, but the sky was bright even in the waning daylight. She checked behind her, where a man walked away, directly in the path she'd passed. She shook her head at the notion he'd passed through her. If he'd been in her way, she would have run into him.

When she returned to the hotel, a man wearing work clothes and a patch that designated him as a building engineer was opening and closing the door to her bedroom from the parlor. With his back to Sebastian he used a measuring tape and a level to check the door.

Sebastian's voice was louder than it needed to be. "I stayed in a room like this only a month ago, and we didn't have any issues with the doors. This suite is unacceptable."

"With the Pacific Coast League All-Star game coming to town, the other suites in the hotel are currently occupied," the engineer told him. "And there is no physical reason for the door to open on its own. The latch is in good repair. The frame is square." He turned and tipped a finger to his forehead toward Kathleen. "Ma'am."

Sebastian raised his voice another notch. "Then why won't the damn door stay shut?"

The engineer shot a glance at him, then at Kathleen and shrugged. "Ghosts?" He smiled sheepishly.

"Don't give me that bullshit. I want to speak to the hotel manager."

"I'll send him up," the engineer said. He passed Kathleen on his way to the door, a sympathetic smile on his lips. "You have a good day, ma'am," he said, and let himself out.

"We can't have the door opening and closing by itself for the next two weeks," Sebastian sputtered. "And kids racing in the hall. Call Margot and ask her to find us another hotel."

Kathleen set her tote bag beside the sofa and took a seat in front of her computer. So much for telling him all the exciting things she'd discovered at City Hall. She was back to being a flunky. "It's after business hours. I can send her an email, but she likely won't get it until tomorrow."

Sebastian tugged his ear and opened the minibar.

Great. Bad enough the man had a temper. She knew from experience with her father that adding alcohol could make things worse, except when Sebastian turned around, he was popping the top of a can of cola.

"I ordered dinner," he told her. "We have a lot of work to do and I didn't want to waste time."

He ordered dinner? Instead of delegating that task to her, his lackey?

"I had to guess at what you might want," he continued. "Is there anything you can't or won't eat?"

"I can order my own…" she started. She paused to regain her composure. "I'm fairly adventurous when it comes to food. When in Rome, you know. I like to taste local cuisine when I travel. At home, I tend to be in a rut with salads and chicken. Oh, and the occasional pizza."

He managed a smile, the first one she'd seen from him. Okay, he was a lot more attractive when he did that. But he was still a jerk.

"I ordered Gulf fish and steak. If you prefer one over the other, feel free, or if you want to try a little of each, we could split the entrees."

"Either would be fine with me," she said, typing the email. "I met a chatty man at the Planning Commission. The Historic District is excited for the renovation of one of their gems."

A knock interrupted her. Kathleen rose to her feet, and Sebastian opened the door to a rotund gentleman in a sports coat with the hotel logo. He introduced himself as the hotel manager.

"I understand you're having problems?" he said to Sebastian.

"The door to my colleague's bedroom won't stay shut," he said. "And since you're here, I've heard children racing up and down the hallway, laughing and playing games. I haven't been able to find them to ask them to stop. We have work to do, and I don't appreciate the distraction."

The manager chuckled. "I'm afraid you've met our ghosts. There are no children staying on this floor."

"You don't expect me to believe that," Sebastian said. "Or perhaps the children are from another floor?"

"That might well be true." The manager smiled at Kathleen. Checking to see if she believed his ghost theory? "We often have reports on this floor of similar disturbances. Some have reported seeing the children, only to have them disappear at the end of the hall. As for the door, the engineer assures me there is nothing mechanically wrong with it to account for the problem you are experiencing."

"Thank you for taking the time to stop up," Kathleen told him. "I'll be sure to put something in front of the door to keep it closed when I retire for the night."

In the hallway, room service arrived with a cart full of food.

While Sebastian turned his attention to taking care of room service, the manager lowered his voice when he spoke to Kathleen. "I'm not sure blocking the door will make much difference. Please don't be alarmed. The ghosts that haunt our hotel are benign and won't harm you. Those guests who have reported sightings said they were never frightened by the presence. However, if another room becomes available before the end of your stay, we will do our best to accommodate your request to move."

Apparently, she appeared less skeptical about ghosts than Sebastian. Kathleen gave the hotel manager a smile. "Thank you."

"Have you ever heard such crap?" Sebastian said as he carried a plate to the parlor table. "Ghosts. A poor excuse for bad management."

"He did say he'd give us a new room if one became available," Kathleen said.

"We'll be gone before then." He waved a hand over the plates, waiting for Kathleen to choose which plate she wanted.

"I'll take the fish," she said.

Which is what he'd hoped. Sebastian was hungry for the thick steak and potatoes.

They sat to eat, and Kathleen filled him in on her trip to the Planning Commission. More of the enthusiasm he'd seen on the plane bubbled from her. While she talked, she picked up a pen and drew on her napkin to illustrate something she'd seen on the plans she'd found online. She seemed to know what she was doing, so where was the catch? What was Barrett's motive for assigning her to this project? Was he throwing up roadblocks to Sebastian's promotion?

Sebastian glanced toward her bedroom door, the one that wouldn't stay shut. Would he be looking at a sexual harassment suit when they returned to Chicago? Kathleen had a sweet, wholesome look to her. People would believe anything she said.

Sebastian had never abused a woman, and he wasn't about to start now.

"Am I talking too much?" Kathleen asked.

He'd missed most of what she'd said. "Not at all. I'm afraid I have a lot of balls in the air at the office, and I've scheduled contractor meetings here. I apologize if I seem distracted." He took a bite of his steak and waved his fork. "Go on."

"I had some ideas for Ms. Walton based on the information I've been collecting. You said she wants to restore the home to its original grandeur." Kathleen's eyes sparkled and she leaned forward.

He was not going to have a junior associate telling him how to draw his designs. He'd better stop her before she got carried away. "First of all, when a client says they want to restore a home to its original grandeur, they seldom mean 1800's, in this particular case. She's going to want running water and electricity and modern appliances, for instance. Second, I am running this project. I'm happy to listen to your ideas, but all design decisions will be made by me. Are we clear?"

She straightened in her chair, the smile slipping from her face. "Yes, sir."

Better she learn right away who was in charge of this expedition. Kathleen had already exhibited a cheeky personality. Maybe Barrett was counting on Sebastian to tone down her natural exuberance.

Except he liked that about her.

Her phone rang. Kathleen picked it up from the table and then shot Sebastian a sheepish look. "It's my sister."

"Then you should answer it," he said.

She smiled timidly, picked up the phone and wandered into her bedroom, but she didn't bother to close the door.

Sebastian dug into his dinner. The Cajun seasoning gave his food extra flavor, more than the fare he was used to in Chicago. That was the thing about New Orleans, it was a different world. Where else could a hotel blame their shortcomings on a ghost?

Kathleen spoke in hushed tones, and then she broke into a throaty laugh that sent ripples of awareness across his skin. Moments later she walked out of her room, smiling, her hair hanging around her face in soft red curls.

That hair—vibrant, colorful. When it wasn't tied back, it took on a life of its own. Now he remembered her from the elevator at Winslow Designs. She'd been hard to miss.

"I told her I'd meet her Friday night," she said. "She mentioned a place in the French Quarter."

Sebastian focused on his steak, trying not to stare at Kathleen.

"And I asked her about our ghost problem." Kathleen's mouth twitched and her eyes sparkled in a way he was coming to recognize as flippant. "Her husband is a ghost chaser."

Sebastian set his fork down, wiped his face with his napkin. Another attempt at a joke? "And what does the ghost chaser husband recommend?"

"He says the ghosts in New Orleans never bother anybody, and most places down here actually like to keep them around. He says it adds character when a hotel is able to say it has unseen occupants." In a practiced motion, she slipped something from her wrist and pulled her hair back.

His fingers itched to tug one wayward curl free. He wanted to tell her to leave her lovely hair loose.

And then he remembered his diversity training.

"I still think it's a poor excuse for bad management," he muttered.

Chapter 5

The only way to do great work is to love what you do.

Ten-foot ceilings. Floor to ceiling windows. Three-piece crown molding at the ceiling with matching corbels supporting the mantel over the fireplace. Kathleen had done her research, had seen the photos, but nothing compared with standing in the palatial room, even subdivided as it was.

She pictured opening the walled-off room next door into double parlors with arched entranceways. Built-in cabinets. A Victorian color palette. Stained glass insets in the windows. Twelve-inch baseboards. Embellishments on the archways. She felt like a kid on Christmas morning.

"Kathleen?"

Sebastian called her back to the apartment as it was, painted contractor white. She retracted the handle on the cooler they'd rented from the hotel, filled with water and sports drinks. "I was reading about one of the plantations last night," she told him. "About a restoration where they went with the original method of notched and pegged joints. Not a single nail holding it together. Are the walls here constructed with bricks between the posts? Not the newer walls, of course, but the original walls?"

Sebastian leaned against the doorframe, arms folded. "Yes, these are brick walls."

She was babbling again, but this house—this was why she'd gone into architecture. Forget all the glass and metal and modern lines. This house had been standing for centuries and was likely to last several more. Kathleen preferred the ornamentation of wood. This house told a story with its classic lines and floor to ceiling windows. The shutters and mixed column styles that supported the balconies—no, not balconies. When balconies were supported by columns, they were called galleries here in New Orleans.

"Anytime you're ready," Sebastian said with a hint of sarcasm.

Right. He wasn't interested in the ideas of a junior associate.

"You can start sketching this room and I'll do the apartment next door. We'll do the measurements on the first floor before we move upstairs."

She'd show him she could do this. Kathleen nodded and held out her clipboard, walking the perimeter of the room to assess the best place to begin working. She roughed out the apartment, adding outlets, windows and doorways.

Sebastian rejoined her and gave her sketch a nod of approval.

"I'll take the measurements, you write them down," he said, pulling out the tape measure. "Make sure to make note of bearing walls, columns and beams."

Kathleen scowled at his instructions for what was considered basic knowledge, but held her tongue.

A welcome breeze blew through the open windows. Humidity tugged curls from her ponytail, and while Sebastian climbed the ladder, she pulled a skinny elastic headband from her pocket to hold back the tendrils.

She glanced up at him, at the fit of his chinos across well-formed glutes, at the gap between his polo and his belt as he reached to the ceiling to measure the top of the window. At the dimples that smiled on his low back. Skin. Her woman-in-a-drought fingers itched to touch him.

He fixed the top of the tape measure to the top of one of the window moldings. "You want to grab that?"

The well-formed glutes or the skin that peeked out? No, with his back to her, he couldn't know what had crossed her mind with his innocent question. Kathleen licked her lips. A trickle of perspiration crawled down the side of her face. She set down her clipboard and crossed the room to pick up the dangling tape measure. The heat in this room was stifling. She peeled off her button-down shirt to the camisole she wore beneath. Another trickle of sweat slipped between her breasts and she poked her cami to soak it up. Naturally, he picked that moment to glance down at her.

And why was she fantasizing about her boss again? *Sebastian Brooks is a jerk.* Except in casual clothes, he looked more human, and he had his moments.

"Kathleen?"

Right. She was taking measurements. She crouched to read the tape measure.

"Only two-piece molding at the windows," he said. "Don't forget to add the three inches for the housing on the tape measure."

As if she didn't know. Again she scowled. "Got it," she replied.

He released the tape and it whizzed down. Kathleen backed away while she transcribed the numbers and Sebastian descended the ladder.

"You need a break?" he asked, standing much too close.

Kathleen's nerve endings jumped and her heart rate spiked. Worst of all, a flame stroked her womb. She needed an outlet for her pent-up hormones, and quickly, before she made a fool of herself with her boss.

"I could use something to drink," she said. "Won't Ms. Walton want the air conditioning on when she arrives?"

"She won't be staying here," he said. "Not until the renovation is done."

His low voice raised gooseflesh. Kathleen didn't want to walk away from the nearness of the man, from the way his words soaked into her. Sebastian Brooks was the wrong man, but after three months of celibacy, her body was begging for whatever attention it could find.

"Will you grab me a lemonade while you're over there?" he asked.

Back to being the gopher. Kathleen tamped down her unwelcome reaction to Sebastian and took a step away. And then another. Better. She reached into the cooler and pulled two bottles of lemonade from the melting ice, stopping to press one of them to her neck. Better still.

She handed the second bottle to Sebastian and their fingers touched. He smiled and, as if he hadn't felt the same zing that ran through her, thanked her and turned away. Kathleen rolled her eyes, frustrated by her apparent lack of control over her response. She was hot, and she was sweaty, and even if, in her wildest imagination, Sebastian might be interested in her, she couldn't present a less attractive image of herself if she tried. Winslow Designs also had a non-fraternization policy she'd do well not to forget.

He was a man, she was a woman in a drought. Nothing to see here. She'd been curbing her appetite for three months. She could control her urges until a better option came along.

———◆———

The lemonade washed down Sebastian's dry throat. Kathleen had an earthiness about her, and the way she'd pressed her bottle to her neck and closed her eyes had gotten his attention, the same way he'd noticed when she'd pressed her form-fitting cami between her breasts.

Her cheeks were flushed with the tropical heat, and wisps of hair framed her face. The urge to press her against the wall, a wall that would be torn down, and kiss that sassy mouth irritated the life out of him. That wasn't how he treated women. Sebastian stopped to wonder yet again if Barrett had assigned Kathleen to derail his promotion.

If Sebastian had been doing the as-built with Renee, if Renee even knew how to do an as-built, she'd be dressed more appropriately. In a sensible cotton blouse and linen pants. Not stripped down to a cami and capris. She'd be wearing makeup designed to minimize the perspiration rather than going without and glistening like… like…

Except Renee was an interior designer, not an architect. "Why did you get selected for this project?" he asked.

Kathleen's eyes widened for a moment, surprised. "You told me it was because of my work on the house in Highland Park, among other things. Didn't you make that decision?"

"No, I didn't. I'm used to working with people who have more experience."

Her hands went to her hips and her eyes flashed again. Storm warning. He was growing to like those storms.

"Listen, buddy, I'm a damn fine architect and you've got me chasing and fetching for you. I realize that's my job, but you don't have to be so condescending."

Buddy? His mother was the only one who still called him Buddy. He was going to get the truth from her, and right now. Sebastian closed the distance between them. "Why did you call me Buddy?"

Her eyebrows jumped again. More surprise?

"Buddy? Bud? Mack? Sir? Oh, excuse me. I should have called you *Mr. Brooks.*" Her nostrils flared, still in a temper, but he wasn't letting her off that easy.

"No. You said Buddy. Why?"

She opened her palms. "The first thing that came to my mind that wasn't an epithet?"

He took a step closer, nose to nose. "I don't believe you."

"What's wrong with Buddy?"

She said something more under her breath. Had she called him an asshole? If she had, she'd given him grounds for dismissal with her insubordination. "What did you just say?"

She didn't reply.

"Is my father behind this?" He spoke before he could stop himself. Could he afford to fire another associate without it reflecting poorly on him?

"Your father?" she asked warily.

Sebastian took a step back. Had he overreacted? He wiped his face with his hand and glanced at the ceiling, at the walls that would be torn down, and then at the redhead who filled the space he'd vacated between them.

She stared into his eyes, searching for answers he couldn't give her. Her nostrils flared and her chest rose and fell with a deep breath. "It's hot, my temper's short, and I have some really great ideas you aren't even willing to listen to."

"This is my project." His words came out as a rasp. "And I have a lot riding on it. I can't afford to coddle you."

"Coddle me?" she repeated with narrowed eyes.

He needed to back the hell up. Not only to regain his composure, but to keep from pulling her in and kissing her. Something about her fire attracted him in directions he couldn't afford to follow. "It's hot. My temper's short," he repeated. "I may have overreacted."

Her tongue darted out to wet her lips and his body responded. Not in the casual way he responded to Renee, in a spike of testosterone that bordered on painful.

The heat had to be responsible for his lack of coherent thought. This was a test, he was sure. Barrett had assigned him a spitfire to gauge how he reacted, a chance to redeem himself after the lies his last associate had told. He wouldn't let Kathleen get to him again. His eyes were drawn to the pinpoints in her cami. "You should dress more appropriately tomorrow," he told her. "Ms. Walton's people could show up at any time. We want to look professional."

"Yes, sir." She picked up the blouse she'd been wearing and fought to get her arms into the damp fabric.

"Are you ready to get back to work?"

"Yes, sir."

He looked at her lips once more, shook his head to remind himself kissing her would be a bad idea, and turned away.

Chapter 6

Don't be busy, be productive.

Kathleen and Sebastian went to neutral corners when they returned to the hotel room, opposite sides of the parlor coffee table, hiding behind their computers. Kathleen's temper continued to simmer.

That damn house was hot. She had a blouse she could have thrown back on if "Ms. Walton's people" had decided to put in an appearance. Nothing was wrong with the outfit she'd chosen to wear to do the as-built survey, and if he thought she was going to put on a skirt and blouse to crawl around floors and climb ladders, he'd better think again.

She'd called him an asshole, the memory of which crawled over her skin and made her cringe. Kathleen knew better. She'd given him grounds to fire her.

She'd assumed Sebastian had selected her based on the work she'd done at Winslow Designs. His outburst at the site today indicated it hadn't been his choice, which made her more uncomfortable.

He hadn't chosen her. He didn't want her here. He'd fired the last associate who worked with him, and he clearly didn't want Kathleen on his project now. She'd have to prove she could do this job, and she had to control her temper.

Eye on the prize. If she got promoted, she'd be able to buy a house that much sooner.

And what was that part about his father? Wouldn't most people laugh if someone stumbled on a childhood nickname? As far as nicknames went, Buddy didn't seem to be offensive. Funny he'd been more pissed off by that than the fact she'd called him an asshole. Maybe he *hadn't* heard that remark. She chuckled and he looked up, as if he'd forgotten she was in the room.

"Sorry," she said.

Let him work on his precious designs. She'd draw her own plans, bring her own vision to life, and add it to her portfolio for when he fired her, too.

With a sigh, Kathleen crossed the room to retrieve her phone from her purse on the table behind him. If he didn't want her input, didn't want to talk to her, she'd listen to music instead. She looked over his shoulder, at his computer, but he didn't have his drafting program open. She took a second look. He was browsing diamond rings.

"What do you think?" he asked when he caught her looking.

Damn. She'd been unprofessional yet again. "Ummm…" She looked at his face. He didn't look mad. He looked like he really wanted an opinion.

"I was thinking of buying one for a friend," he said.

"A friend?" Was he kidding? "Shouldn't your friend be doing the ring shopping with his fiancée?"

"No, I meant I wanted to buy one to give to a friend."

"A friend?" she asked again. Was he gay? Was this a trick question? "People don't normally give engagement rings to friends," she said warily. "If this is for a woman, she might think it means something more than 'hey, since we're such good friends and all.'"

"Well, yes. I was considering proposing."

Was this guy nuts? "Proposing? To a friend?"

He shifted in his seat. "Am I not being clear?"

To hell with keeping her opinions to herself. She was already doomed for calling him an asshole. "Most men, when they propose, are excited about the prospect. They gush about the woman and how much they love her and can't wait to spend the rest of their lives together, blah blah blah. At the very least, I'd expect you to describe the woman as your girlfriend, or significant other, or something a little more personal than 'a friend'."

He chuckled. "It's not like that. She's not the emotional sort. It's more of a business arrangement."

Her jaw dropped. This guy wasn't serious, was he? "You're proposing as a business arrangement? Is this a joke? I don't get it."

He minimized his browser. "If you don't like the ring…"

"For what you're suggesting, it's probably perfect. Something to barter with. I'd suggest a solitaire."

"I suppose you'd want a profession of undying love from a man along with a Cracker Jack ring."

Jerk. "I'd want input into what jewelry I'd be wearing for the rest of my life, and no, I wouldn't marry a man I didn't love."

His laugh was derisive. "Love is an ideal. The stuff movies are made of. In reality, love is nothing more than respect for another person. I respect her a great deal."

Kathleen folded her arms and walked to her seat on the opposite side of the table. "Yeah, I respected my last boyfriend, too, but not enough to marry him. I want more from a husband."

"Like?" he rolled his hands to get her to continue.

"For starters, not a gaudy, pretentious ring. If it were me, I'd want rose gold with a classical design. I do believe in love. I've seen the real thing with my brother and his wife, and my sister and her husband." She shook her head and sat, hanging her earbuds around her neck. "No, if I'm getting married, it's got to be the real deal, like what they have."

"The romantic. How sweet." He closed his laptop and rose to his feet. "Make sure you send what we have so far to the team in Chicago so they can get started on the construction designs. I have contractors stopping by the hotel for bids. In the meantime, I'm going to find the exercise room, get my thoughts in order." He disappeared into his bedroom and closed the door behind him.

A business arrangement?

And she'd actually considered kissing him, taking advantage of his man-ness to break out of her dry spell. To be fair, romance had not been part of her fantasy, but she'd prefer a man with a little imagination.

A man who wanted to propose to a 'friend' as a business arrangement was likely to be a dud in the bedroom. Purely transactional. Climb on, poke around a bit, climb off. And didn't *that* sound like fun? Not.

Kathleen nestled her earbuds in and started her classical playlist to quiet her mind. She opened her drafting program and studied the design Sebastian had saved to the cloud. Hadn't he mentioned Aria Walton wanted to restore the home to its original grandeur? And yet all of his options had decidedly modern touches. Not unexpected, but not in line with what Kathleen perceived to be the client's wishes. Then again, Aria Walton was a repeat client, and Sebastian knew better than Kathleen what she wanted.

She scrolled through the samples she'd put together, at the different styles available, and then she checked the example historical floor plan she'd gotten from City Hall. She saved Sebastian's design to her hard drive and modified it to add the double parlors with arched entranceways she'd envisioned when she'd first walked into the home, the built-in cabinets. She added period millwork adorning the lavish formal dining room.

The door slammed shut and Kathleen jumped. A man sat on the sofa. His clothes looked oddly out of date, although they suited him. His cream-colored pullover shirt was made of linen, open at the neck. His trousers had extra buttons for suspenders. There was something about his face, his eyes. Something fuzzy. Or it was eye strain from a long day and staring at her computer? She checked the lamps, wondering if they were set to the highest light level.

"Very nice," he said. "Have you considered dentil crown molding?"

She tugged her earbuds out and glanced around the parlor. Sebastian *had* said contractors would be stopping by. "Are you one of the contractors?"

"You might say I'm one of the original architects." He had a hint of an accent. French? She didn't know Sebastian was working with a local architect, but then, why would she?

"May I offer my suggestions?" he asked.

If he had Sebastian's ear, she had nothing to lose. Sebastian certainly wasn't interested in her ideas. When Sebastian decided he'd had enough and fired her, would this man give her a job?

Kathleen turned her computer so he could take a closer look. "Sebastian wants to put the kitchen back where it was originally, at the back of the house," she said, using the mouse as a pointer to show the plans she'd drawn. "And here. I saw a beautiful picture of a double parlor, and I thought this might be a perfect spot to add an arched entranceway." As she spoke, she added two more arches on each end of the wall. "Columns with scrollwork separating the arches."

"And the corbels at the fireplace," he said. "Something unusual, I'm thinking. Faces, maybe, instead of the profile you've selected?" He looked up, and the door to the hallway swung open.

"That's odd," Kathleen said. She rose from her seat. "And here I thought my bedroom door was the only one that didn't work right." She turned to address her visitor, but he was gone. Both the bedroom doors were closed. If he'd gone into one of the rooms, she would have heard the door close, wouldn't she? Gooseflesh rose on her arms. The clothes, the speech patterns, had her visitor been a ghost? She checked the hallway.

Sebastian came toward her in shorts and a gray t-shirt, dark with sweat, a towel around his neck and wiping his forehead.

Great. If he wasn't already entertaining thoughts of firing her, Sebastian would have even more motive if he caught her modifying his designs when he'd made it clear his were the only ones that mattered. Kathleen hurried to her computer and closed the program.

<hr>

Sebastian had decided to shop for rings to set his mind straight, remind him of his goals. Renee had always been the perfect date—elegant, intelligent, attentive. And when whatever social event they attended together was over, they settled on which apartment to go to, ended the evening in bed, and then parted ways until the next event.

If she accepted his proposal, he'd need a prenup, one where they'd keep their separate apartments. He didn't want to deal with someone else's things in his space, much less the ugliness of waking up beside someone. Renee understood him.

Kathleen's comments about the ring put a kink in his idea. She had made one valid point, however. Renee would probably prefer to select her own ring. He could use that as a bartering point. Provide her a budget and let her choose.

The more Kathleen had expressed her opinion, the more uncomfortable he'd become. Kathleen didn't understand, didn't know the challenges he faced. Her pedestrian concepts of love were unrealistic.

She was distracting, and that was what sent him to the exercise room.

Why was she peeking down the hall?

Sebastian entered his bedroom from the corridor, not wanting another confrontation. By the time he showered, she might have gone to bed and he could retrieve his computer from the parlor. Aria Walton would expect at least a preliminary design tomorrow, and they still had work to do onsite.

Another day in that big empty house working beside Kathleen McCormick.

Between his father's phone call and Barrett's veiled implications that Sebastian might not be ready for promotion, he was under more pressure than ever to get this renovation completed ahead of schedule. He'd prove he could work with any associate, including Kathleen, but if she hurled accusations at him the way Shep Collier had, he could kiss his promotion goodbye. Barrett might have sided with him once, but Sebastian might not get the same consideration a second time. And if Kathleen went the harassment route…

Why couldn't he get the image of her in that tight cami out of his head? There was a time and a place for intimacy, and a jobsite wasn't one of those places.

He was never going to finish his designs if he didn't regain his focus. He let out a groan of frustration and stripped down.

"Are you okay?" Kathleen called out.

Sebastian reached for a towel and slung it around his hips.

What the hell was wrong with him? He wasn't a horny adolescent. He was a grown man, in control of his actions.

"Sebastian?"

"Yes?"

"Are you hurt?"

Kathleen had the power to burn him. "I'm fine, unless you need to see for yourself?" He stared at the locked door, half hoping she'd walk in, but then she'd have her lawsuit, for sure.

"Just checking," she said, her voice retreating.

He pulled off his towel and looked down. Oh, he was hurting, all right. He was going to need that shower. A cold one.

"I'm going to run downstairs and see if the room situation has changed," Kathleen called out.

"All right." As he said it, his door to the parlor opened slowly—the door he was sure had been locked. "Kathleen?"

No, she'd gone. She'd said she was leaving. Unless it was a trick.

Sebastian approached the door cautiously, hiding behind it as he glanced around the parlor. Nobody there.

He gathered up his computer and carried it into his bedroom. Until he got Aria's designs done, he was better off eliminating his distractions.

———◦———

Kathleen stood beside the concierge desk, waiting for the hotel manager.

The concierge returned a moment later. "I'm sorry, he's left for the evening. Is there something I can help you with?"

"This is going to sound strange," she said, still not sure she hadn't dreamed the whole thing.

"Probably not as strange as you think," the young woman said.

Kathleen chuckled. "Okay. I came to ask about the ghost."

"Which one?"

"You mean there's more than one? Oh, wait. He said something about children playing in the hall."

The concierge smiled. "We have at least twenty-five documented ghosts in this hotel."

"Documented?"

The concierge shrugged. "We've had paranormal researchers in to check things out. Tell me which one you've seen. Or tell me which room you're in and I can give you an educated guess."

"A man? I'd guess in his 40's. Big moustache, linen shirt. Canvas pants. He looked like a regular person. Not at all what I'd expect in a ghost. I was more worried he might have broken into the suite, or that he had an appointment with my boss, except for the way he came and went. And the period clothes. And the fuzzy edges." She sounded like a whacko.

"Are you on the fourteenth floor?" the concierge asked.

"Yes."

"Then my guess would be you've met Victor Mercier."

"And is Mr. Mercier living or dead?" Kathleen asked.

"Mr. Mercier died in 1863, I'm afraid," the concierge said.

"In the hotel, I'm assuming."

The concierge directed Kathleen to a couple of seats in the lobby. "Victor was a younger son who was more interested in life in the city among the social elite than he was in sugarcane. In those days, the plantation owners sent their children to France for their education. Victor's daughter came back to Louisiana in 1862, after her tour in post-revolutionary France, filled with righteous indignation against oppression.

"Her education gave her an eyes-open view of the slaves who worked the plantation, and she insisted her grandparents free their slaves and pay those who chose to remain a living wage. America wasn't quite as enlightened at the time, and Victor's parents told him to keep his daughter away from the slaves to prevent an uprising. Victor was only too happy to commission a home in New Orleans, where he could be with 'his people.'

"Plantations were a family business, handed down from generation to generation, and he was happy to let his older brother take the reins. Victor brought his daughter to New Orleans while their city residence was being constructed. His wife remained at the plantation to guard his family interests. After the Gettysburg Address in 1863, she came to the city to bring them home, but Victor wasn't interested in his legacy. His daughter wanted to return to the plantation where she could do more good helping the slaves who had been given their freedom, but Victor preferred the pampered life to the hard work of a plantation. His wife argued that without the plantation, there was no money to support Victor's city lifestyle. Afraid of losing his inheritance and the life she'd grown accustomed to, she ultimately killed him. She took their daughter and escaped to France.

"Victor is a social ghost. Those guests who have met him aren't aware he's a ghost until he vanishes."

"I certainly didn't realize he was a ghost," Kathleen said. "Until suddenly he wasn't there. Is he the one opening my bedroom door?"

"Most likely. Now that he's shown himself to you, you're likely to see more of him."

Kathleen gave a nervous laugh. "Not sure I want to, and my boss certainly would not be amused."

"I'm sorry for the inconvenience and, unfortunately, we won't have another room available until next week. You were fortunate to get the suite you have. There's a chance we could move you on Monday."

"I appreciate your efforts, but I'm not sure we'll be able to stay on," Kathleen said.

The concierge offered a sympathetic smile. "I understand, but chances of you finding two available rooms anywhere in town on such short notice aren't good. New Orleans is hosting the Minor League All-Star game and it's tourist season. The city is inundated with guests."

Kathleen rose from her seat. "Thank you again." She shook the concierge's hand and returned to the suite, entering through the parlor.

Sebastian's computer was gone and his bedroom door was closed. Apparently she was dismissed for the night.

Chapter 7

Success is the byproduct of hard work.

Aria Walton had loved Sebastian's work for her home in Illinois. Could he create magic a second time? He had a pulse on what she liked, even if what she'd requested for this project didn't match what they'd done before. With such a short turnaround time, he wouldn't be able to present her with complete designs tonight, but he'd know if he was on the right track with what he had to show her.

Standing in the center of the second-floor hallway of her home, he pictured the apartments that occupied the rear wing of the house as the master suite overlooking the courtyard and accessible by the outside staircase, with a walk-in closet and built-in shelves to accommodate her unusual amount of clothes and shoes. He considered what to do with the other three apartments. He'd rendered one as an upstairs lounge, complete with wet bar—widen the entrance and frame it in wood. The other apartments were studios. They'd convert neatly back into bedrooms.

The designs he'd drawn up last night would be a good starting point.

Sebastian descended the curved staircase—a crime they'd closed it off—and opened the exterior entrance at the bottom in the vestibule that separated the doors to each of the two full-sized apartments on the first floor.

He walked outside, onto the lower gallery porch where Kathleen sat on a step adding details to the as-built survey. Head bent over the printout, her hair was caught up in a ponytail again along with a headband. She'd taken his suggestion dressing today too far, wearing long pants and a white short-sleeved shirt that showed another light blue cami underneath. Perspiration glistened on her forehead and her face was flushed enough he felt a twinge of guilt for making her cover up in the tropical heat. A breeze made the loose strands of hair that escaped her headband dance around her face. She swiped them away and looked up.

She'd put in the hours, done the work. While he'd been working on his presentation last night, he'd seen by the changing file times she'd been updating the survey in the cloud. "Thank you for your hard work."

She didn't smile. "Just doing my job." Her voice was hoarse.

She picked up her bottle of water and took a drink. It had to be warm. The ice in the cooler had melted before noon, two hours ago. He was hot and tired, and he was wearing shorts and a polo. If she got heat stroke, it would be his fault.

"Let's head back to the hotel. I need to clean up before I meet with Aria and you have a date with your sister."

Kathleen pushed to her feet and held the clipboard to her chest. "Do you need anything from me for your presentation?"

He retrieved the cooler and dumped out the now warm water while Kathleen locked the house.

"If you could email me the samples you gathered and the plans I prepared—you'll find that in the cloud— that should cover tonight's meeting. Once Aria gives me her input, we can marry the rest of the information we've gathered today with my design drawings to make sure everything's in order."

"Yes, sir."

Kathleen sounded washed out. She hunched over the clipboard as they walked toward St. Charles Street where the Uber would pick them up. Sebastian wheeled the cooler along.

"You okay?" he asked.

Another wan smile. "I'm fine."

When the car arrived, she climbed in, leaned back and closed her eyes.

"I know I've been working you hard. Not everyone can keep my pace."

She straightened, tucking the clipboard against her hip. "Am I not keeping up?"

"You are." She was the best associate he'd ever worked with, the distraction factor aside.

"If you want to work after your meeting, I could skip dinner with my sister. How long do you think you'll be?" she asked.

He laughed. "Are you looking for an excuse?"

"No."

She looked at him and again he worried about heat stroke. She'd hardly spoken to him since lunch, and one thing he'd learned about her, she had a tendency to prattle on. "Maybe you should stay in. Rest."

She grabbed his wrist. "Do you see him?"

"See who?"

"He wasn't there a minute ago," she said in a hushed voice.

What the devil was she talking about? "Who?"

"The man beside the driver. Do you see him?"

Sebastian leaned forward, in case the headrest was blocking his view. The only person in the front seat was the driver. "Man?" Was she hallucinating? The heat was oppressive, and the humidity didn't help matters. She was thin, which might make her more susceptible to heat exhaustion. "Make sure you get a bottle of cold water when we get back to the hotel."

Kathleen let go of his wrist, but she continued to stare at the headrest, at the passenger seat.

They stopped in front of the hotel, and as they climbed out of the car, Kathleen stopped. "I know," she said angrily, looking at the passenger side of the car.

"You know what?" he asked, wondering what had prompted this latest outburst.

She looked at Sebastian. "That you can't see him."

"Can't see who?" He checked the crowd on the street.

She shook her head and stalked into the hotel.

"Let me see if the hotel can recommend a doctor. I'm sure you're not used to the tropical weather."

Kathleen punched the elevator button and set her hands to her hips. "I said I'm fine. Now, if you'll let me know what time you expect to be back, I'll make sure I leave my sister in enough time to work."

"Take your time."

They rode to the fourteenth floor in silence. Kathleen let herself into her bedroom. Sebastian entered through the parlor. A moment later, her suite door opened and she set her clipboard on the table, opened the mini bar and grabbed a bottle of water. She drained it, closed her eyes and stood there a moment while her skin visibly rehydrated.

"I'm going to take a quick shower," she told him. "And then I'll update the electronic copy of the preliminary construction drawings before I leave." She started for her room and then stopped. "Wait, you asked me to email you the samples and the designs. I'll do that first."

She sat on the sofa, opened her laptop on the coffee table and clicked away.

"You sure you don't want to take the time to rest?" he asked.

"I'll be ready to work after dinner," she insisted. "After your meeting." The spark was back in her eyes. Not quite the lightning he was used to, but enough to reassure him the water had restored her.

<hr>

Kathleen peeled off her sweaty clothes. Damn man and his dress code. She'd make sure the ice in the cooler was filled to the top next time they went to the house.

She checked her door to the parlor—locked, she wasn't in the mood for any unexplained open doors—and retreated to her bathroom. Under the shower head, the grime washed away, the barely warm water refreshed her skin. Ten minutes later, she felt almost human again.

She stepped out of the shower and grabbed a towel from the rack, wrapped it around herself and wound a second towel around her hair turban style. In her bedroom, she selected a print cotton skirt with a white background and a blue sleeveless top, laid them on the bed and bent over to towel dry her hair. No sense trying to style it in this climate, the humidity would puff it out and curl it up no matter what she wanted her hair to do. She'd tame her hair with mousse and keep it pulled back.

When she straightened, the door to the parlor stood open.

"Not funny," she said under her breath. The ghost, Victor Mercier if the concierge was to be believed, sat on the sofa in the parlor, one leg crossed over the other. She threw her hair towel to the floor and crossed the room to close her door. "Don't mess with me right now, ghost," she told him.

"Excuse me?" Sebastian, crouched beside the mini bar, rose. His eyes took her in from top to bottom.

So much for a refreshing shower. She was heated up all over again. Kathleen tightened the tuck of her body towel, glared at the ghost who sat on the sofa laughing, and slammed her door. She dropped onto the bed and rubbed her forehead.

You're in a drought. He's a man.

You can wait.

She looked at the door again. Yes, she could wait, but Sebastian was right there. And the look in his eyes— he definitely liked what he'd seen. Would he knock?

Of course he wouldn't. He was too proper, not to mention his business meeting with a beautiful movie star in less than an hour. Even if she thought he might take advantage of a situation if she offered—her pulse quickened as she considered opening the door and dropping the towel—he didn't have time. He wouldn't miss such an important meeting. And Siobhan was waiting for Kathleen.

"Damn you, ghost," she whispered.

The room echoed with laughter. "Too late, Cherie."

With one last look at the door, which was firmly closed, she carried her clothes into the bathroom to dress. She wasn't taking any chances.

Half an hour later she exited from her bedroom to the corridor to make sure she didn't have to look at Sebastian again. *Sebastian Brooks is a jerk.*

Except he'd been concerned about her on the way back from the house. Hell, she'd been concerned about her. She'd sweltered inside the hot house. Even the breeze coming through the long windows hadn't helped. No, he was a jerk.

She stopped at the concierge desk and asked the woman to call her a cab.

In another fifteen minutes, she was in the French Quarter crowded with tourists, the congested traffic all but impassable. The short trip took longer than she'd allotted, and the cab let her off two blocks from the restaurant when he found himself blocked into the narrow side street.

Kathleen admired the double gallery townhouses lining the streets, the ferns and flowers hanging over the edges of the iron scrollwork railings. All the pictures she'd seen didn't do justice to the beautiful city. The street names were marked with tiles on the buildings, as well as with street posts. Bicycle rickshaws pedaled by, and hansom cabs competed with cars for street space.

She found the street she was looking for. Halfway down the block, a sign hung over the sidewalk to show her where the restaurant was located. Kathleen stopped to snap photos with her phone. When she reached the restaurant, she stopped and took more photos. The entrance wasn't a door, as she'd expected. A cobbled carriageway led past a bar on either side and into a courtyard. A hostess stand was halfway between the street and the courtyard.

"Are you meeting someone?" a young woman asked.

"Yes, my sister."

The hostess looked at Kathleen's hair and smiled. "Yes, she's arrived. I'll take you to her table."

A fountain bubbled in the center of the courtyard. Wrought iron tables dotted the large stone tiles that made up the patio. Siobhan rose from one of the tables and pulled Kathleen into a hug.

"It's so good to see you," she whispered.

"You have no idea how good," Kathleen replied, hugging tight. She took the seat with her back to the carriageway entrance, ordered a hurricane from the waiter who'd followed her in, and squealed with delight. "This place is gorgeous."

"It's not fancy, but it will give you a taste of the local cuisine," Siobhan replied. "And now you need to tell me everything about the project you're working on, and this jerky boss of yours, and what happened with Brutus?"

"I told you, Brutus broke up with me—his name is Russ, by the way. Just one of the many reasons I pissed him off, not addressing him by his given name. I wasn't prepared for how bad I'd feel. I didn't think I was using him, but he made me feel like I was being selfish and shallow."

The waiter returned with her drink. She glanced at the menu and ordered étouffée. Siobhan ordered the jambalaya. Creole food. When in Rome, or New Orleans, as the case may be.

"You have to let me taste some of yours," Kathleen said when the waiter left.

"Of course."

"How's Jared?" Kathleen asked redirecting the conversation to her absent brother-in-law.

Siobhan leaned forward. "He's fine, and you already asked about him. I want to hear about you."

"Well, for starters, there's a ghost in my hotel room," Kathleen said. "Jared was right, he's friendly enough, but he nearly gave my boss a free show right before I left. He likes to open doors, and he opened mine. Luckily, I was wearing a towel."

Siobhan laughed. "Jared will get a kick out of that. And your boss? What did he say when he saw you in nothing but a towel?"

"Not a word." Kathleen took a sip of her drink. "The man confounds me. He's a jerk, make no mistake, but there's something about him. He gave me the once over, but wouldn't you if you saw someone standing in a towel?"

Again Siobhan laughed. "And?"

"He'd never take advantage of the situation. He's too uptight." She lowered her voice. "I've been three months without a man. *Anything* looks good right now, but no, I exercised some self-control and closed the door."

"Except you said there's something about him," Siobhan pointed out.

"I also said he was a jerk." Kathleen took another sip. "This drink tastes good."

"A New Orleans specialty. Have you tried the beignets yet?"

"No. I've barely had time to go to the bathroom. My boss is a workaholic."

"Remind me to thank him for letting you have a night off." Siobhan clicked her glass to Kathleen's. "So back to Brutus?"

"Russ," Kathleen corrected her. Regret washed over her. "We probably went into the relationship too fast. I'm willing to take the blame. When he was assigned to watch over me, when that cop who killed Mary went after Kevin and me, I guess I was annoyed I couldn't move without someone watching me every minute of the day, so I teased him." She wagged her eyebrows. "He was so easy."

"You're terrible." Siobhan laughed again.

"I thought we were having fun. We were having fun. Then he started getting all serious on me. He accused me of using him and I felt so bad that I tried to make the relationship work, I swear. He's a good guy. He took me to meet his parents. We went on a vacation together."

"But you never invited him to Friday night dinner at Ma's."

Kathleen shook her head. "I couldn't do it. In the first place, Kevin would have had a fit. After a policeman killed Mary, he would have been suspicious of the whole department. Can you imagine what he'd say if he knew I was dating a policeman?"

Siobhan sipped her drink and raised her eyebrows. "You don't give our brother much credit. He might not have liked it, but I think he would have been happy if you were happy. But go ahead. Blame Kevin for your inability to invite your boyfriend to dinner at Ma's."

Kathleen lowered her eyes. "I know."

The waiter set their entrées in front of them. "Can I get you ladies anything else?"

Kathleen smiled at him. The waiter appeared to be close to her age, and he was attractive. His chestnut hair had blond tips, and he had dark, soulful eyes.

"Nothing right now," Siobhan said as she reached across and squeezed Kathleen's hand. The waiter retreated.

"I saw you undressing that boy with your eyes," Siobhan said.

"Woman in a drought, meet an opportunity." Kathleen giggled.

"Or is that the hurricane talking?"

Kathleen sighed. "It's so hard to meet people. I keep telling myself to wait for the right guy to come along, someone I can spend quality time with, but I'm dying for a little fun in the sack." She pushed the food around her plate. "Am I a terrible person?"

"You're asking the wrong sibling," Siobhan said. "You know my history. Fortunately for me, Jared's accident made it impossible for us to jump into bed right away. We had plenty of time to get to know each other first. That was the best thing that could have happened to me. On the other hand, Amy jumped Kevin before he even knew she liked him and look how deliriously in love they are."

Kathleen leaned over the table again. "You think that'll happen to me? I mean, you guys are my role models. I'd given up on Kevin ever finding a girlfriend, and then almost overnight he's head over heels. That whole thing happened so fast. And then you and Jared. I *want* to have a relationship like that, but I spent two years with Russ. He was a great guy, too nice a guy. I just couldn't picture forever with him. You know what I mean?"

Siobhan nodded. "You just be you. Don't settle for less than you deserve. And yeah, maybe Russ was a nice guy. Maybe he was even fun in bed." She raised her eyebrows and laughed. "But there's more to relationships than that. Take it from someone who knows."

"God, I miss you," Kathleen said. "I'm so glad to have my sister back." She looked over her shoulder. "Can I play with the waiter in the meantime?"

Siobhan tilted her head back and laughed so hard she had to wipe tears from her eyes.

Chapter 8

If you wait for opportunity to knock, you'll miss your chance.

Apparently, the restaurant Aria Walton had selected was the same place Kathleen met her sister. That wouldn't have been so bad, in theory, if Kathleen didn't continue to distract Sebastian.

Every damn day was something new with her. From the cami that showed off her curves yesterday, to seeing her in the towel tonight, he couldn't seem to concentrate, even with a gorgeous movie star sitting across the table from him.

Kathleen and her sister left the restaurant arm in arm, giggling and laughing like schoolgirls. He leaned back to glance through the carriageway, to where they hugged and said their goodbyes.

When he reported in, he'd tell Barrett Kathleen wasn't serious enough, not focused. Sebastian would send her home.

"Sebastian?" Aria brought him back to the meeting.

"Sorry. I thought I saw someone I knew." Someone he was beginning to wish he'd never met.

"I was telling you I love the plans. I haven't had much time to look over everything, but what I've seen is perfect. You know how much I love an open floor plan, but these arched entrances give the rooms just enough relief, enough separation."

"Arched entrances?" He opened his computer and pulled up the email Kathleen had sent him, the one he forwarded to Aria.

"And the Eastlake accents on the square entrances add the perfect touch of ornamentation. Can you show me the samples again? I'm still wondering which window molding works best with the coffered ceiling."

"Coffered ceiling?"

She sat back, staring at him. "Why are you repeating everything I say?"

Sebastian zoomed in on the plans, his blood pressure rising. The design Kathleen sent wasn't the one he'd drawn. No wonder he sounded like a fool. "I think there's been a mix-up. These aren't my plans. I asked my associate to send them, but she apparently emailed the wrong ones."

"Now, I know you're a brilliant architect, but I can't imagine improving on these. Oh, we need to work out the finer points, but I absolutely love these. She? You say your associate drew them?"

"I hope so." Either that, or she was opening them up to a lawsuit by stealing someone else's designs. Goodbye promotion, and potentially goodbye job. He had to fix this. Fast. "It looks like the restaurant has WiFi. Let me show you what I designed for you."

Aria shrugged. "Okay."

He opened his file from the cloud and scooted closer to show Aria his work, the open floor plan she'd asked for. The details she'd liked in the Lake Forest house. "We can bring in those Eastlake accents you liked," he said, dragging his mouse to the corners in the drafting program, "and I'd added medallions for the ceiling light fixtures to give it an old world feel."

"And if I want the coffered ceilings, that looks cluttered, don't you think?" She smiled at him, a practiced smile that didn't feel sincere. "Your design is what I asked for, but I do like this other one better. I'd love to meet your associate, to see what else she might have to suggest."

Sebastian tugged on his ear to ease his irritation. If Kathleen hadn't left the restaurant, he'd likely have fired her on the spot. Fortunately for him, Kathleen was already gone. Or unfortunately.

Aria liked Kathleen's designs better.

The client came first. Sebastian drew a cleansing breath and forced a smile. He'd give Kathleen the opportunity to hang herself. "We could meet at the house tomorrow. She can walk you through her ideas. I know you're eager to get this project running. Will tomorrow work for you?"

Aria woke up her phone and checked her calendar. "Is eleven o'clock okay?"

"We'll make it work."

"Excellent." She pushed away from the table and Sebastian rose to his feet. She gave him a distant hug and air kissed his cheeks. "Until tomorrow then?" she said.

"We'll see you at the house at eleven."

So much for sending Kathleen home. She could count herself lucky Aria liked the designs.

Sebastian settled the bill, packed his laptop and left the restaurant. Why could he never find a cab in the French Quarter other than rickshaws or hansom cabs? Cars jammed the narrow street and tourists packed the sidewalks. He slung his computer bag over his shoulder and pulled out his phone to request an Uber driver as he stalked his way to Decatur Street, where the traffic should at least be moving. He looked for a landmark and requested a pick up from Café Du Monde.

Had Kathleen deliberately sent the wrong designs, either to make him look bad or, as it turned out, to upstage him? Was this Barrett's plan? If Barrett had done the designs himself and told Kathleen to present them as hers, it might be an effort to forestall Sebastian's promotion—or worse.

Sebastian paced outside the café. He'd looked like an idiot in front of the client.

An Uber driver pulled to the curb and ducked to look through the window. Sebastian compared the plate and the photo, nodded, and climbed into the car.

"You're going to the Folies?" the driver asked.

"Yes."

The driver pulled away. "Dropping lots of people off in the French Quarter tonight. You know, the All-Star game is in town this weekend. Seems like baseball fans are making a vacation out of it."

"I don't follow baseball," Sebastian retorted.

"In town on business?"

"Yes."

"How you like the Folies?" the driver continued. "Any trouble with ghosts?"

Don't mess with me right now, ghost. And what had Kathleen meant by that?

"I don't mean to be rude," Sebastian said, "but I'm not in the mood to chat."

"Got it," the driver replied.

Ten minutes later, Sebastian stormed into the hotel and punched the elevator button. As he rode up, he was vaguely aware of a couple on the opposite side of the elevator who inched away from him.

When the elevator stopped at the fourteenth floor, he'd regained a modicum of composure, although his temper still burned hot. He entered the suite through the parlor door. Kathleen was curled into the corner of the sofa, eyes closed. Sleeping?

"Miss McCormick, are you familiar with the chain of command?" he barked.

She startled awake, glanced around the suite, then focused on him. She rubbed her eyes. "Yes, of course. Why?"

"The plans you sent me were not the ones I prepared."

She leaned forward, blinked several times and shook her head, then woke up her computer. "I'm sure they were. The only other thing in that folder in the cloud is the as-built we've been working on." She clicked around and her eyes grew round. "I sent the wrong plans."

"Yes, you did."

"I'll contact Ms. Walton and apologize."

"You will not." He set his laptop bag on the coffee table. "Who drew the plans you sent?"

Her cheeks grew red. "I did."

"You did?"

She nodded. "I'm sorry. I was playing around with some ideas I had. I never meant…" She rose to her feet and stumbled, shook her head again, reached for the arm of the couch and dropped back down.

"Why didn't you bring your ideas to my attention?"

"You weren't interested." She looked up again, still blinking.

"Are you drunk?" he asked.

"No. I only had one drink." She frowned and made another attempt to get up. She stumbled.

A ploy? Sebastian crossed the room and took her arm to ease her down. Her skin was cool and clammy, and when he let go, his fingerprints remained. "One drink?" he asked.

"Yes. That's all. I swear."

"Alcohol?"

She scowled. "A hurricane. A New Orleans specialty, or so I understand."

"And only the one bottle of water since we left Aria's house?" he asked.

She furrowed her brow and then nodded, quickly followed by blinking her eyes as if she couldn't focus.

Dehydration. Sebastian opened the minibar and pulled out a sports drink. He opened it and thrust it into her hands. "Drink."

While she did as he said, he folded his arms.

She paused to take a breath, then took another drink. "Was she very angry?" she asked when she'd drained the bottle.

"I'm going to ask you again who prepared the designs you sent me."

She scowled. "I did. I said I'm sorry. It was an honest mistake."

"Are you trying to undermine me?"

"Wha…?"

He huffed. "You might have lost us a significant contract, not to mention a repeat client." Sebastian glared at her. "As it turns out, she likes your plans better."

A smile lit up her face. "She did?"

Damn it all. He tugged on his ear, unable to displace his annoyance. "Why did you draw your own designs?"

"I thought about what I'd do. I was just playing around. I never meant for my designs to go anywhere."

He dropped to the chair opposite the couch. "Why didn't you speak up? Tell me what you were thinking? Show me what you had in mind?"

She folded her arms. "You've been fairly dismissive, reminding me I'm a junior associate without any experience."

"Which you are." He scowled. "A very talented junior associate, which I'd do well to remember. You're certain Barrett Winslow didn't send you here to make me look bad?"

She chuffed. "Aren't you the golden boy? How am I supposed to make you look bad?"

"Something's not right with this whole setup." He wiped his hand across his face. "You may have heard I had difficulties with the last associate I worked with."

"I'd heard something."

Heat exhaustion *might* account for her mistake. Whether her actions were deliberate or not, he couldn't afford to underestimate Kathleen. "I have one piece of advice for you. Check your work. Accuracy is your most important asset. Do you understand?"

"Yes, sir."

"Then let's go over your plans. We have a meeting tomorrow morning at eleven."

"We?"

"Yes. Aria Walton wants to meet the architect who drew those designs. If you're going through with this presentation, you'll need to be prepared." He opened his laptop bag and removed his computer. "The success or failure of this project is now in your hands unless Ms. Walton says otherwise. You understand?"

The sparkle returned to her eyes. "Yes sir."

He took another bottle of water from the minibar and handed it to Kathleen. "Let's get started."

***

Sebastian had leaned back and closed his eyes—she was sure he only meant to close them for a minute—some time after midnight.

The ghost of Victor Mercier had joined her around one o'clock, commenting on her drawings and making suggestions.

At three a.m., Kathleen raided the minibar for whatever rehydrating drinks were left. The adrenaline that had kept her going was dying off, but she was too excited to sleep.

"I don't like faces holding up the mantel," she told Victor, "even if they are angels. And I'm pretty sure the client would think they're creepy. She does chick flicks, not horror movies."

"What is chick flicks?" the ghost asked.

"Romance movies. Boy meets girl, boy loses girl, they make up and live happily ever after."

"He's awake, you know," Victor said.

Kathleen checked Sebastian. "His eyes are closed."

"What do they call that? Looking through one's lashes? He's wondering who you're talking to."

"Why can't he see you? Hear you?"

"Limited imagination."

Kathleen laughed. "I've never seen imagination open a door. And I'm still not happy with you for that little stunt."

"You are just what he needs. A breath of fresh air in his dull little world."

Kathleen started to respond, then stopped herself. If Sebastian was awake, pretending to be asleep, she had to be careful what she said. "I disagree."

Victor waved a finger at her. "I only said limited imagination. When you see the plans he draws for himself, there you will see what makes the man tick."

Sebastian opened one eye. "Who are you talking to?"

"He told me you were awake," she said.

"Who?"

"The ghost."

Sebastian stretched his arms over his head and leaned forward. "I don't believe in ghosts."

"What do you believe in?"

He raised his eyebrows. "Hard work. I suggest we retire to our respective bedrooms to get some sleep so we're ready for the presentation tomorrow."

"Go to bed, Cherie," Victor said.

"You're not going to play anymore games with the doors, are you?" she asked.

"I'm not the one playing games," Sebastian replied.

"I wasn't talking to you."

"Oh. Right. The ghost." Sebastian looked around the room. "Not much of a gentleman if you deprive a lady of her privacy. If you ask me."

"I didn't ask you," Victor replied. He took a step toward Sebastian. "And you aren't much of a gentleman if you can't see the beauty of the woman who stands in front of you."

Sebastian continued to scan the corners of the room, stopped when his attention landed on Kathleen once more. "Good night."

"Good night," she replied.

"Foolish man," Victor muttered.

"Stop it," Kathleen whispered.

Victor's laugh faded as he disappeared.

"Stop what?" Sebastian asked.

She shook her head.

"The ghost again?"

"He's gone now."

Sebastian studied her. "I hope it's the heat exhaustion that has you imagining things. I'm not sure Barrett Winslow would like having someone who is mentally unsound on his staff."

Jerk.

"Are you sure there isn't something you want to tell me?" he asked.

She wanted to tell him a lot of things, every one of which would get her fired. Instead she smiled sweetly. "Not a thing."

Chapter 9

Alone we are smart. Together we are brilliant.

Kathleen was up early Saturday morning. She slipped down to the lobby, got directions for where to find beignets from the concierge, and returned to the suite with her purchase by eight.

She should have known Sebastian would be awake and waiting for her. He spared her a glance and continued working on his computer.

"My sister said beignets are a taste of New Orleans. I thought I'd pick some up," she said, taking her seat on the sofa across from him.

"Donuts, covered in powdered sugar. Too messy."

"I can order room service, if you'd rather," she suggested.

"I already have." He sat straight and looked at her. "We might miss lunch, considering the timing of our appointment with Aria. I'll leave it to you to decide on dinner tonight. There's a Lagasse restaurant down the street, or we can order in and keep working."

The workaholic was offering her a night outside their suite? And he was offering to let her order her own food, or at least choose where she wanted to eat. Probably another test. "Maybe we should see how the meeting goes and decide from there."

"Smart decision. And be sure to take extra bottles of water today." He leaned over his computer. "Let's go over the designs. I know you didn't see much of the second story, so I've taken the liberty of adding my plans to what you drew for the first floor. I'm giving you the stage, Kathleen. Show her your vision of the first floor and let her tell you where she wants modifications. Then I'll take her around upstairs and present my ideas for the second floor. After today, we'll be dealing with emails and phone calls. It's important we get it right."

"I understand."

"It's also important we email her the most current plans. The right plans."

Kathleen sighed. "I understand."

"I won't tolerate another mistake, Miss McCormick. Do I make myself clear?"

Her muscles flinched. "Yes, sir."

"Now, these are my suggestions."

He rose from his seat when someone knocked. Sebastian opened the parlor door to room service without missing a beat. "Built-up, two-piece moldings around the doors to match the windows and twelve-inch baseboards on the second floor." He raised an eyebrow, inviting her to offer an opinion.

Kathleen folded her hands in her lap and remained silent.

Sebastian thanked the room service attendant and closed the door behind him. "I ordered for both of us. Eggs and fruit. Help yourself."

She speared him with a "I have my own breakfast" look and took a bite of her beignet. Powdered sugar sprayed across the coffee table and she couldn't help but laugh, making the mess worse. He was right. Donuts, and an overabundance of powdered sugar.

"When in Rome?" he asked sardonically.

She took another bite, grinning. "Yep." She spooned a bowl of berries and settled on the sofa. One beignet was enough. It was warm, it was tasty, but he wasn't kidding when he pointed out they were messy.

While they ate, they made a list of questions for Aria, things to double check, program considerations and suggestions for exterior changes.

He checked his watch an hour later. "I'm going to run downstairs to find the manager. I'm sure you don't want any more mishaps with your door. While I'm gone, you might dress for the meeting. Something similar to what you wore last night to meet your sister might be appropriate, and functional in this heat."

She watched him leave, struggling not to say something nasty about his imposed dress code. He wouldn't appreciate *her* telling *him* what to wear. Then again, she wasn't accustomed to doing client meetings.

When she looked at the sofa he vacated, she groaned. The ghost was back.

"What?" she said.

"I'm enchanted you are able to see me," he replied.

"I'm not so enchanted you exposed me in front of my boss."

He waved a hand in the air, a blur of the light. "You were covered up. I've seen others in this suite show much more. I was merely trying to help things along."

"He's my boss. You can stop helping. Why are you haunting me?"

He leaned forward. "Because you can see me. You can hear me."

"You're making my life more difficult, if that's even possible."

"I've heard you might know someone who can help me."

She narrowed her eyes. "Help you what?"

"What is the saying? Go into the light."

"You can't find it by yourself?"

Victor smiled, a sad smile that made Kathleen want to cry. "I cannot."

"I know someone?" she asked, and in the same moment, she remembered Siobhan's husband, but how could she arrange for Jared to come to the hotel while Sebastian was there? Sebastian would follow through on his 'mentally incapacitated' threat. "You've been haunting this hotel for what? A hundred and fifty years? In all that time, you've never found your way to the light? Never found someone to help you?"

"Most people can't see me. The parlor tricks, the opening and closing of doors, that isn't enough for some people to recognize they are not alone. And those people who do see me?" He held out his arms. "Apparently I am not frightening, although I have tried to be at times. The hotel sees no urgency to remedy our plight, those of us who reside here."

"So I've heard."

"I would ask your help, Cherie. I have been waiting a long time to rejoin my family."

Kathleen snorted. "Your wife? The one who killed you?"

He waved off the notion. "*Alors*, she did not mean it. She was quite distraught when she realized what she'd done. And my daughter. I wish to be reunited with my daughter."

"My boss is trying to move us to another suite. I won't have access to this one when that happens." She tried not to think about the fact she'd seen Victor outside this room, in the cab.

"There are no rooms available to you," Victor said, tugging on his moustache. "Or, if there were, the reservation system does not appear to be functioning properly."

"You can do that?"

"I can do many things. One hundred and fifty years is a very long time to be wandering these halls."

The chirp of a security card signaled Sebastian's return.

"I don't know if I can help," she said quickly.

Sebastian walked in, took a look at her, at the sofa across from her.

"I thought you might take the time to change your clothes while I was gone," Sebastian said.

Kathleen rocked her head as she mimicked his words inside her head.

Victor laughed and she shot him a dirty look.

"Were you talking to someone?" Sebastian asked.

"Myself." She rose from the sofa and retreated to her bedroom.

Kathleen had twisted her hair behind her head into a neatly tucked bun. She'd taken Sebastian's advice and worn a skirt and sleeveless blouse, a similar style to what he'd seen her in last night. She looked professional, neat, and he had the urge to muss her hair to make her look more natural.

While they waited outside the house for Aria to arrive, Kathleen's blue eyes sparkled and her hands fidgeted, a sure sign she was nervous. She should be. He meant for her to understand the pressure of being on the front lines, for stealing his thunder.

Kathleen began to pace, and when a car stopped at the curb, she clasped her hands tight and rounded her shoulders. Then she tilted her head back and took a deep breath. By the time Aria got out of the car, Kathleen was smiling brightly. Too brightly.

Aria approached Sebastian, leaned in, and gave him air kisses to each cheek.

"Aria Walton, may I present my associate, Kathleen McCormick. Kathleen is the one who drew the designs you saw." He waved a hand Kathleen's direction.

Kathleen's eyes grew wide and her shoulders were tight. Her response was textbook panic. Star struck?

"Kathleen," Aria said in a practiced voice. "How nice to meet you. I absolutely loved your ideas. Of course, I have a few suggestions I'd like to run by you."

Kathleen swallowed hard and for a moment Sebastian wondered if she'd curtsy before royalty. She took another deep breath.

"S-so nice to m-meet you. I'm a big fan. Can I tell you how much I loved you in that remake of Pillow Talk?"

Aria's face relaxed into a patient smile. "I'm gratified."

Kathleen dropped a pen, and when she stooped to retrieve it, she couldn't seem to grasp it. Sebastian crouched beside her, picked it up and handed it to her. When her eyes met his, her loss of composure was obvious. He squeezed her hand to reassure her.

"Shall we go inside?" Aria asked.

Sebastian hovered a step behind Kathleen, leaned forward and whispered in her ear. "You've got this."

She straightened and her back rose with yet another deep breath.

"This house is amazing," Kathleen said. "When I walked in, I could immediately see all the wonderful ways we could open it up. Sebastian mentioned you preferred an open floor plan, and I tried to stick with that as much as possible. The double parlors would give you plenty of room to entertain, and the dining room right here gives you the space to dine and mingle at the same time." She clutched her binder to her chest.

Kathleen appeared more composed, more in her element now that she was sharing her vision. This was what it was all about. As she waved her arms and pointed out what she wanted to do, from tearing down a wall to highlighting the features of the house, Sebastian was drawn into her vision. Aria appeared to be, as well. Kathleen presented her ideas with passion. Had he ever felt that way about a project?

Yes. When he'd been in her position. When he'd had only a design group head to pitch to. Was that only five years ago? Now, instead of imagining the space, he took a more practical approach. Clients didn't always know what they wanted, and Aria was a perfect example. Sebastian had thought he understood her tastes, but Kathleen had embraced the soul of the house they were renovating, and that's what she was selling.

When had Sebastian lost the thrill of sharing his visions? He felt like a puppy who'd been trained to repress its nature. Excitement was frowned upon. The job was about winning over the client.

Kathleen opened her iPad and showed Aria the sample library, pointing out her suggestions along with other options for the same areas. Aria was fully engaged.

They moved upstairs, Sebastian's turn to present. As he walked through his suggestions, Aria glanced to Kathleen. "What do you think?" she asked on several occasions.

"He spent much more time than I did up here," Kathleen told her. "I think he's got it right. Don't you?"

Yes, his ego was tweaked, but Kathleen was working with him. Not undermining him.

Sebastian showed Aria his plans for the master suite and the walk-in closet. He'd added a dressing room, and between the natural light and the spa-like fixtures, he'd regained her interest. He knew what she wanted.

Aria framed her hands as if envisioning the shelves and the cubbies for her shoes. "I love it, but then you knew I would." She looked around the empty apartment, then at the rendering on the iPad. "This is going to be perfect. The two of you, you work well together. Kathleen, you did an outstanding job on the first floor, and Sebastian, you understand me and my need for space. Now, let's talk about what I'm still missing, what I want to see."

"Our hotel is just up the street. We might be more comfortable there. We can sit and discuss the options," Sebastian suggested.

"That would be brilliant," Aria said. "My driver is waiting outside. He can take us over."

She led the way out of the house. Sebastian locked up, and when he got to the car, he slid into the back seat beside Kathleen. She practically bounced with excitement, grabbed his hand and squeezed—a silent squeal?

She'd done well. He'd been excited at his first presentation, too, and his first presentation hadn't been with a famous movie star.

When had presentations become routine?

Don't let it go to your head.

Sebastian's father had agreed Winslow Designs would be good experience, preparation for taking over the family business. Every contract Sebastian had won since his father deemed a 'lucky break.' His father's efforts to temper Sebastian's excitement had turned into expectations of failure, until Sebastian found himself working longer hours, networking with the right people, all in an attempt to prove to his father that he was good at what he did.

He'd proven himself to Barrett Winslow, and still he wasn't good enough for his father. Sebastian was so close to a promotion he could taste it, but watching Kathleen today, he stopped to wonder if that was what he wanted.

Somewhere along the line he'd lost sight of his dreams while he was chasing ambition.

Once he got that promotion, he could go back to doing the things he wanted to do. He was a successful architect, whether his father wanted to believe it or not. Sebastian had worked too hard to get where he was to walk away from it all now.

Did he want to walk away from Winslow?

Chapter 10

Good business stems from good relationships.

They'd reached the time of night where giddiness kicked in and everything was funny. Kathleen looked at the crown molding profile Aria Walton—*The* Aria Walton, Kathleen was still squealing inside—had said she wanted to see a sample of, and giggled. The straight runs were standard, but at three o'clock in the morning the corner piece looked to Kathleen like a poop emoji.

"What's so funny?" Sebastian asked.

She cleared her throat and tried to sober up. "Nothing."

He straightened and crossed his arms. "Clearly something's amusing you."

And then she laughed, picturing a meme of Queen Victoria with the words, "We are not amused."

Sebastian's smile was more of a smirk, as if he fought his humor. "Are you going to share?"

"It's late," she said, stopping to catch her breath between laughter. "That magic hour when everything sounds funny. The profile of the molding, an oddly phrased remark, a typo in my notes."

He leaned over his computer once more. They weren't kidding when they told her he was a workaholic. Did the man never laugh?

"Are you always so focused?" she asked.

"If you expect to get ahead in this business, you need to be." He looked at her, then leaned back. "I was like you. Once. I could look at an old warehouse and see loft apartments. See abandoned schools and picture a mall of boutique shops. A boarded-up mansion as a civic center." His smile turned nostalgic.

"You should do that. Old buildings have such potential. Why did you change your mind?"

He shrugged. "The real world caught up to me. Those abandoned buildings? There isn't enough money to do the renovations, or people lack the vision…" Sebastian scowled. "I've had great opportunities at Winslow, the kind that have given me new goals. I'm on the fast track to be promoted."

"So that's what it's all about? Sacrificing what you want to do in favor of a promotion?"

He narrowed his eyes. "I wouldn't say I've sacrificed my vision," he said slowly. "I'd still like to resurrect dead buildings. A promotion may give me more opportunities to choose my own projects." He leaned back, a more relaxed smile taking over. "You remember Hurricane Katrina? That was my first trip to New Orleans, the reason I pursued a license here. While the goal might not have been restoration, rebuilding homes for people who'd lost everything gives you a real sense you've done something worthwhile."

The arrogant, dismissive Sebastian Brooks doing humanitarian work? Had she misjudged him?

"And now the only restoration I get to do is homes like Aria Walton's, clients with big pockets." He shook his head. "It must be the witching hour if you've got me harking back to my old dreams."

"You could still volunteer," she said quietly.

"Barrett has my nose to the grindstone. Not enough hours in the day. Once I get this promotion, I hope to be able to manage my schedule to do more of those types of projects."

A piece of her heart softened toward Sebastian. "Then I hope you get that promotion."

———⁂———

For a split second, Sebastian imagined he saw a man behind Kathleen, hazy and not quite in focus. The man's dark hair was tied back and he had a full moustache. His clothes were out of date—a hundred years out of date. Her ghost? The late hour was playing tricks on him, and Sebastian had to laugh at his own imagination.

"What's so funny?" Kathleen asked.

"You're probably right when you say the late hour distorts everything into a joke."

"You should laugh more often," Kathleen said. "My ma always says laughter is one of the secrets to our souls. It makes us whole."

The secrets to our souls. Like the ones she'd shared with her sister at the restaurant? "You know, I'm not as stiff as you think I am," he said before he had a chance to consider his words.

The look in her eyes told him he'd caught her by surprise. "I never said you were stiff."

"Didn't you?"

She closed her computer, studying him intently. He liked 'intently.'

Blame his response on the intimacy of the late hour or blame it on the presentation she'd given this afternoon, but he suddenly wanted Kathleen to tell *him* all the things he'd overheard her tell her sister. "Do you know where I met Aria for dinner?" he continued.

"No, I don't think you told me."

"I met her at a creole restaurant in the French Quarter. Coincidentally, the same restaurant where you met your sister."

Her eyes grew round. She shook her head as if to convince herself she was misunderstanding his implication. But it was true. He was there.

"No," she said. "I would have seen you. There would have been a hullabaloo over an Aria Walton sighting."

"Celebrity sightings aren't unusual in New Orleans. You didn't see me because we were sitting back to back, you and I."

She put a hand to her heart and her cheeks flushed that pretty shade of red that made her freckles stand out.

"I don't believe you," she said.

He was enjoying her discomfort more than he should. Kathleen had a way of upending his world, and he relished returning the favor. He hadn't felt so alive in… five years? "Your sister's hair is a darker red than yours, more the color of a copper penny."

She crossed her arms. "Okay, so you saw us."

Did he dare to continue? To let her know he'd overheard most of their conversation? Her words had distracted him, made him look inattentive to the client. No, he wasn't done making her squirm. "You apparently changed your mind about propositioning your waiter."

Kathleen shot to her feet.

Sebastian rubbed his eyes. Why had he provoked her? They had been working too long, past the point of coherent thought. They both needed rest. He glanced at her, at her horrified expression. He wasn't too pleased with himself, either. He was the senior project manager, she was his associate. Better to keep that in mind.

"Before tonight, I'd planned to send you home," he told her. "I don't think you're right for this project."

Her hands went to her hips. "I have been working my ass off, and you know it."

Sebastian rounded the coffee table to stand beside her. "Yes, I do know, but you're a distraction, and I'm still not sure what your game is." He shook his head. "I *have* seen you in the elevator at Winslow. With your hair down." He wound a curl around one of his fingers. Okay, maybe he shouldn't have gone there. His heart pounded an unfamiliar rhythm. He was too close. Was that why he could *see* her response? Kathleen had told her sister she was a woman in a drought.

Her voice was raspy. "So you're going to fire me?"

"I can't. Aria wants you on her project." The late hour had apparently affected his voice as well, or the lack of distance between them. She had a way of clouding his vision, his common sense.

Sebastian wove his hands into her hair and kissed her. She sighed against his lips and returned the kiss, sliding her hands around his waist as she took a step closer, pressing her body to his. He slid his hands to her waist, pulling her tight.

And then he stepped away. Now she had grounds for her sexual harassment claims. He'd fallen right into her trap. "I'm sorry."

"No," she whispered.

He might have thought he had the upper hand when he'd told her he'd overheard her, but he was right back on his heels, reeling from the effect she had on him. "That shouldn't have happened. I apologize."

"Don't you dare." Kathleen filled the void he'd created between them and kissed him, intertwined her fingers with his. She lifted his hand to shoulder height between them. "You're not sorry any more than I am." She brought his hand to her breast. "Okay, so you overheard me talking to my sister. What are you going to do about it?"

He cupped the breast reflexively, ran a thumb across the pebbled peak, and then stepped away again.

"I'm going to walk away," he said. "I'm your boss and I won't open myself up to charges of inappropriate behavior."

Kathleen laughed. "And if I'm the one who initiates said inappropriate behavior? That puts you in the clear, doesn't it?"

Could he believe her? He shook a finger at her. "Winslow Designs frowns on fraternization between employees. This is a bad idea."

"Oh, that's right." Blue lightning flashed in her eyes. "I almost forgot about your friend. The one you want to give an engagement ring to. I'm sure she's much more predictable. Like you. Always does what she's supposed to."

What was he thinking? He intended to propose to Renee. He had no intention of—what exactly was he doing with Kathleen? "That's right."

Kathleen nodded, tears in her eyes. "If you'll excuse me, I think I'll go find that waiter. Someone more my speed who knows how to have fun."

Something kicked inside him. Images of Kathleen kissing another man, inviting him to touch her, clouded over Sebastian's good sense once more. He couldn't let her go. Couldn't send her to another man, and yet he didn't dare take her himself, as much as he wanted to. "No, you're going to stay here and we're going to work on the feedback on the construction designs we've received from Chicago."

She swallowed hard, straightened her shirt and sat. "Yes, sir."

Sebastian wiped a hand across his face, turned, and adjusted his pants. He'd probably killed his chances for promotion with one impulsive decision. Kathleen had the power to sabotage his career, and yet he couldn't find the sense to regret kissing her.

Chapter 11

Don't follow someone else's path. Blaze the trail.

Kathleen's eyes were bleary. She'd gone to bed somewhere around four a.m., and now, five hours later, she and Sebastian were back to work in the suite's parlor.

She'd tried to sleep, but she'd spent too much time trying to figure out why Sebastian had kissed her. He had to be messing with her head after what he'd overheard at the restaurant.

And what had she told Siobhan? Other than she wanted to take the waiter home, that is, but she'd been joking.

Sebastian's kiss, on the other hand, was no joke. For a moment, she'd been convinced he could be impulsive, and then he'd pulled away. No, more like he was getting even with her for being too outspoken. He'd definitely gotten even, and then some.

She stared at the floor plan. Something didn't feel right about the feedback she'd received from the Chicago team when comparing the drawings to what she remembered from the house.

Why couldn't she concentrate?

No sleep. Yeah, that was part of it. She'd replayed Sebastian's kiss on a loop all night. He might have been kidding when he started out, but things had gotten pretty heated pretty fast. Or maybe that was her body-in-a-drought talking. And he *knew* she was in a drought.

What was the female equivalent of blue balls?

She looked up and found Sebastian staring at her. "What?" she said curtly.

He winced. "You'd mentioned the plantations," he said. "Asked about notched and pegged joints."

Kathleen tilted her head. What was he driving at?

Sebastian raised his arms over his head in an exaggerated stretch. "You could check with the concierge about a plantation tour while I try to put Aria's plans together. It's Sunday. You deserve a day of rest."

"What about you?"

His smile bordered sarcastic. "I don't have the time to spare. Aria wants…"

"Which is why I should help."

He winced again and tugged on his ear. "Actually, I think I could get more done without you, not that you haven't done an excellent job."

So why did she suddenly feel like she wanted to cry?

"You could call your sister," he suggested. "Spend some time with her."

He was preparing to fire her, she knew it.

"Who knows," he went on. "You might be inspired by something and give Aria another suggestion for her house."

"From a plantation?" she asked skeptically.

"You never know. The tours probably leave early, so you might want to look into it."

He wanted to get rid of her? She'd go.

Kathleen sighed and gave him a forced smile. "Fine." She marched into her room and changed into shorts and a short-sleeved shirt, grabbed her phone and her purse and stormed out.

In the lobby, she checked with the concierge and managed to secure a seat on a tour that would be leaving within the next half hour. While she waited, she called to see if Siobhan could join her.

"Oh, honey, I wish you'd have told me sooner," Siobhan said. "Jared and I are running to Baton Rouge today."

"Sorry, I only just found out I was released for the day." She frowned and lowered her voice. "And maybe permanently."

"What did you say?"

Kathleen forced another smile. "Nothing. Just tired and overworked. My boss has me upside down. My body clock is off, my mood is off." Her hormones were off, too, but she didn't need to mention that. She looked up to see a tour guide holding a sign in the lobby. "Looks like the van is here. I gotta go."

"Talk to you soon?" Siobhan said.

"Yep. I'll let you know if the boss decides to give me more time off." Or decided to fire her before they left New Orleans.

⁕

The look on Kathleen's face when she left made Sebastian feel like a jerk, but until he could regroup, she was better out of his way. No more slip-ups. They were on a tight deadline to deliver something Aria could approve, and he was having enough trouble concentrating without Kathleen sitting across the table from him.

He leaned into the sofa, closed his eyes and tilted his head to the ceiling.

Okay. He'd kissed her. Lapse in judgment due to the late hour. He'd be more diligent to make sure it didn't happen a second time. Except he couldn't get the taste of her out of his mind, the feel of her in his arms.

How long had it been since he'd made a pass at a woman? There was Renee, once, but that was less of a pass and more of a negotiation. A convenient arrangement.

Renee had never responded to him the way Kathleen had.

Sebastian shook his head and focused on Aria's plans. Something felt wrong.

He scoffed. His whole life was wrong, but he was too damn distracted to pinpoint how to fix it.

He reached for his briefcase and retrieved his flash drive, plugged it into his computer, and opened the plans for the house he wanted to build for himself. That always helped to center him. Would he ever finish tweaking the floor plan?

Sebastian added Eastlake moldings to the front porch, similar to what he'd seen here in the Garden District, then tried dentil molding like Kathleen had added to Aria's house. What would Kathleen add to his plans?

And he was back to thinking about Kathleen again.

He went to the second floor of his layout, the two loft rooms, and began adding scaled furniture. The loft would give him distance from the everyday living space, the perfect place for an office. A desk. A bookshelf. A drafting board.

Without thinking, he dragged random pieces of furniture into the second loft room on the opposite side of the staircase, and then looked at what he'd done.

A crib?

Sebastian pushed his laptop away, staring at the screen. Did he want kids? From what he knew of Renee, she certainly didn't seem interested in children. For that matter, Renee probably wouldn't be interested in a cozy Craftsman house. She'd want a showplace, like his father had built, the kind of place you could get lost in.

He didn't want a showplace.

What about his promotion?

He'd earned the damn promotion on his own merits. As long as he kept his nose clean, and that meant staying away from Kathleen, Winslow didn't have a valid reason to deny him his right. It was too late to produce a wife now anyway. Promotion decisions were likely already made. They would be announced a week from tomorrow.

Sebastian tugged on his ear and closed his laptop. He glanced at the opposite sofa, the place Kathleen occupied when she was working.

Kathleen would appreciate his Craftsman house, he was sure of it.

With a groan of frustration, Sebastian jumped to his feet. Kathleen was off limits, even if he wanted to be with her, which he definitely didn't. She was impulsive and unruly and would wreak havoc on his neatly-ordered life. Any fraternization with Kathleen would derail his career faster than Shep Collier's design flaws.

And he couldn't stop thinking about her while he was sitting in this hotel parlor.

He was going to Aria's house. Maybe if he went over there he could concentrate.

Chapter 12

You can't have a bad day with a good attitude.

When Kathleen emerged from her bedroom to the parlor at nine o'clock on Monday morning, Sebastian wasn't there yet. She took the initiative to order breakfast for the two of them—see how *he* liked having someone order *his* food—and when she turned on her computer to check emails, she discovered one from him. He'd already gone out.

He might have told her.

The knock on the parlor door was too soon for breakfast to have arrived. When she opened the door, Aria Walton smiled at her. Kathleen still wanted to squeal, but she was supposed to be professional. No fangirling allowed.

"Is Sebastian here?" Aria asked.

Kathleen stepped aside. "No, he had a meeting with the Historical Landmark Commission. Won't you come in?"

Aria smiled at her and sashayed past. "I wanted to follow up on my revisions to the plans. As long as they are doable, I'm ready to approve them. How quickly do you think we can get this started? I have to leave town this afternoon, so I thought I'd stop by on my way to the airport to make sure everything's in order."

"We have to wait for contractor drawings, but we can get a preliminary demolition permit while we're waiting. That would allow us to pull down the millwork and have it stripped and re-stained, and any repair work to the floors to begin."

Aria took Kathleen's hand. "I have to tell you, I'm very excited. When Sebastian found out you'd sent the wrong plans, he had a hard time recovering. He isn't used to being off balance. But I'm glad you screwed up."

Kathleen cringed. "It was an honest mistake. I had a mild case of heat exhaustion and wasn't thinking clearly when I sent that email."

"You saved the project," Aria whispered conspiratorially. "Don't get me wrong, Sebastian is a fine architect, but he lacks the imagination you showed with your designs. May I say something that might be out of line?"

Kathleen's heart skipped a beat. "I guess so?"

"One of the reasons I like to work with Sebastian is because he's so sober-minded. When you're in my position…" She hesitated, then chuckled. "Men tend to want to try for the Hollywood movie star, if you know what I mean. Sebastian has never been anything but professional. It's refreshing, if a bit sobering, but I appreciate that he's all business."

Kathleen lowered her eyes, aware of her own tendency to be star struck in Aria's presence. "Yes, I can see how that might be a problem. And I apologize if I've acted like a ninny."

Aria squeezed Kathleen's hand again. "No, I'm used to that. What I'm getting at—and this is the inappropriate comment—is I've seen the way you look at him. He's too wrapped up in his job, too uptight. That makes him a great architect, but in my experience, those types make lousy lovers."

Kathleen laughed. Hadn't she thought the same thing? And yet that kiss last night… "I'm sure I wouldn't know about the latter."

"No, but you wish you did. The way you responded to even the most innocent touch, when he handed you your pen. A woman like you deserves a man who will be as passionate and outgoing as you are."

Kathleen took a step back. Did she look at Sebastian the way Aria said? "I assure you, our relationship is strictly business. He's my boss."

"Right." Aria brushed at her sundress and fluffed her hair. She smiled. "You'll tell him to let me know if my revisions are workable? And I'll expect a start date in his next email. It's been a pleasure meeting you, Kathleen. More than you know." She opened the door and walked out with a finger wave over her shoulder.

And what was that supposed to mean? Kathleen had *not* been ogling Sebastian, had she? She'd been too nervous during her presentation to pay attention to the boss in the room, although once they'd gone to the second story…

He'd used her plans. Added her designs to his for the presentation. Okay, so she'd pictured him pressing her against a wall, telling her she'd saved the day with her sketches for the first floor. Kissing her face, her neck, her mouth, his hands all over her.

She'd totally been ogling him. Was that why he'd kissed her?

No, he'd been messing with her. Sebastian Brooks wasn't likely to kiss her a second time. Aria was right. He was too absorbed in his work to notice Kathleen other than her pathetic case of hero worship.

Sebastian Brooks was a jerk.

Sebastian returned to the suite triumphant.

The Historic Landmark District Commission had given preliminary approval for the renovation and, as Kathleen had predicted based on her visit to City Hall, they were eager to see this project started.

He and Kathleen went through the building codes to make sure the plans were in compliance and started the permit applications while contractor drawings were being pushed along with the Chicago team. The project was moving forward at an accelerated rate.

So why was Kathleen so subdued? Her usual exuberance was missing. Because they were doing the mundane tasks? Or had she been offended by the kiss—a kiss he still couldn't get out of his head?

"I thought you might like to visit an oyster bar for dinner," he suggested. "When in New Orleans, and all of that."

She grimaced. "Sorry. Not a fan of oysters. I have to draw the line somewhere."

Did he dare pursue what was bothering her? Yes. He had to know. What would she do with what happened the other night? "You seem a little off. Are you well?"

She gave him a wan smile. "Yes, I'm just very tired. We've been putting in long hours."

"Maybe you'd like another visit with your sister and an early night, for a change."

Her eyes lit up, and he was jealous again of the bond she shared with her sister. What was it like to have someone you cared that much about? Someone you could share confidences with?

"They've been busy. I was hoping to see my brother-in-law," she said, "but he's on a job in Baton

Rouge. I can email the project I had for him and hopefully he can take care of it on his own. Honestly? I'm too tired to go out."

Then it wasn't the kiss. Sebastian considered pointing out the long hours he was used to keeping and how she'd need to suck it up if she wanted to get ahead, but the words felt empty. *There's more to life, Dad.* Hadn't he said that once upon a time? And here he was, a breath away from selling the same all-work mentality to Kathleen.

"I'll order dinner in," she said. "What about you? You want something or are you going out?"

Kathleen by candlelight, in a hotel suite, her hair curling around her shoulders. No, without work to distract him, staying in tonight would be a bad idea.

"I think I'll check out Lagasse's place. You sure you don't want to come along?"

"I'd fall asleep in my soup," she joked with a tired smile.

"Get some rest then, and I'll see you tomorrow."

<hr>

Kathleen's circadian rhythm was messed up. She woke up sometime in the middle of the night and pulled back the curtains to her balcony overlooking St. Charles Street.

The door to the parlor opened slowly and she rolled her eyes. "Oh, you're not starting this again, are you?" she asked the ghost.

"Dance with me," he said, bowing, a soft glow surrounding him in the dark room on the other side of the door.

"And how will we do that? I can't touch you, can I?"

"Sadly, no, but you can see me, and you have enough imagination to pretend. Amuse me. Until I can find my rest, haunting these hallways is dreadfully boring."

"You're a terrible flirt. It's no wonder your wife killed you."

"No, Cherie, she killed me in the pursuit of money. You might be surprised to know that despite our separation, I remained true to her." He held out a hand. "One dance? You can turn on that device that plays music."

"My phone? It'll wake Sebastian."

"With those things in your ears, he won't hear."

"Will you?" she asked.

"But, of course."

Why not. Kathleen retrieved her phone and earbuds from the nightstand. She scrolled through her playlist, to the classical songs she used when she needed to concentrate. "A waltz?" she whispered, creeping into the parlor. She checked the room to be sure Sebastian hadn't remained behind.

"A gavotte."

She chuckled. "I don't know how to gavotte. I don't even know what it is other than a reference in a Carly Simon song."

"Close your eyes and I will guide you. Take my hand," Victor instructed her.

"Figuratively speaking, of course."

"Close your eyes," he said again.

She played a track from Handel's Water Music, raised her arms from her sides to a four o'clock and ten o'clock position and closed her eyes. This was silly. She wanted to twist and shout, to blast her favorite rock and roll song, and yet a sense of peace washed over her.

As if in a dream, Victor guided her. He turned her in a circle and guided her steps, told her how many steps to take and when to hop.

"Excellent, Cherie," he whispered.

She gave in to the sensation, gliding through the open spaces in the parlor with her ghostly partner and humming along to the music in her ears. He stopped, and Kathleen opened her eyes. "Not yet," Victor told her. "You haven't finished your dance."

She closed her eyes again and imagined the touch of his hands on hers, leading her through the next steps. From behind, she was sure she felt his hands on her waist, gliding in time to the music. And then he turned her to face him, realigning her arms at four and ten. She bent to each side in time with the music, letting the tune carry her until her ankle brushed the coffee table. She opened her eyes to get her bearings and found herself in Sebastian's arms.

She stepped away quickly. "Oh." And then she remembered what she was wearing—her pajamas. A cami and running shorts. Sebastian wasn't wearing much more, shorts and a t-shirt.

"I couldn't resist stepping in when I saw you dancing," he said. "I hope you don't mind."

She swallowed hard.

"Unless you were dancing with your ghost?" he asked, brows up.

Victor was nowhere to be seen. "I'm afraid the ghost is a bit of a prankster. I didn't mean to disturb you."

Sebastian stepped into her personal space once more. "In case I haven't told you, you've done excellent work on Aria's project. I should have taken you out to celebrate your first presentation."

Now he wanted to compliment her work? "You offered, and you didn't think they recommended me for this project based on my looks, did you?" she groused.

"Didn't they?" he asked.

"What's that supposed to mean?"

He was an inch away, but she was determined to hold her ground—her body, sensing a man in close proximity, begged her to step into that last inch between them. Her responses were at war with her good sense.

Her good sense had never been dependable in a fight.

Sebastian brushed her hair behind her shoulders. "You are very attractive."

A stiff compliment if ever she heard one, and yet he stood before her, an opportunity to quench her thirst.

He's a jerk AND he's your boss. She wasn't getting drawn into his dark sense of humor again.

Except he'd told her she'd done good work. He'd taken care of her when heat exhaustion put her down for the count. Half-naked in the dark, he called to her sense of adventure. Forbidden fruit. Kathleen licked her dry lips, eye to eye with Sebastian Brooks, in a standoff.

He'd said he was worried about being accused of sexual harassment, but if she made the first move… She kissed him before she knew she was going to.

What good sense?

Hands on his hips, she pulled him closer. He molded to her, his hardness against her belly. Sebastian wove his hands into her hair and met her tongue, stroke for mesmerizing stroke. His hands roamed her back and cupped her bottom before he groaned and pulled away, forehead to forehead.

Was he going to leave her hanging again?

"You were going to chase down a waiter," he said, his voice husky. "For one night?"

She nodded and he kissed her again, then met her dreamy gaze.

"One night?" he repeated, less of a question and more of an offer.

Yes, please. She nodded again.

"You and me?" he said. "No lawsuit?"

She smiled. "No lawsuit." She drew a finger across her chest. "Cross my heart."

His hands slid under her cami, traveled to the front and cupped her breasts. He eased her to the sofa and pulled the cami over her head. "So beautiful," he whispered, before he lowered his head to lick her happy nipples.

She flattened her hands against his chest and arched her back. "We're going to have to move to the main event," she said. "I'm dying here." She reached for his shorts and released his erection.

Sebastian stopped her. "I don't have a condom."

"I'm on the pill."

"Yes, but is that safe?"

She rolled her eyes. "I haven't been with anyone since my last relationship, and he and I were both tested. So unless there's something you plan to share with me, I'm clean."

Still he hesitated.

"Damn it, Sebastian. If you leave me hanging again, I will bring that lawsuit. Take a chance. Have a little fun. We can forget this ever happened tomorrow. I want you inside me. Now."

Apparently that was all the invitation he needed. He yanked down her shorts, pushed her to the sofa and slid into her with a growl.

She was doing this. With her boss. On a sofa. It was wrong on so many levels, and yet her body was high-fiving her, thanking her for bringing on the relief. Kathleen leaned forward to kiss him and his eyes opened. He looked shocked for a moment. Startled. Had he been imagining his 'friend?'

"You need to keep those eyes open," she told him. "We're in this together, you and me, and I want to make sure you're with me."

He stopped and tried to pull away, but she grabbed his butt and held him in place. "Too late," she told him.

He closed his eyes again.

"Look at me."

Sebastian opened his eyes and she moved beneath him, drawing him in, easing back, setting the pace for their horizontal dance. Reminding him what they were doing. His body responded, moving in an ancient rhythm that came as naturally as breathing. Gently at first, as if he was afraid he'd hurt her.

"Don't you dare hold back," she whispered. "I want to feel you. All of you."

"My pleasure." His voice sent shivers all through her body as he renewed his efforts with more enthusiasm, filling her, stretching her, pounding deep inside her.

Oh yeah. This is what she needed. Her body hummed with delight. "Yes," she whispered, her own eyes rolling back with the way he made her feel.

He dipped his head and laved her breast, returning his gaze to hers as he braced himself over her, driving her to the edge.

And then he stopped.

"What?" she gasped.

"I could swear I heard someone laughing. A man."

Kathleen groaned and rolled out from under him. "Honest to God." She sat up and pulled her cami on.

"What?" he asked.

"And you accuse me of lack of focus."

"Didn't you hear him?"

"So now you hear the ghost?"

And then she heard the laughter. Victor.

"You were right," she told Sebastian. "This was a mistake." She leaned over to retrieve her discarded shorts and Sebastian flipped her to her knees.

"No," he said. "You wanted this, we're going to finish this. One night."

He positioned himself behind her and slid home. "Tell me you want me."

Her body thrilled with the invasion. "I want you."

"All of me." He drove into her again and again.

His passion ignited hers and she cried out as her world shattered into a million pieces. What do you know? There was more to the unapproachable bastard than he let on. He groaned, his climax lighting up all her nerve endings a second time. He shuddered and slowed, but he didn't withdraw. Sebastian leaned over her and kissed her shoulder, continuing to thrust gently so as not to dislodge himself.

"Kathleen," he whispered.

He was with her, then. She smiled, moving in rhythm with him, as gentle as a touch and far more intimate. His hands snaked around her sides and cupped her breasts, tweaking her nipples.

"Kathleen," he whispered again. He pulsed inside her, and then again. Sebastian took hold of her hips, pushed himself upright. His strokes became more deliberate. She knew he'd finished, felt the aftermath inside her with each motion, and yet he was still hard—or hard again, renewing his efforts.

The waiter probably couldn't have done that. Russ never had.

"Rock my world," Sebastian whispered. "I need you again."

"Yes," was all she could say. Still wound tight, it didn't take long until she was on the verge again. He slid a hand around her hip, toward their connection, and stroked her wet nub. Fireworks went off inside her brain, and when she could breathe again, Sebastian was groaning and shuddering a second time.

This time, he fell out. Sebastian shifted to the sofa beside her and pulled her into his arms. He leaned back, eyes closed. "Damn, woman."

She wanted to return the compliment, but she was speechless. Sebastian may have hidden his passion down deep, but it was most definitely there. If she wasn't careful, she might actually grow to like the man.

* * *

Sebastian woke up curled around something soft and warm. He opened his eyes and discovered it was Kathleen. They were still on the sofa, stretched out along the length of it.

He'd spent the night with her. Sleeping with her. Sticky with what they'd done together.

One night.

He rolled over and fell on the floor.

This was bad.

He wiped a hand over his face and glanced around. What if she'd been lying and she wasn't on the pill? What if she filed that sexual harassment lawsuit?

He'd filled her full of his DNA and, God help him, he wanted to do it again.

Sebastian scrambled to his feet and retreated to his bedroom, where he paced. He couldn't remember ever losing control like that, he'd never gone twice without stopping, and he'd never spent an entire night with a woman.

Sex with Renee was satisfactory—hell, he'd been willing to consider making that the standard for the rest of his life.

Had been?

He shook his head to clear it. Renee represented stability and structure, the things he needed to succeed. Yes, the sex was merely transactional, but he knew what he was getting into with Renee. Kathleen represented mayhem. Unstructured, undisciplined, wild.

Renee represented the clean lines of a skyscraper, able to sway gently against the wind when storms hit. Kathleen represented the storm, tearing his world apart.

He'd worked too hard to sacrifice his efforts now, when that promotion was within his grasp.

One night.

He peeked into the parlor. She had curled up on the couch, her hair like a red bird's nest rioting around her head. Sebastian's cock twitched to join her again, but they'd made an agreement, he and Kathleen. One night. Any more of a relationship with her would be messy, personally and professionally. It was time to get his head back in the game.

Chapter 13

There's no place for romance in the workplace

Kathleen rolled over—and fell to the floor.

Where was she? One minute she'd been looking out over St. Charles Street, and then she'd been dancing with a ghost, and then...

Telling Sebastian exactly what she wanted him to do to her. In graphic detail.

Her stomach fluttered, her drought ended. But the need remained. Who knew men could go twice in a row like that?

She crossed to his closed bedroom door and knocked, fully prepared to climb him, or push him down on the bed, or whatever it took to get him inside her again.

Talk about your still waters running deep.

When he didn't answer, she tried the door and it opened. He wasn't there.

One night.

He had contractor appointments this morning, and she'd slept late.

She retreated to her own bedroom to shower and dress for the day.

When she returned to the parlor, she opened her computer to check for emails. Maybe he'd left her instructions.

Or a severance package.

His absence was palpable. The excitement about the project subdued. The apathy she'd felt with Russ provided a sharp contrast to the stimulation Sebastian provided.

"You look distressed, Cherie," Victor said, appearing on the sofa across from her.

"I don't know how to help you," she told him. "And I don't appreciate you amusing yourself at my expense."

He waved a ghostly hand in the air. "Life is wasted on those who will not live it." He leaned forward. "And you *can* help me."

She patted her chest. "I can't. I sent Jared an email and he said he'd come when he could. I don't even know if he can help you."

"And if I was your mother, on my deathbed, and this Jared was a doctor, would you have me wait until he was available?"

"A hundred fifty years, Victor. You can't wait another week?"

He grew large in front of her. "One hundred fifty years of one more week. Until I'm able to move on, I have no choice but to amuse myself at the expense of others, *non?*"

Kathleen picked up her cell phone and dialed Siobhan.

"Hey, I'm at work. I can't really talk," Siobhan answered. "What's up?"

"The ghost. He's impatient. Is there any way for Jared to get here sooner?"

"What about the boss? I thought you were trying to keep a low profile with the ghost thing so he wouldn't think you were a nutjob."

Kathleen checked her emails and opened the one from Sebastian, the schedule for the next couple of days. "The boss is just going to have to spare me for a few minutes. He doesn't need to know. We should be able to take care of things from my room."

"I'll see what I can do and let you know. Maybe we can run over at lunchtime. Gotta run. Love ya, bye."

***

Sebastian sat at a table in a bar on Bourbon Street waiting for the contractor he was scheduled to meet. He checked over the first set of drawings from the team in Chicago, writing notations in block letters. He stopped when he reviewed the arched doorways Kathleen had added. They were a nice touch, one he hadn't thought of. She was good, in more ways than one.

In spite of his shower this morning, he couldn't seem to escape the scent of her, and his fingers tingled, remembering the feel of her skin.

"Can I get you something to drink?" a waitress asked.

"Manhattan," he said reflexively. He checked his watch as she walked away. Eleven o'clock in the morning? He raised a hand to call the waitress, but she didn't see him. A drink would help him get his mind back in the game. Kathleen had a way of disrupting his thoughts.

He couldn't date Kathleen, even if he wanted to. In the first place, he didn't have time for a girlfriend. In the second place, they'd both get fired for fraternizing. And in the third place, he already had a girlfriend. Kind of.

Renee was the perfect woman. He pictured her dressed in a smooth gray silk sheath, her dark hair cut short, creamy skin—the contrast might have accounted for why he'd commented on Kathleen's freckles and her make-up. Renee's makeup hid every imperfection, every blemish. She had a practiced smile, one that, by comparison with Kathleen's, didn't seem quite genuine.

No, Renee was the perfect woman. He'd already made the decision to propose to her when he got back. A proposal would boost both their careers. Hadn't Renee mentioned the same reluctance to promote an unmarried woman? And Barrett had mentioned the stability of a wife would aid Sebastian's career growth.

Sebastian's promotion was within reach.

The waitress brought him his cocktail. Drinking at this time of day felt wrong, but after the night he'd had with Kathleen, the disorder she'd thrown into his life, he needed it.

A tall man approached the table in blue jeans and a light blue denim shirt. Embroidered over the pocket was the Pierce Brothers logo.

"Mr. Brooks?" the man asked.

Pierce Brothers was bidding on the finish work. Sebastian rose to his feet to shake the man's hand. "Troy Pierce, I presume?" He motioned to the seat.

The waitress reappeared, smiling and flipping her hair. "Can I get you something, sugar?" she asked Troy.

"A sweet tea would be perfect," he told her, giving her a broad smile.

She returned the smile, did a funny sort of wiggle, and walked away.

Interesting. Sebastian assessed the carpenter across from him. Was it the earthy quality about him or the man's looks that had the waitress flirting with Pierce? Would Kathleen be attracted to him?

Sebastian tugged his ear. Why did he care?

"Somethin' wrong?" Pierce asked. "You look angry."

"No. No." He managed a smile. "Sorry, I'm preoccupied this morning. Why don't you tell me what your company can do."

The waitress set Pierce's tea in front of him and asked Sebastian if he wanted a refill.

"Not right now," he told her.

The waitress glanced at Pierce and turned up the wattage on her smile. He gave her a wink and she walked away again.

Pierce presented his marketing material along with testimonials from satisfied customers. He and his brother were based out of a suburb of New Orleans and were currently doing renovations at one of the plantations out of town. They'd done work in the Garden District as well as the French Quarter. And their quote was reasonable.

So why couldn't Sebastian get the image of the waitress flirting with him out of his head? Would Pierce make the same impression on Kathleen?

What the hell was wrong with him?

One night of the best sex he'd ever had, that's what. Sebastian closed his eyes and remembered the weight of Kathleen's hair against his chest, the firmness of her breasts in his hands, the look in her eyes as she'd come apart.

"Mr. Brooks?"

Sebastian wiped a hand across his face. "You know what? Your quote looks great, your references are great. The client's on a tight deadline. What's your availability?"

"We do have this plantation job to finish up, which is taking the bulk of our time over the next month or so, but beyond that, I'm sure we could schedule your job as a priority."

Sebastian opened his phone to his planner and showed Pierce the time frame they hoped to keep to. "We're working at an accelerated pace, and assuming demolition is completed here," he said pointing to the date he had marked on his calendar, "construction can begin here. We'll want an interior decorator onsite as quickly as possible, as the client wants to move in by this date." He pointed to Aria's target.

"That is awful quick," Pierce said, "but I think we can meet your timeline."

"Think?" Sebastian cocked an eyebrow.

Pierce relaxed into a lazy smile. "I'm sure."

Sebastian put his phone away. "Then we'll be in touch, Mr. Pierce."

They rose from their seats, shook hands, and Pierce left the bar.

Sebastian ordered another drink. No flirty smile from the waitress, she was all business.

One night.

He'd made a mistake by giving into temptation with Kathleen, but they'd agreed it would be one night. An anomaly. It wouldn't happen again.

When the waitress set his drink in front of him, Sebastian forced himself to think about Renee. She was the key to this promotion. Smooth, sleek, cultured. Sex with her was... when was the last time they'd had sex?

It had been after a cocktail party and they'd gone to her place. She'd had a business call half an hour later, apologizing and pointing out they only needed ten minutes, right?

No, they rarely needed that long. She undressed herself, he undressed himself, he mounted her, did his thing, and then left. All very straightforward. Most times, she wasn't even interested in a kiss for fear of mussing her lipstick.

Not like the way he'd ravaged Kathleen's mouth, her hands tugging on his shorts, him slipping her cami over her head and bowing to her gorgeous, full breasts. Did Renee even take her bra off when they had sex? He couldn't remember.

He'd popped off twice with Kathleen, without ever leaving the heat of her body, definitely more than ten minutes.

Ten minutes. Hop on, hop off. For the rest of his life. A week ago, that had been enough.

He couldn't propose to Renee, even if it cost him the promotion.

Would it? No, he'd earned this promotion, with or without a wife, no matter what Barrett said, no matter what his father said. Except Barrett was the one making the decision.

Kathleen McCormick threatened to derail him.

Sebastian wiped his face, paid the tab and headed to his next proposal meeting.

Chapter 14

A man should never neglect his family for business – Walt Disney

Jared and Siobhan called from the hotel lobby as Kathleen finished eating her room service lunch. While she gave them her room number, she hooked the swing lock on her hotel room to block it open and went back to her computer to shut it down.

Sebastian had several meetings scheduled, or so he'd told her, but would likely expect to work when he returned. If Jared and Siobhan were still here, he'd have to wait. She was good and done with this ghost.

Jared tapped on her door and pushed it open. "Hey, baby."

Kathleen stepped into a hug. "Thanks for coming." She hugged Siobhan while Jared surveyed the room.

"The concierge says they've had paranormal researchers in the hotel before," Jared said. "And the rumor is when they sat down to discuss what they'd found, management said they'd get back to them. And never did."

"Victor wants to move on," Kathleen told him. "Wouldn't they have tried to help him regardless of whether or not management invited them back? Isn't that their job?"

"Their job is to document the haunting, not necessarily to act on it. That's where people like my daddy and I come into play." He leaned over his knees. "Can I point out you don't look too concerned about this ghost? The first time Siobhan saw one, she was none too pleased."

"He's a pleasant enough gentleman, not frightening, although he has shown he isn't above a practical joke at my expense to amuse himself." Like asking her to dance and then disappearing so Sebastian could cut in. Had Sebastian seen him?

"That doesn't surprise me. You say his name is Victor Mercier?"

"That's what I gathered from the concierge. He's apparently one of the more popular ghosts."

"More than a residual haunting, then. He isn't going through the motions leading up to his death?"

Kathleen raised her eyebrows. "No. He seems to know who he is and where he is, and he wants to move on, to be reunited with his family."

"When does he appear to you?"

"Whenever the hell he feels like it, usually at inopportune times. He has a thing with opening and closing doors."

"A manifestation to call attention to himself. People look at the door to see why it's opening, and those with open minds will see him. The more cynical part of the population will see a malfunctioning door."

Like Sebastian. "Do you think he'll show up if I call to him? He did ask me to help, told me I knew someone, so I would assume he knows who you are and, therefore, maybe he knows you're here?"

Jared's eyes widened. "Interesting. Most ghosts tend to be shy around me, mistrustful." He walked the perimeter of the room, then closed his eyes. While Kathleen watched, an aura brightened around him.

"Have you seen that before?" Kathleen whispered to Siobhan.

"Seen what?"

"The way he glows?"

Siobhan chuckled. "Only in bed." Her brow furrowed. "Wait a minute. Do you mean literally glowing?"

Kathleen pointed to him.

"I don't see anything out of the ordinary," Siobhan said.

"Victor Mercier," Jared called out.

Victor appeared and Siobhan clutched Kathleen's arm. "I don't think I'll ever get used to this," she whispered.

"*Enfin!*" Victor said. "*Etes-vous la luz?* Can you guide me to the light at last?"

"I can try," Jared replied. "Do you have any family you can call on who might walk you home?"

"Helene?" Victor turned in a circle, his voice hollow as it echoed in the suite.

Jared's shoulders rose. He chanted something that sounded like a prayer.

"What's he doing?" Kathleen asked Siobhan.

"Asking for protection," Siobhan whispered. "Something's wrong."

A flash of light brightened the corner of the room.

A woman's voice reverberated. "No."

Jared closed his eyes, his aura growing brighter. "This spirit seeks peace. Let him walk into the light."

An icy breeze lifted the hair on Kathleen's neck.

Siobhan clung to Kathleen. "I should have stayed home. I hate this stuff."

Shadows moved in the corners, and a wisp of a cloud floated toward Victor.

"No," the woman's voice grew louder. Kathleen cupped her ears with her hands.

"Helene?" Victor asked.

Two ghostly hands reached for him from the light. A woman appeared like a hologram, dressed in a long gown with a full skirt, her hair wrapped into a crown of braids.

"*Ma Cherie,*" Victor said, his voice strangled with emotion. He rattled off a string of words in what Kathleen presumed to be French.

Jared cringed, ducked his head. "This man wishes to be reunited with his family on the other side."

The breeze grew in strength, lifting papers from the nightstand, billowing in the curtains. Kathleen's brush slid across the dresser and fell to the floor.

"*C'est impossible.*" The female ghost, presumably Helene, raised an arm and pointed toward the window.

"*Mais la luz,*" Victor said, moving toward the light in the corner. He turned his face to the light, as if it was the sun, and held out his arms. The light seemed to absorb him.

"NO!" the female ghost shrieked. She circled like a tornado until the wind stopped as suddenly as it had started. Both Victor and Helene were gone.

"Where'd they go?" Kathleen asked.

Jared dropped to a knee, the glow gone.

"That's not anything like what you did back in Illinois," Siobhan said softly.

"Each ghost is different," he said.

She went to his side, placed a hand to his shoulder. "You're burning up!" She pulled him to his feet and pressed her hand to his forehead.

"Lots of ghosts in this hotel. They all want to speak."

"Did she take him home?" Kathleen asked. "Into the light?"

Jared shot her a wary glance. "She said that wasn't possible."

"Then where did they go?"

"Do you have a bottle of water?" Siobhan asked Kathleen.

A ghostly sigh echoed in the room while Kathleen retrieved a bottle from the parlor.

"And who is that?" Siobhan asked.

"My guess? Helene," Jared said.

"He went into the light, didn't he?" Kathleen asked. "I saw him. It. Whatever."

Jared gave her a tired grin. "I believe he did, but I can't be for sure." He took a pull from the bottle of water.

"I'm worried about you," Siobhan said. "I haven't seen you like this before."

"I'll be fine in a few minutes," he said. "It's the extra energy you're feeling." Jared held the bottle up to Kathleen in a toast. "Thank you."

"Do you want to lie down? Rest a while?" Kathleen asked.

"I'd be more comfortable somewhere else," Jared said. "There's too much energy in this hotel, and they all know I'm here."

"Didn't you bring your ghost cleansing stuff with you?" Siobhan asked.

Jared took her face in his hands and kissed her. When he pulled away, he had a big smile on his face, and Siobhan looked dazed. He glanced at Kathleen. "You're welcome to come home with us," he told her. "It's a short drive to Vacherie."

"What? For the day? Overnight? I'm sure you both have to go back to work, and if I stayed, I'd have to find a way back in the morning," she said. "And I have a lot of work to do, still."

"I'm concerned about the woman. Helene. Do you know who she is?" Jared asked.

"His wife, I think."

"Then she should have walked him into the light. Why wouldn't she do that?" He asked the question rhetorically.

"Maybe she was still angry with him."

"Angry?" Jared asked.

"Apparently she's the one who killed him, but he said he'd forgiven her, that he didn't blame her, that it was a crime of passion and he didn't believe she meant to."

Jared groaned. "I should have asked you what you knew about him first. Careless on my part."

"Why?" Kathleen asked.

Jared frowned. "If she killed him, she might not want him to move on. As long as he hadn't found his peace, there was no consequence. Now that he has, she'll have to answer for what she's done."

Kathleen wrapped her arms around herself, gooseflesh rising in spite of the New Orleans heat. "So what does that mean?"

Jared shrugged. "Time will tell." He winced. "And I need to leave this place until I've had a chance to build my strength."

"You go on ahead," Siobhan told him. "I need a minute with Kathleen."

Jared nodded. "There's a jazz band playing in the beignet shop. I think I'll go settle there for a bit." He hugged Kathleen. "You'll let me know if you hear any more from Victor?"

"Do you think I will?" she asked.

"This job doesn't come with any guarantees."

Kathleen kissed his cheek. "Thanks for making the trip. I know you're busy."

"It's what I do. Especially for family." He squeezed her hand and waved to Siobhan. "Half an hour, and then I'm going to come and throw you over my shoulder to haul you home."

Siobhan giggled as she closed the door behind him. "And he means it," she told Kathleen. "As for you, I can see the change in you. I want details."

Kathleen raised her eyebrows. "What change?"

"More relaxed?" Siobhan gave way to a silly grin. "When I met you for dinner Friday night, you were bouncing off the walls, and you told me why. It wasn't the waiter. Who was it?"

Kathleen's cheeks heated.

"There. I knew it." Siobhan put her hands on her hips. "Spill, little sister."

She'd been so eager to tell Siobhan about Russ. Why couldn't she tell her about Sebastian?

"I don't have Jared's extra set of skills, but I'm sensing something wonky here. Kathleen Elizabeth McCormick, I have a very uncomfortable feeling."

Kathleen tugged Siobhan to sit on her bed. "He was sitting behind me at the restaurant, the night you and I met for dinner."

"He?" Siobhan's eyes widened. "Do you even know who was at the table behind you? Because I do. Aria Walton. She was with a man, one of those cool, arrogant types. We don't make a big deal about movie star sightings down here. A bunch of them own homes in the Garden District. Are you going to tell me…?" She shook her head. "No, you saw her and now you're messing with me."

"That cool, arrogant type with her—that was my boss."

Siobhan clutched Kathleen's forearms. "You did the horizontal mambo with your boss? No. Kathleen, that guy looked like the type who has no soul. You couldn't have found someone who might actually have fun with you?"

Kathleen giggled. "I would have agreed with you a couple of days ago, but something happened. We've been working ridiculous hours and my sleep cycle is seriously messed up. Victor opened my bedroom door and invited me to dance, and next thing I knew I was dancing with Sebastian. And then I was *dancing* with Sebastian."

Siobhan straightened and folded her arms. "Sleeping with the boss is never a good idea."

"We made an agreement. One night. And once we decided to go through with it, I wouldn't let him do the bump and run. I made sure he was right there with me, and Oh. My. God. Buried inside that cool customer is a red hot…" She closed her eyes, reliving the way he'd touched her, the way she'd been sure he would pull out after the first round, amazed to discover it was only an intermission.

"You would have been smarter to tackle the waiter," Siobhan said. "One night or not, working with him is going to be uncomfortable, especially now that you've seen his inner beast. Red hot generally indicates once is not enough."

Kathleen laughed. "We'll only be here another week, tops, and I can control myself that long. Especially without a playful ghost throwing us at each other."

"So you say."

"I'm pretty sure that cool, arrogant asshole will be the man who walks back into this parlor. Yeah, I'm sure I can leave that alone."

"And if you've rattled his cage? If he suddenly can't live without you?"

Kathleen laughed again. "You haven't met Sebastian Brooks."

Siobhan's phone chimed a text. She checked the display. "Jared says his brother is in the city. He apparently quoted a job today. Want to say hello?"

Troy Pierce was every bit as handsome as his brother, without the scars that gave Jared his rugged looks. They'd had fun together at the wedding, but Troy was a player, something that had been obvious that night and not someone Kathleen wanted to tangle with.

Siobhan tugged her hand. "Won't hurt to say hello."

"You're trying to distract me from what happened."

"You know it."

Kathleen laughed. "I'm not going to sleep with Jared's brother."

Siobhan returned the laugh. "Not asking you to, but those Pierce brothers were definitely blessed when they were handing out genes. Won't hurt to take in a little eye candy, huh?"

Kathleen hesitated. "Is Jared going to be okay? The ghosts can't hurt him, can they?"

"He's been working too hard and he's probably run down. Don't you worry." Siobhan hugged Kathleen.

Siobhan's phone chimed with another text.

"Jared says they're outside the hotel. Come down and say hello to Troy, then you can run back up here to do whatever work you still have to take care of."

What could it hurt? Troy definitely fit the eye candy description from what she remembered, and she could use a reminder that Sebastian had just been the next, closest man to ease her drought. "Okay."

Moments later, they walked through the revolving doors and down the steps toward the street. Live oak trees overtook the parkways, roots lifting large segments of the sidewalk. Kathleen stepped carefully to where Jared and Troy stood waiting for them.

"Still as pretty as ever," Troy said, pulling Kathleen into a hug. He leaned in to kiss her and she turned her head, offering a cheek instead. She wasn't interested in being part of his harem.

Kathleen scowled as she stepped out of his embrace. "I'd say the same," she teased, "except boys aren't supposed to be pretty, are they?" Yes, he was as handsome as they came, but the sparkle in his eye was as roguish as she remembered, always working the crowd for an easy lay.

"Let's go for a drink," Siobhan suggested.

"I really can't," Kathleen said, taking hold of Siobhan's arm and squeezing to send a message. "I still have so much work to do."

"All work and no play," Jared said. "One drink can't hurt."

"I'm afraid in this case, it might." She hugged Siobhan once more, then turned to Jared. "And I do appreciate you making the trip."

"I hope Victor was able to move on," Jared said.

"I haven't seen him again. It seems whatever you did worked. Kathleen turned, and tripped on a jutting edge of the sidewalk. While she windmilled to recapture her balance, someone pushed her toward the street.

Two arms wrapped around her, righting her and pulling her back to safety.

"What the hell?" Kathleen cried out. She looked up to see who she had to thank for saving her from falling into the traffic on St. Charles Street.

Sebastian.

Chapter 15

Don't be afraid to take a chance. The greatest failure is not trying.

Saving Kathleen from falling into traffic nearly sobered Sebastian. Nearly. He'd had way too much to drink for one shot of adrenalin to do the trick.

"What the hell?" Kathleen said again, hands on her hips, looking from her sister, to Troy Pierce, to what appeared to be the other Pierce Brother.

The sister stepped up to take Kathleen away from Sebastian. "Are you okay?" she asked.

"Who the hell pushed me toward the street?" Kathleen asked.

Sebastian glanced around, certain he'd been hallucinating. He *was* drunk, after all. Yes, he'd seen a woman dressed in period clothing extend both arms and give Kathleen a shove, but a second later, the woman was gone. Vanished. He wiped a hand across his face to clear his vision, but whatever he thought he'd seen was gone.

"No one pushed you, sweetie," her sister said. "You tripped."

Kathleen turned toward Sebastian, her mouth drawn tight. "Thank you."

"Yes, thank you," the second Pierce brother said.

"Mr. Brooks," Troy Pierce said. "Nice to see you again, and I'd like to thank you…"

Sebastian reached back and threw a fist at the man who'd kissed Kathleen moments earlier. He immediately grabbed his injured hand and bent over in pain.

Troy crouched into attack position, but his brother held him back.

"What was that for?" Troy growled. He shrugged free of his brother and took a step back.

Kathleen grabbed Sebastian by the arm and steered him toward the hotel. "What the hell?" she said yet again.

Sebastian did his best to narrow his eyes, but his vision wasn't working as well as it should be. "Saw him try to kiss you. You didn't appear to appreciate the gesture. Thought you might need help."

Her lips pursed again and she turned toward her sister. "Siobhan Pierce, Jared Pierce, Troy Pierce. My boss, Sebastian Brooks."

"We've met," Troy said, holding his jaw.

"Troy is my sister's brother-in-law," she told Sebastian. "Apologize."

And yet she'd clearly been uncomfortable when Troy had tried to kiss her, not a warm family gesture.

Her hands went to her hips again as she gave Sebastian a pointed look. Then she offered an apologetic smile to her company of friends. Or family. Or whatever they were. Okay, he might have misread her expression. Didn't mean he was sorry he'd slugged the guy. Troy had kissed Kathleen. No one should be kissing Kathleen except for Sebastian.

"Sorry if I misread the situation," Sebastian grumbled, even though he was sure he hadn't.

"Go sleep it off, buddy," Troy told him before he took Kathleen's hand. "You going to be okay with this guy?"

Kathleen was giggling again. Because Troy had called him buddy or because he'd taken her hand?

"Yes. I'm sorry, Troy," Kathleen said, withdrawing her hand. "It was nice to see you again, but we should get back to work now." She hugged Siobhan and the other Pierce brother one more time. "I'll let you know if I run into any more…" she cast a glance at Sebastian once more. "…incidents."

"You sure you're going to be okay?" her sister asked, sending Sebastian a "don't mess with my sister" look.

"I'll be fine." She waved them off, took Sebastian by the arm and dragged him into the hotel.

"Care to explain yourself?" she asked under her breath as she guided him into the elevator.

"I saw a woman push you into the street," he said. "Or I think I did. Long skirt." He circled the top of his head. "Braids on top, except she disappeared." He opened his hands. "Poof."

"And Troy?"

"Well he did try to kiss you. And you didn't look like you wanted him to. Why did you let him kiss you?" His eyes were out of focus again. "I want to kiss you."

"Not while you're in that condition, you don't."

They arrived at the suite and she unlocked the parlor door. Sebastian headed for the mini bar, pulled out a beer and popped the top.

"Haven't you had enough to drink?" she asked.

"Memo for next time. Don't do contractor interviews on Bourbon Street." He tossed down a swig of beer and his head started to swim. No, he wasn't in any condition to work, or to have an intelligent conversation with Kathleen.

"Agenda," he said, and cleared his throat. "I'm going to finish this beer, and then I'm going to bed. Tomorrow, we are going back to the project to double check some of the dimensations." He cleared his throat again. "Dimensions."

Her eyes shone with—fear?

"Unless there's something else you want to do?" he asked.

"Nope. Not with you. Not in that condition."

Right. He started for his room, held up a finger and looked at her once more. "Oh, and I heard from Chicago. They want us to finish up here and head back early, so we need to make sure everything's set here. You got that, Red? They've got us on a flight home day after tomorrow." He pointed a finger at her. "Don't screw this up."

"I have no intention of screwing this up."

He turned toward his bedroom, swinging the bottle at his side. "Just sayin'. Last associate I had screwed up."

He closed the door behind him, set the bottle on the dresser and leaned over, studying himself through bleary eyes. Not a pretty picture. Sebastian flexed his fist. Probably shouldn't have punched Troy, either. Now he'd have to hire Pierce Brothers if only to avoid a lawsuit. And yeah, he owed Pierce an apology.

Who was that other woman? And why had she pushed Kathleen toward the street? Except he'd watched her dissolve right in front of his eyes.

Sebastian shook his head. There was no woman. It was a figment of his imagination.

⸻ ◦ ⸻

On the plus side, Kathleen had gotten a full night's sleep, uninterrupted. Also on the plus side, she and Sebastian were going home tomorrow.

Sebastian had slugged Troy. Part of her wanted to laugh and thank him, the other part of her wanted to run and hide. Sebastian had been stinking drunk.

She showered and dressed, donning capris and a sleeveless blouse. When she opened her bedroom door to the parlor, there was no sign of Sebastian.

Kathleen set her computer on the dining table, plugged her earbuds into her phone and tucked the phone into her pocket. Earbuds around her neck, she opened the minibar.

Tomato juice. Sebastian would need that this morning, and she'd order eggs. How had he eaten them the other day?

Why was she worried? The jerk was wasted when he got back yesterday. There was no excuse for that.

She flung open the curtains, letting in the morning sun. His senses would be exaggerated this morning, and she intended to make sure he felt each and every one. She crossed to the balcony and opened the doors, flooding the parlor with more sunlight.

Eight o'clock. Sebastian hadn't slept this late during their entire trip. Certainly he'd be up shortly. Kathleen checked her email before she placed the call to room service and sat down to work, tucking her earbuds in. Led Zeppelin would get her heart pumping this morning. She bounced in rhythm to *Black Dog* and pulled up Aria's construction plans on her computer. Sebastian had said there was an error in the dimension string. She needed to see if it was her fault.

A tap on her shoulder startled her. She tugged out her earbuds and rose to her feet.

"You're going to go deaf," Sebastian said quietly. He smelled of hotel soap and shaving cream, and he was dressed in khakis and a polo.

She took her phone from her pocket. "It's not that loud, is it?"

He squinted against the sunlight and pulled the sheers across the windows.

"Your hearing might be a little oversensitive right now." She tried not to smirk. "I hope the light isn't too bright for you."

His scowl told her he knew she meant to make him suffer this morning. "Are you ready to go to the house?" he asked as he glanced at the sofa—the same sofa he'd had her pressed against night before last.

Okay, she wasn't immune to the man. "I ordered breakfast," she told him. "There's a can of tomato juice in the mini bar. It might make you feel better."

He seemed fixated on the sofa. Yeah, she was having a hard time forgetting their 'one night' too, but she wasn't about to get involved with an alcoholic.

"Sebastian?" Kathleen said, snapping her fingers at him. "Are you in there or are you still drunk?"

"Damn New Orleans. I should have known better than to try to conduct business in a bar." He cradled his head and squinted at her. "Is something wrong?"

Other than he'd come staggering back to the hotel and threw a punch at an innocent man? "Not a thing, boss."

She turned from him and he grabbed her arm.

"What did I miss?" he asked.

She glared at him a moment, struggling to hold her tongue, but he'd asked. "I don't know anything about you," she began. "And if you want to get stinking drunk, that's your business, but I prefer not to be around when that happens, especially if you're going to come out swinging."

"This is the second time you've brought up my drinking. I don't usually over imbibe, and I apologize if that bothered you. As for your friend, I've already apologized to him. Even offered him the job as a peace offering, but he didn't think it was a good idea, under the circumstances."

"That's your business, not mine." She yanked her arm away.

"You didn't look like you appreciated his attentions. I thought I was protecting you, even if I might have taken it too far." He followed her. "Unless I was mistaken. Maybe there's something more between your sister's brother-in-law and you."

Jealousy? She set her hands on her hips. "There's nothing between Troy and me. It was a friendly kiss. A greeting."

"Didn't look friendly from where I was standing."

"Troy's a player," she said simply.

"He made a play for you?"

"At my sister's wedding." She sighed. "We stood up together, me and Troy. He's an attractive man, but Troy has a tendency to keep his options open at all times. He's fun to be with, nice to look at, but the night of the wedding, he kept working the crowd. Flirting. Taking numbers." She shook her head. "That's not the kind of man I want to be with."

"Then I wasn't wrong about your response to him. So what else are you angry about? There's something you aren't saying." He took a step closer. "The drinking?"

She turned away.

"Who?" he asked gently.

She clenched her teeth. "My father."

"And?"

"Let's just say it never ended well for any of us." She retrieved the can of juice from the minibar.

"Past tense? Present tense?"

She handed him the can, her muscles taught with unpleasant memories. "He left us a long time ago, and good riddance."

"Noted, and I assure you, this isn't a regular occurrence with me."

She studied him a moment, his hazel eyes bloodshot. Could she trust him?

A knock signaled the arrival of their breakfast. Kathleen opened the door and the waiter wheeled in a cart. Sebastian reached into his pocket for the tip.

The waiter set the plates on the table, bowed as he took Sebastian's tip and left.

Kathleen took her seat and dug into her breakfast. The sooner they got this over with …

"Kathleen?"

She wasn't ready for small talk, or any other kind of talk. "I stocked the cooler. You'll need sports drinks to replenish your electrolytes," she told him. "We're good to go as soon as we've finished breakfast."

He nodded and they ate in silence.

Chapter 16

"Roll with the punches. Tomorrow is another day." – Jerry Maguire

Kathleen looked up to the ten-foot ceilings in Aria's house, stroked the corbels under the mantel. She had that dreamy look in her eye, the one that told Sebastian she saw beyond the contractor-white walls.

Sebastian had been that way once.

She circled in the center of the apartment, and when she faced him, she straightened. "You'd mentioned a problem with the dimension strings," she said. "I double checked the measurements on the construction plans to the as-built and I couldn't find anything wrong."

There was something wrong with his head, something that wasn't alcohol related. "One of the contractors I interviewed yesterday asked about the kitchen wall. He pointed out the discrepancy to me."

She pulled out the tape. "Which end do you want?"

"Kathleen." He whispered her name, not intending to say it at all.

She tilted her head when she looked at him. She'd done her best to be all business—and so had he—but the air between them crackled. Her cheeks pinked when she met his gaze, the way they had the other night when she'd called his name 'in the moment.'

She saw the house, the potential buried in the brick walls they would uncover. The loving way she'd touched the wood around the fireplace—it was sexy as hell, but they'd agreed to one night.

Kathleen held out the measuring tape. "Did you want…?" she swallowed the last word as her gaze dropped to his lips. "How do you want to do this?" she asked, her voice husky.

A slow smile creased his face. She had to know exactly what he was thinking.

"Would it be inappropriate for me to tell you I find your imagination incredibly sexy? The way you look at the walls, the fireplace?"

"How do you know what I'm imagining?" she asked, a shy smile turning up the corners of her mouth.

They stood three inches apart.

"I used to look at buildings that way," he went on. "Until Barrett Winslow taught me it wasn't my vision that mattered. It was the client's. But sometimes—" he closed another inch between them, "sometimes the client needs to see your vision to know what they're missing."

"I don't like Barrett Winslow very much right now," she whispered.

"I've been pretty pissed off at him, myself, but right now? I'm grateful to him."

Kathleen's eyes widened and she stepped back. Sebastian stepped forward, into her. "He threw mayhem in my life when he assigned you to this project."

"We all need a little mayhem sometimes."

He cupped the back of her head and kissed her, flooding him with all the memories of the other night, the sensations, the colors that went with them. "I keep wondering if it was an anomaly," he said. "That one night. It couldn't have been that good, could it? Am I misremembering? Or was it because we shouldn't have done it?"

"Oh, definitely forbidden fruit," she said.

"If anyone in the office found out…" he said, and stepped away.

"You might not get your promotion?" she asked. Kathleen took a deep breath. "I won't get in your way, if that's what you're worried about, and I'm not about to give up my paycheck. We probably won't even see each other at work, you up there in your fancy office and me downstairs at my lowly draft board."

He nodded, and yet he had visions of her in his office, bent over his desk, arching into him, calling out his name.

She reached for the waistband of his pants. "We could see. If it was really as good as we remember it." Her fingers worked his belt buckle. "Here, in someone else's house. More forbidden fruit?"

As much as he wanted to, this was a bad idea. "I can't," he said.

Kathleen dropped her hands and tilted her head again, as if trying to read him.

"I told you I was planning to propose…" he said, his voice tight.

"Yes, you did." She said. "A business arrangement as I recall."

"It wouldn't be right. This."

"Because you love her," Kathleen said.

"No. Because it would be dishonorable."

"I'm not sure about the rules when it comes to your 'business arrangement,' but I respect your sense of honor." She turned away. "I apologize."

"Don't."

Kathleen narrowed her eyes. "Don't apologize?"

Sebastian looked away, tugging his ear. "She'd mentioned it a time or two, thought it would help both of us advance our careers." He shook his head. Had Renee manipulated him? All the things he'd given up came clearly into focus. "I can't do it."

"I think you've said that already."

"No," he corrected her. "I can't propose to Renee. Not after what happened."

Kathleen's tongue darted out to moisten her lips, a lusty glow shining in her eyes. "What happened?"

"You happened." He turned away. A relationship with Kathleen couldn't turn out well. One or both of them would lose their jobs.

"We have one more night," she rasped. "What happens in NOLA stays in NOLA?"

"I thought that was Las Vegas."

She shrugged. "Same difference."

"We're in someone else's house," he said, searching for excuses.

"Someone might walk in," she replied.

Except Aria had left town. She had agents in the city but the chances anyone would stop by— No, the chances of being interrupted were pretty slim, and Kathleen was standing in front of him, wanting him as much as he wanted her, he was sure of it.

Sebastian finished loosening his belt buckle and backed Kathleen to the wall. His pants dropped to the floor when they got there and he hiked up the skirt of her sundress. He slipped his fingers into the sides of her silky panties and drew them down before crushing his mouth to hers.

"One more time?" he growled against her mouth.

"Or two," she said on a sigh.

He cupped her bottom and lifted her off the floor. She circled his waist with her legs and he slid into her, stumbling to hold them both upright.

"You feel so damn good," he said.

"Back atcha."

She slid against the wall and he fell out.

"This isn't working."

"Floor," she said.

They moved to the floor together and as he braced himself over her, they locked eyes. They weren't in a hurry. They had nowhere else to go. And he wanted more than the quick ten minutes Renee allotted him.

"What?" she asked.

He grinned as he eased down her body, touching her through the dress, massaging her breasts, and coming to rest between her legs. He kissed each thigh and then kissed her where it mattered, slowly, tasting her.

She arched into him, her hands grasping the sides of his head as she moaned.

"Good?" he stopped to ask.

"Don't stop."

He gave her a playful lick. "More? Like this?"

"Damn you, you're going to kill me here."

She'd already done him in. This vibrant, colorful woman had reminded him of everything he'd lost in his drive to be better than his father, to prove himself to a man he would never be good enough for. She'd breathed life back into him. Sebastian blew where she was wet and she wriggled with another groan, and when he closed his mouth on her once more, she cried out.

Now. He had to be inside her now.

Sebastian settled between her legs quickly, driving home as she dug her fingers into his shoulders, then lower as she pulled him deeper. All the while, he gazed into her eyes, blue eyes that could shoot lightning at him or surround him like the Caribbean. Kathleen's eyes, reaching into his soul and drawing him out.

Kathleen, moving with him, demanding his passion, sharing her own.

No, it wasn't an anomaly. She rocked his world again, sending shudders through him with the force of his release, making him cry out in a way no one else had done before.

And then she giggled.

"I can't breathe," she said, her voice muffled.

He'd collapsed on top of her, and yet she hadn't pushed him away. He was still buried inside her, the way he'd been the other night, and like the other night, she felt so good he didn't want to pull out. If he moved, the way he had the other night, could he do it again?

The dull thud that remained inside his head answered for him. No.

Sebastian rolled off Kathleen and rested an arm across his forehead. "You're going to kill me, woman."

"We have tonight," she said. "Before we have to go back and pretend none of this happened. Before we have to abide by the non-fraternization policy."

Could she forget? He opened one eye to look at her to see if she was joking. And yet they had to forget. If anyone at the office found out, they'd both be fired and he could kiss his promotion goodbye.

Sebastian sat up and rested his arms on his knees. Whose dreams was he chasing? Who was he trying to prove something to?

"Sebastian?"

He couldn't look at Kathleen. If he did, they'd never get the work done. "Still a bit of a headache," he said.

Kathleen sat up and adjusted her dress. "I hear oysters are good for a hangover."

"You said you didn't like oysters."

She shrugged. "When in New Orleans. Can't hurt to try one." She pushed to her feet. "Let's get this done." She extended a hand to help him up. "Suddenly I'm anxious to get back to the hotel. Did I mention oysters are supposed to be good for more than headaches?"

He cocked an eyebrow. "Are you suggesting I might need an oyster for something other than a headache?"

"Not based on my experience, but imagine the possibilities." She wagged her eyebrows and Sebastian did something he hadn't done in far too long. He laughed.

———◆———

With the final kink worked out, Kathleen emailed Aria the plans to approve. They'd missed lunch, but it was too early for dinner. Sebastian suggested they take a walk along the river, get out of the hotel room for a while. Kathleen had been only too happy to comply.

As much as she would have preferred crawling into bed with Sebastian for the rest of their time in New Orleans, she needed to clear her head. After Russ's accusations that she'd merely used him to satisfy her desires, she wasn't eager to repeat that mistake.

Except she liked Sebastian.

What if he was a rebound man? They had red-hot chemistry, but would it last?

The breeze coming off the Mississippi River was refreshing, counteracting the heat and humidity. She and

Sebastian walked hand in hand enjoying a comfortable silence. That was new. She'd always felt she had to fill the quiet with Russ, that he expected her to say or do something.

And why was she comparing Sebastian to Russ? The two men couldn't be more different. For starters, Russ was the consummate nice guy and Sebastian was a jerk.

Except Sebastian wasn't a jerk. Not really.

She glanced at him and her hormones jumped. Good thing they weren't in that hotel room, or maybe not such a good thing. The way he made her feel, she'd drop her panties for him behind the nearest bush.

This was way more than her body in a drought. Sebastian made her feel things—things she'd never felt with Russ—but they'd talked about this. They couldn't be together. They'd lose their jobs.

Forbidden fruit is always sweeter.

No. This was more than that. It wasn't the thrill of being caught. If that were the case, she'd go ahead and drag him behind one of those bushes.

Just her luck. She'd fallen for a man she couldn't have.

As if he could read her mood, Sebastian tugged her into his arms and smoothed her hair off her face.

"You okay?" he asked.

She smiled and nodded.

He kissed her, right there on the riverwalk, rubbing her back and pressing against her.

Yeah, she wanted to ravish him behind a bush, right here in public, but the fact she didn't act on that impulse was more revealing than she cared to admit.

She enjoyed his company.

"What are you thinking so hard about?" he asked.

No, she didn't dare tell him. She felt maudlin and weepy and more emotional than she ought to be. Low blood sugar? "I'm thinking I'm hungry," she said. "How about that oyster bar?"

Sebastian kissed her once more and leaned back, his hands on her hips. "I have to say this is the best business trip I've ever been on."

She scoffed. "You probably say that to all your associates."

"Only the red-headed ones." He grinned, took her hand and led her back to Decatur Street.

They arrived at the restaurant ahead of the dinner crowd and were seated right away. Kathleen couldn't bring herself to order oysters, and got a fish boil instead. The Cajun spices tingled her lips and tongue with each bite.

Sebastian insisted she try one of the oysters from his plate, as she said she would. He laughed as he showed her how to let it slide down her throat.

He'd been laughing a lot today, and smiling, too. It was a good look on him. Had she ever thought he was only marginally attractive? The way he was tonight, Sebastian was a different person. Approachable. Fun. Sexy as hell. And he hadn't had an adult beverage all night.

They had one more night together and she couldn't wait to get back to the hotel.

Between the spices and the anticipation of more play time, Kathleen tingled everywhere.

Her stomach fluttered when they climbed into the Uber, but not in a fun way. She rested a hand there and a belch bubbled up. She covered her mouth, and the belch was followed by a groan from deep down inside.

Sebastian slung an arm across her shoulders and nibbled at her neck. "When we get back to the room," he whispered, "we're taking the night off. And your clothes. And my clothes."

Another bubble rose inside her and she swallowed hard to fight the feeling it was more than gas.

"Unless you're not okay with this," he said, straightening.

She covered her mouth again and fought her gag reflex.

"Kathleen?"

She swallowed the gross taste of the burp. "I'm thinking that oyster was a bad idea."

"You're not feeling well? They didn't bother me."

Her stomach rumbled more loudly, and this time he heard it.

"Oh," he said. "Maybe you need to… uh… let it back out, if you know what I mean."

The Uber stopped in front of the hotel. Kathleen shot out of the car and ran for the elevator, one hand over her mouth to hold back another belch that might be more than a belch. Sebastian unlocked the parlor door and she darted inside, to her room and the bathroom.

She sat on the toilet and grabbed the garbage can, evil things spewing out of her from both ends—hot, painful things. In the same position ten minutes later, she considered dying might be a better alternative.

Sebastian knocked on the bathroom door. "Are you okay?"

"I will be, once I purge whatever demon took hold of me," she said with a groan. She rose to her feet and cleaned up her bottom half. That part appeared to be over. She dumped the garbage can into the toilet and went to the sink to wash her face—too soon.

She knelt before the toilet, emptying more of the contents of her stomach.

"What can I do?" Sebastian asked from the other side of the door.

"Let me die in peace."

The door opened a crack and he peered into the bathroom. "Sometimes it's better not to pretend you're Roman," he said.

He was cracking jokes? The unapproachable, buttoned-up Sebastian Brooks? "Who are you and what have you done with my boss?" she asked.

He knelt beside her and gathered her hair in his hands, holding it back with one hand as he pressed a palm to her clammy forehead.

"Did you get it all out?" he asked.

On cue, she heaved again, although nothing came up. "Just let me die."

"Sprite? Coke? Gator-Ade?" he asked.

"Water."

He cupped her elbow and helped her to her feet.

"Why don't you crawl into bed? I'll bring your water."

Kathleen stripped to her undies and did as he said, shivering while she pulled the covers to her chin. A few minutes later, Sebastian walked in with two bottles of water, wearing nothing but his boxers.

"Sorry, but I don't think you're going to get lucky tonight," she said.

"You don't think I know that?" He smoothed her hair. "Slide over. You're trembling. I'm coming in to provide body heat."

She took a drink from one of the bottles, inched back on the bed and Sebastian settled in, holding her tight. He smelled so good, and she smelled like… vomit. He pressed a kiss to her forehead.

"Close your eyes. Go to sleep," he told her.

"Umm, there's a man in my bed."

"You got a problem with that?" he asked.

"Yeah. Usually that means play time, and I'm not up to it right now."

He snuggled her closer. "I've got you, Red. Sleep."

Kathleen rolled over, slowly as to not upset her stomach further, and Sebastian nestled against her backside, one arm wrapped protectively around her.

"How come you're not sick?" she mumbled.

"Either I have an iron stomach or it wasn't the oysters. You ever consider it might have been your fish?"

"Sebastian?"

"Yeah?"

"I'm sorry I called you an asshole."

He chuckled. "When was that?"

"Might have been our first night here. I don't remember."

He hugged her tight. "Neither do I."

<hr>

The pain that woke Kathleen helped to explain her episode the night before. She knew she was due for her period, but she hadn't had debilitating cramps like this since high school, before she was on the pill. She curled in tighter to herself, trying to ease the spasms before she made the trip to the bathroom.

"Kath?" Sebastian's mouth was against her ear, his voice raspy with sleep.

"It's okay. I'm okay. Go back to sleep," she told him.

He tightened his hold on her.

"Seriously, dude," she said. "I need to get up."

He rolled back and opened his eyes.

Kathleen doubled over, clutching her gut.

"You're still sick," he said.

"No, I've got cramps."

He eased to his elbows. "What can I do?"

She couldn't remember such a drastic hormone shift since she'd started taking the pill, but clearly her body was out of whack. She wanted to hate Sebastian, to tell him to leave her the hell alone, but the man had held her hair back last night while she bowed to the porcelain god. He'd crawled into bed with her to warm her up, and he hadn't made one inappropriate move.

This was Sebastian Brooks. Could he have loosened up so much in the short time they'd been together?

"You've already done a lot," she said.

"I-uh, I've heard that sometimes having sex can ease cramps," he said, and shrugged.

And he'd heard right, but did she dare? "It might get messy," she said.

"A warm shower?"

She straightened, taking a deep breath. No cramps.

"A warm shower and sex?" Sebastian wagged his eyebrows.

She managed a smile. "Maybe."

The slow smile on his face did more to ease her cramps than anything she'd tried yet this morning. Heat pooled in her womb.

"Let's give it a try," he said, his voice low and yummy. He climbed out of bed and took her hand, leading her to the bathroom.

Sebastian turned on the shower and slid his boxers to the floor, ready for action. Another lurch in her womb let her know she was ready, too. He released the clasp on her bra and knelt before her, easing her panties off—no blood yet—then thrust his hand into the shower to test the water.

"Anytime you're ready."

She stepped in and he followed her, drawing the curtain closed behind him. He reached for the bar of soap, held it under the water, and gently washed her back, and then her front, and then her goody bits, slowly and with great care to caress those same goody bits until she was panting for air. No more cramps, only hot, blinding need.

He kissed her, slowly, gave her the soap and guided her hand to the hardest part of him. So hard. She stroked him and he growled.

"Careful, or I won't be able to help you with those cramps."

"You've already done more than you know," she said, her heart squeezing.

He turned her to face the wall and kissed her shoulders while he cupped her breasts. "So beautiful," he whispered against her ear. And then he was inside her, moving slowly. Caressing her inside.

"You're like a furnace," he said, his voice rough. His hands roamed her body, gliding with the water, waking up every nerve ending with his gentle touch.

Kathleen pressed her hands to the wall to keep from melting into a puddle. He felt so good.

"Better, baby?" he asked, his voice tight with need.

"Yes," she whispered.

He pulsed inside her, took hold of her hips and pressed deep inside. Warm water sluiced over them, his hands gliding up her sides, to her breasts, back to her waist, and then he groaned, carrying her right along with him.

Before she could catch her breath, he'd turned her to face him and kissed her thoroughly, their slick bodies sliding together.

"Kathleen." He whispered her name as he pushed her wet hair off her face.

The way he said her name wrapped around her heart. This was the feeling she'd been missing with Russ, a feeling of being cherished.

And then she remembered who she was with. Once they boarded that airplane, they'd have to leave this behind—whatever this was.

'This' was pretty spectacular. She'd inadvertently been giving up little parts of herself, sharing, in spite of an unapproachable boss who'd tried his best to keep her in her place.

She was in her place now. She'd been in her place last night. In Sebastian's arms. A couple of hours from now, that wouldn't be possible, not if they wanted to keep their jobs, and she needed her job if she wanted to buy a house.

The water turned cold and they both giggled as they threw open the curtain and wrapped themselves in towels.

"I'm not ready for this to be over," she whispered.

The towel tied around his waist twitched and she grinned. Kathleen tugged his hand toward the bed. "I'm feeling much better. How about we try this lying down. What do you think?"

Sebastian picked her up and deposited her in the center of the bed. He kissed her face—her forehead, her cheeks, her chin, and then her mouth. He opened her towel and suckled at her breasts.

"So beautiful," he said again.

He kneeled beside her and she yanked off his towel. Yep, he was ready again.

"Again," she said. "And you don't have to be so careful this time."

He grinned. "You are a demanding woman, aren't you?"

Her pulse kicked up. "Saving up for when we go back," she told him. "I thought I was in sensory withdrawal before. This is going to be even harder."

He chuckled. "Glad you noticed."

She swatted his backside playfully. "I'm not talking about body parts."

Sebastian kissed her again and stared into her eyes. "Right there with you, Red."

He surprised her by sliding home in one smooth stroke. She took everything he offered and held him tight.

Chapter 17

*"Chains of habit are too light to be felt until they are too
heavy to be broken." – Warren Buffett*

They'd been back in Chicago a little over a week
and Sebastian hadn't seen Kathleen other than a
quick glimpse on the elevator. When he'd seen
her, he had to bury his attention in his phone to
keep from staring.

His life was well-ordered, structured, his goals
lined up with an action plan to achieve them in the most
efficient manner. Kathleen was messy and impulsive. She
didn't fit into his plan, and yet she'd reminded him that
his goal to be a partner by the time he was thirty had
fallen in line with Barrett's architectural ideas, not what
Sebastian wanted to do.

He couldn't stop thinking about her.

In half an hour, they were scheduled for a status
meeting on the New Orleans project. Kathleen would be
there, the first intentional time he'd spend with her since
their return. Surely their time in New Orleans would be
nothing more than a pleasant memory for either of them.

Or an obsession he had to overcome.

The contractors in New Orleans had begun
removing the millwork and checking the floors for
spongy spots. There would be more trips to New
Orleans, but Kathleen wouldn't be going.

Sebastian was tempted to buy her a ticket, out of his own pocket. The pressures of his job had felt lighter when he was with her.

A knock on his door drew him out of his contemplations.

"Renee." He crossed the room and air kissed one of her cheeks. "How nice to see you."

"You'd mentioned you wanted to get together when you got back from New Orleans," she said. "You said there was something you wanted to discuss. When I didn't hear from you, I wondered if something was wrong."

Right. He'd fully intended to propose upon his return from New Orleans to improve the optics for promotion. A business proposition. He'd even started writing clauses for a prenup before the trip, one of which stipulated they keep their own condos, maintain their separate lives. In all the years he'd known Renee, they'd never spent a whole night together. Never wanted to. Not even in college.

An unexpected tug below the belt reminded him of the nights he'd spent intentionally sleeping beside Kathleen.

"Well?" she asked.

Sebastian's gut clenched. A proposal wouldn't matter at this stage. Promotions would be announced on Monday. And he didn't want to marry Renee. "You're right, I did suggest dinner, but I've been tied up with this project. I'm sure you understand."

She gave him a porcelain smile, one that looked like it might shatter if it grew any larger. Had she always smiled that way?

"That's one of the things about you and me," she said. "We understand each other, don't we? I hope you don't mind me stopping by your office before the meeting like this, but I wanted to confirm I'll be at your birthday party tomorrow night. Do you want to get together before then? In case there was something you wanted to share with your family when we're all together."

Something to share? A thousand conversations circled in his head, all the times Renee had made subtle references to marriage and the professional benefits of having a spouse. Yes, they'd reached him on a subconscious level, but today, he recognized those manipulative comments for what they were. She'd been angling for a proposal for… how long? And he'd nearly fallen into her trap.

It wasn't going to happen. What was more, he needed to find a way to keep Kathleen in his life, even if it meant more business trips out of town, requesting her on his jobs. She'd opened his eyes to so many of the things he'd overlooked in the past several years.

Sebastian needed to set Renee straight. He closed his office door, leading Renee to a chair across from his desk.

"We've been friends a long time."

She smiled. "Of course, Darling. We've always understood one another."

"I get the impression…" He paused when Barrett appeared in the window beside his office door knocking on air to ask if he could interrupt as he let himself in.

"Forgive me for barging in," Barrett said. He took Renee's hands. "How nice to see you. This conversation looks cozy. I hope that means this boy is stepping up, but can it wait until after our status meeting?"

Boy. Sebastian rounded his shoulders and grimaced.

About time you made something of yourself, boy, instead of pretending to be some hotshot with a fancy office.

"I'd like to get an early start," Barrett continued. "Everyone else is already in the conference room. Something's come up this afternoon that I have to attend to so I'd like to cross this status meeting off my list."

"Of course," Renee answered for Sebastian. "We'll be right there." She rose from her seat and the men followed her down the hall.

Half a dozen people sat around the mahogany table, including Kathleen. His pulse kicked up a notch being in the same room with her. So different from Renee.

His associates knew Renee from other projects she'd been subcontracted for. Everyone except Kathleen.

"I'm sorry, I don't know you," Renee said, zeroing in on Kathleen.

Kathleen rose from her chair. "I'm Kathleen McCormick."

"Kathleen was part of the design team in New Orleans," Barrett said by way of introduction. "Kathleen, this is Renee Quinn. She's going to be the interior decorator once the construction is completed."

"Design team?" Renee repeated. She turned to Sebastian. "I thought there were only two of you in New Orleans." She held a hand out to Kathleen, princess style, as if she expected Kathleen to kiss it instead of shake it.

"That's right," Sebastian said.

Kathleen gripped Renee's hand and shook it. The flinch on Renee's face indicated Kathleen might have squeezed harder than was necessary.

"Nice to meet you," Kathleen said.

Renee lowered her voice and leaned toward Sebastian. "Just the two of you?" She blinked a couple extra times.

Sebastian broke a lazy smile, all too familiar with those extra blinks. Renee rarely showed a lack of composure. The blinks were her only tell.

Barrett started the meeting, projecting the designs on a screen. Sebastian offered narrative, indicating the progress they'd made already and finishing with the timeline for the next steps.

"Millwork is being removed, tagged and repaired," he said. "The contractors are restoring damaged floors. We'll need to be on site here." He used a laser pointer to highlight, "and here. Renee, Ms. Walton will be expecting you here," again he pointed to the timeline, "and for the next couple of weeks following that. I'm assuming you already have a copy of this itinerary and have Aria on your schedule?"

"Yes, she is a top priority," Renee said.

Forty-five minutes later, Barrett wrapped up.

"Excellent work," he said. "Ms. Walton is a high profile, high revenue client. She has a very tight turnaround schedule, so I'm asking people to be available to step in should Sebastian need assistance. Any questions?"

"Let me know what you need," another project manager said.

"I have availability if you need me," another associate said.

"Excellent," Barrett said again. "Thank you all for coming."

People pushed away from the table, talking as they made their way for the door.

Renee hovered, making a show of checking her phone and then looking through her purse until she and Sebastian and Kathleen were the last ones remaining in the conference room.

"Since I haven't met you before, I assume you're a junior associate? Or are you an intern?" Renee asked.

"I'm a junior associate," Kathleen answered simply.

"I'm surprised they'd send a junior associate on a project like this," she said to Sebastian, fluttering her eyelashes toward Kathleen. "Whatever does a junior associate do for two weeks on location? It must be terribly boring."

"I do have family down there," Kathleen said, smiling brightly. "But Sebastian kept me busy. I didn't get much time to visit."

He recognized the smartass-ness coming out and wondered if she'd take a shot at Renee, the way she'd taken a shot at him. Part of him wanted to rush to Renee's defense, but another part of him wanted to watch Kathleen at work.

Before he could say anything, Renee set a possessive left hand on Sebastian's shoulder.

"Oh," Kathleen said. "You must be the friend he was telling me about while we were in New Orleans, when you were looking at..." She glanced at Sebastian.

He shook his head, trying to send her the 'stop talking' vibe. If Renee knew she'd almost succeeded in getting him to the altar, she'd pursue him that much harder.

Renee dropped her hand, clearly not sure what to make of the colorful woman in front of her. "Yes. And we're hardly friends, Sebastian and I. We've been close for a long time."

"Well, I'd asked him about that, you know, when he was telling me he was thinking of..." she cast a glance at Sebastian, her eyes sparkling with mischief. What was she up to?

Kathleen cocked an eyebrow. "I thought the use of the term friend was lukewarm."

"Kathleen was instrumental to the project," Sebastian told Renee, redirecting the conversation. "Aria chose Kathleen's designs over mine."

"You presented an associate's designs?" Renee asked. "A junior associate? That's hardly protocol, is it?"

"Funny story," Kathleen said. "I'm not sure if you've ever been to New Orleans, but the house wasn't air conditioned, and I must have suffered heat exhaustion. I inadvertently sent Aria my designs instead of Sebastian's."

"Mistakes like that can get you fired," Renee said.

"And very well might have except that Aria preferred Kathleen's approach," Sebastian said, trying to steer the women out of the conference room. Neither of them moved. "Which reminds me," he said to Kathleen. "Aria sent modifications we should go over, and she's asked for a Saturday morning meeting. Tomorrow. Are you available?"

"I suppose I can fit it in," Renee said.

Sebastian turned to Renee. "Of course you can join us, if you feel it's necessary, but I was referring to structural changes."

"I'm sure any modifications will impact the materials I'll need to order," Renee said, pressing her lips into a thin line.

"I'm in the middle of another project today," Kathleen said. "We could discuss it before Aria's meeting tomorrow?"

"That would be fine," Sebastian replied.

Kathleen picked up her notepad and walked out.

"I don't like her," Renee said in a low voice. "Can't you find another associate for this project?"

"No, I can't. Aria wants her on the team." He faced Renee, more than a little amused. This was more emotion than he was used to seeing from her, and that included in bed. "You aren't jealous, are you?"

She chuffed. "Of her? Please! But since when do junior associates present designs to a client?"

"It was an honest mistake."

"A mistake? I wouldn't trust her, Sebastian." She checked her phone. "I have to run. I have another meeting, but we must find time to get together. This is the first I've seen you since you've been back. I could stop by your place tonight after my dinner meeting, if you'd like, and you could talk to me about whatever it was you thought was so important before you left."

Except it was no longer important. In fact, it was no longer on the table. "Tonight probably isn't the best."

"Tomorrow night, then. After your birthday party. I'll put a bottle of champagne on ice at my place," she suggested.

The birthday party. He'd invited her as his plus-one when his parents had insisted on a party. He couldn't un-invite her. He'd address the elephant in the room with Renee tomorrow, after the party, but he didn't think she'd want to celebrate what he had to say.

"Skip the champagne," he told her. "But yes, we'll talk more tomorrow."

⋯⋯◉⋯⋯

Kathleen's heart was going to pound out of her chest. *That* was the woman Sebastian had considered proposing to?

She had to get a grip. Seeing him again had been like a taking a bullet, and she was mortally wounded. He was back to being the cool, pompous man she'd met a few short weeks ago.

Sebastian Brooks is a jerk.

Her mantra wasn't working this time. He'd helped her through heat exhaustion, held her hair while she puked, and made love to her when most men ran the opposite direction from a woman.

He didn't 'make love' to me.

Except it sure felt like it. And now? Seeing him with *that* woman? All those little pieces of herself she'd inadvertently given to him represented a gaping hole in the center of her chest where her heart should be.

She splashed cold water on her hot cheeks, on her eyes so no one would know she'd had a mini meltdown and actually cried. With a forced smile, she walked out of the bathroom on the twenty-fourth floor. She could do this.

Sebastian stood beside Renee at the elevator and Kathleen considered ducking back into the bathroom and waiting for the next car down, until Renee shot her a glare.

Renee took Sebastian's hands and air kissed his cheek. *Air kissed?*

"Then I'll see you tomorrow," Renee said.

"The meeting with Aria is at eleven," Sebastian replied.

"Going down?" Renee asked Kathleen, as she stepped into the elevator.

"Yes, thank you."

Sebastian turned toward Kathleen, his expression tense. Yeah, he should be tense. *Jerk.*

Kathleen stood beside Renee, pressed the button for the twelfth floor and moved to the opposite corner. Sebastian walked away before the doors closed. Smart man.

"I suppose we'll see each other again in the meeting with Aria tomorrow," Renee said.

Kathleen flashed a smile. "Yes, we will."

"I'm surprised Sebastian would tolerate insubordination."

"It was an honest mistake." Kathleen folded her arms. "I'm sure he would have fired me if Ms. Walton hadn't liked my work."

"Fortunate for you."

"Yes, it was."

"I don't suppose that could happen a second time without consequences," Renee said.

"I don't suppose."

The elevator chimed arrival at the twelfth floor and Kathleen stepped off. "See you tomorrow." She stalked to her desk, yanked out her chair and sat beside her draft board.

She wanted to rage at someone, but she'd have to wait until the end of the day. Her desk didn't offer enough privacy for her to call someone, and discussing Sebastian with anyone she worked with would certainly get her fired.

Eye on the prize. She might still get a promotion of her own with a raise to go with it. She glanced at her computer, at the rotating background of Craftsman houses, one of which could be hers if she could survive this project.

The phone rang and she picked it up. "Kathleen McCormick."

"We need to talk," Sebastian said.

Kathleen glanced around, keenly aware of the people who worked beside her. "Is there a problem?" she asked evenly.

Sebastian cleared his throat. "Are you free for dinner?"

Not a chance. Not with his princess standing by. "No. I'm not free. I have a standing engagement with my family on Friday nights."

"I need to talk to you," he said.

"We'll be going over the modifications ahead of the meeting tomorrow. Would that be soon enough?" She smiled when she caught the eye of one of her coworkers.

"I'll call you later, on your cell."

"I don't think that's necessary."

Sebastian huffed. "I do."

"As I said, I'm not available to work the extra hours tonight, but I'd be happy to come into the office early tomorrow."

He hesitated. "All right. Be in my office at ten."

"Will do." She hung up the phone, her nostrils flaring.

This was her fault. She was the one who hadn't let him back away. It was supposed to have been one night. She hadn't counted on discovering a real person hiding under that arrogant façade. And yet he'd been that same arrogant jerk during the meeting.

As much as she didn't trust herself to be alone in a room with Sebastian Brooks, she also didn't trust him to be that same, caring man she'd met in New Orleans. Which Sebastian would she meet in his office tomorrow?

Chapter 18

"Go confidently in the direction of your dreams. Live the life you've imagined." – Henry David Thoreau

Sebastian shoved the small box into his pants pocket and looked across the lake from his office window. He knew proposing to Renee was a bad idea. When Kathleen had gone on to describe the sort of ring *she'd* want, something had clicked inside, but even then, the promotion had been more important. Sebastian had established a reputation with Barrett Winslow. If he expected to advance—he was so close to his objective—he had to keep up appearances.

The promotion wasn't the most important goal anymore.

When he'd seen Kathleen in the meeting, he knew their time in New Orleans was more than a pleasant memory. That's why he'd stopped at the jewelry store on his way home last night and found a ring—the perfect ring—a diamond set in rose gold.

What was he going to do with that ring?

Sebastian hung his head. He couldn't propose to someone he hardly knew, but he had to let Kathleen know he wanted more. More time to get to know her. More time to discover what they had together. More time to feel like he was part of something bigger than a promotion or a deadline for success.

"You wanted to go over those modifications?" Kathleen asked from his doorway.

His heart rate accelerated, an idiotic sense of joy just being with her. That, right there, was the feeling he wanted for the rest of his life.

"Come in," he said. "Shut the door behind you."

She did a half turn, closed the door and took a seat, her computer in her lap.

Sebastian sat on the corner of his desk, one hand wrapped around the box in his pants pocket. He couldn't give the ring to her. Not yet.

"You've opened my eyes to a great many things," he said quietly, to be sure his voice didn't carry beyond his office. "And there are many things I need to remedy before this goes any further, but I do want to fix things."

She raised her eyebrows, clearly skeptical. "Fix what?"

"For starters, it seems Renee has been trying to influence a certain decision I wasn't consciously paying attention to. I plan to correct that error." He leaned toward Kathleen. "What I told you when we were in New Orleans still holds true. I am not planning to propose to Renee."

"I'm sure she'll be disappointed."

His hands itched to touch Kathleen. "You were the one who pointed out the ridiculousness of getting married as a business arrangement, but I've been caught up on Barrett Winslow's hamster wheel the last several years. They will be announcing promotions on Monday, and if my name is on the list, I intend to pursue the type of projects I've had to turn down, the ones I want to do."

Kathleen held his gaze, the blue in her eyes deceptively serene. "I wish you all the best. Now about those modifications?"

"I'm doing my best not to kiss you right now," he continued. "Not to back you against the wall the way I did in Aria's house before we left New Orleans."

Her cheeks bloomed with color, highlighting those beautiful freckles.

"Unfortunately, my office is a fishbowl, and the whole world would be watching. I'm asking you to give me another day. I feel it necessary to address the elephant in the room with Renee, the elephant she put there, and then I'd like to spend more time with you, if you'll let me."

"And if someone from the office finds out?" she asked. "I still need my job."

"I'd suggest to Barrett that his employee handbook is outdated, another advantage if my name is on that list on Monday."

Kathleen gave a slight bob of her head and smiled. "Then I hope you get your promotion."

"It would be nice, but suddenly the promotion doesn't feel like the most important thing." He leaned forward, fully intending to tell her how deeply she affected him. Instead he straightened when he looked through the sidelight beside his office door and saw Margot escorting Renee through the security door. "She's early."

Renee didn't bother to knock. She opened the door and walked into his office. "Good morning, darling. I hope you don't mind me stopping by your office first, but I thought we might go over things before Aria arrives." She cast a sideway glance at Kathleen. "Good morning."

"Renee," Kathleen said.

His phone rang, showing Margot's extension, and he picked it up.

"Miss Walton seems to be early, as well," Margot told him.

Since when did everyone show up an hour early for a meeting? "Show her to the conference room," he said.

Sebastian took a cleansing breath and smiled at the women in his office. "Why don't we head to the conference room. It seems Aria is here early, too. Kathleen, if you could check the files I uploaded to the cloud last night, we can finish going over the modifications."

"Yes, sir." She rose from her seat and walked out.

Renee lay a hand on Sebastian's arm to hold him back. "I'm surprised you needed to close your door. There's no one else in on a Saturday morning, is there?"

"Barrett is usually in, and he's not the only one. Is there a problem?"

"Of course not." Renee gave him a tight smile.

He held out an arm. "Then shall we?"

She started toward the conference room. "What time shall I expect you to pick me up tonight?"

No, he had no intention of being trapped in a car with Renee. Not tonight. "I can send a car for you around seven."

They rounded the corner and found Aria hugging Kathleen. Sebastian smiled, remembering how awkward Kathleen had been at their first meeting, and how quickly she'd recovered. Renee bristled beside him.

"Good morning," Sebastian said, taking Aria's hand. "We aren't quite ready for you."

Aria leaned in for an air kiss and raised her eyebrows. "You know how eager I am to get things moving."

Renee extended her hand to Aria, but Aria ignored it, instead hooking her arm through Kathleen's as she steered her into the conference room.

"You remember Renee Quinn?" Sebastian said.

Aria nodded to Renee while still holding onto Kathleen. "How nice to see you again." She turned to Kathleen. "Renee decorated my house in Lake Forest, as well." And then to Renee, "But I expect this project to be completely different. Different state, different type of house, you know what I mean, I hope?"

"Yes, I understand you're looking for Victorian décor," Renee said, taking a seat at the table. "And Sebastian tells me you're anxious to get things started."

They all took their places while Kathleen plugged the projector into her laptop and brought the floor plan up on the screen.

"We haven't had a chance to discuss what you sent over," Sebastian said. "We'd planned to do that this morning before you got here."

"We aren't shooting today, so I don't have to be on set. I hope you don't mind. We can go over everything together, if that's all right?"

"Of course," Sebastian said.

"Now, I was looking at your double parlor," Aria said to Kathleen, "and it's so hard for me to envision all this on paper, you know what I mean? So I was hoping you could show me 3D rooms. What if, instead of the three arches," she rose from her seat to point at the projected image— "we put a narrow wall here—a couple of inches—to give it more separation and leave the one arch?"

Kathleen deferred to Sebastian. "Did you want to…?"

"No, please go ahead. They were your designs."

Kathleen modified the plans to Aria's request.

"Yes," Aria said quietly. "I think I like that better." She turned to Renee. "Obviously, that's going to change what you need to do, as well. I think you'd proposed wallpaper. I'm wondering if painting an accent wall might work better."

"In keeping with your Victorian theme, I think the wallpaper would be your better option," Renee said.

"I suppose." Aria turned to Kathleen. "Now, take me to the dining room. I had some ideas there, as well."

Sebastian sat back and watched Kathleen work, every bit as impressed with her as he'd been during their first presentation to Aria. Kathleen had a successful career ahead of her as long as their relationship didn't muck it up.

He hadn't been happy at Winslow for a long time, and this new development with Kathleen underscored that. Barrett had been shooting down Sebastian's charitable projects for years. That wasn't likely to change with a promotion. No, Sebastian would be the one to go, the one to give Kathleen the opportunity to grow and develop. He'd find a job with another firm where he could put the degree he'd earned to better use doing the kinds of projects he wanted to do.

⸺◦⸺

Kathleen was so busy concentrating on drawing the modifications, checking the projection, Barrett Winslow's voice startled her. When had he come into the room?

"Don't mind me," he said, taking a seat at the table beside Renee. "You're doing fine, Miss McCormick."

He knew her name. She'd never met Barrett Winslow in person.

Mr. Winslow reached across the table to shake Aria's hand. "Glad we could accommodate your requirements, and thank you for giving us more of your work." He patted Renee on the shoulder. "I like to sit in to see how my favorite employees are doing from time to time—and my favorite clients. Don't let me interrupt you, Miss McCormick."

"Sebastian is more familiar with the second floor," Kathleen said. "With Aria's accelerated timeline, he's better able to take over from here."

Mr. Winslow smiled at her and waved toward Sebastian. "Teamwork. That's what I like. Carry on."

Kathleen folded her hands in her lap while Sebastian took over.

How did he do that? Continue working as if the boss wasn't looking over his shoulder? Sebastian drew what Aria requested, offering his own suggestions while Renee took notes on those areas that would impact the interior decor.

When Sebastian stopped to review the flow of the layout, Mr. Winslow stood up again.

"I'm going to leave you to your work," he said. "Aria, always a pleasure. You'll let me know if I can help in any way?"

"Of course," she said. She stood and held out her hand to him. "Sebastian is one of your finest, and I'm so impressed with Kathleen, too."

Mr. Winslow patted Aria's hand before he left the room.

"I'll get the modifications to the construction design team right away," Sebastian said. "They should have them first thing Monday morning."

"Thank you for accommodating me on a Saturday," Aria said. "I know this is all last minute, and I know I've put everyone under the gun. It's so much easier to see the rendering of what I envisioned. Now I can see why you said those things wouldn't work, when in my mind it all seemed so easy!" She squeezed Kathleen's hand. "You're good at this, you know?"

Renee pushed away from the table. "Aria, if you're available tonight, you should join us for Sebastian's birthday party. His father is an architect, too, and their home is quite a showplace. The guest list is a virtual who's-who of everyone you'd want to know in Chicago."

"Well, happy birthday, Sebastian," Aria said. "Is today the day?"

"Yes, as a matter of fact."

"I wouldn't want to intrude. Sometimes a celebrity makes things awkward, or diverts attention."

"I'm sure they wouldn't mind," Renee continued. "Do you think?" she asked Sebastian. "After all, his grandmother is considered royalty here in Chicago. You'd fit right in. Sebastian, tell her she should come."

"I'm sure they'd welcome you," Sebastian said, "if you're available."

"Are you going?" Aria asked Kathleen.

Awkward. And Renee hadn't invited Kathleen, as if Renee were the hostess, but then neither had Sebastian. "Winslow Designs has a fairly strict non-fraternization policy," she said. "I'm not sure if that might be a violation."

"Nonsense," Aria said. "After all the work the two of you did in New Orleans, all the time you spent together? Surely you know each other well enough to be friends. Are you going to tell me Winslow Designs doesn't permit friendship between its employees?"

Maybe. If Kathleen were a man. Or if she hadn't slept with Sebastian.

"Really, Kathleen," Renee said with a dismissive sniff. "Sebastian's family knows me well, knows we've been dating for years. I don't see any reason why anyone would think the two of you were fraternizing."

"If you're free," Sebastian said to Kathleen, "you're welcome to come."

Nice, off-the-cuff, oh-yeah-you-too invitation.

"I—" she started to refuse.

"You'll go with me," Aria said. That way we'll both know someone. Other than the birthday boy, of course, but as the guest of honor, he'll be busy shaking hands and kissing babies."

"Yes, of course," Renee said, her voice strained. "It wouldn't be the same without you, Kathleen."

"Then its settled," Aria said. "Kathleen, I'll have my car pick you up. What's the dress code? Is this a fancy thing or a barbecue with jeans?"

"Business casual," Sebastian said. "I don't think either of my parents owns a pair of jeans."

"I don't think—" Kathleen tried again.

"I insist you go with me," Aria said. "Don't worry, I won't keep you out late. I have an early call tomorrow. We're shooting on Lower Wacker Drive, and the city wants to minimize the disruption to traffic. Unless you want to stay late, in which case I'm sure Sebastian can arrange to get you home."

"No, an early night suits me fine," Kathleen said.

They all exchanged addresses, Aria providing the appropriate level of excitement the rest of them seemed to be lacking.

"Ride down the elevator with me?" Aria said to Kathleen when she was getting ready to leave. "Or do you still have work to do?"

Kathleen looked for direction from Sebastian. What was she supposed to do?

"No need for you to stay. I think we've wrapped everything up."

"I'll ride with you, too," Renee said. "See you later?" She kissed Sebastian's cheek.

"See you tonight," he replied.

What had Kathleen gotten herself into?

Chapter 19

Networking, in person and face to face, is still the most effective form of salesmanship

While Kathleen waited for Aria Walton to pick her up, she glanced around her apartment. The Victorian house was subdivided much like Aria's house in New Orleans. Same high ceilings with crown molding, even if it was a different style. Kathleen's apartment was one of four, two on the lower level of the house and two upstairs on either side of the grand staircase. Like the Craftsman style houses Kathleen loved so much, a stained glass window filtered light to the foyer.

One day someone would buy this house and return it to its original glory, too.

With one last glance to check her hair in the mirror, Kathleen opened her apartment door and placed a hand to her chest. Aria Walton was standing there. *The* Aria Walton. She still couldn't get over it.

Aria wore a pair of ankle-length black pants with strappy high heels, and a sequined, white off-the-shoulder top. Kathleen's print cotton skirt and blue sleeveless shell looked dowdy by comparison.

"Nice place," Aria said, walking inside. "No neighbors conveniently visiting?"

Kathleen had considered telling Jennifer, her friend next door, that Aria would be stopping over. As a flight attendant, Jennifer had her share of celebrity encounters and wouldn't cause a fuss, but Kathleen had thought better of it. "I assumed you'd prefer your privacy."

"You are so normal! I miss normal. I'll bet Renee won't be as thoughtful, and I'm still annoyed she wouldn't even let you ride in the elevator alone with me. I've been dying to talk to you all day, but first..." she stepped back, assessed Kathleen's appearance and gave a nod of approval. "He won't be able to take his eyes off you."

"He?" Kathleen asked, knowing full well who Aria was referring to. "I don't know. I should change."

Aria reached out. "No, you look fine. Really. So what's going on with you and Sebastian? It was pretty obvious he was mesmerized during your presentation."

"I may have mentioned we have a non-fraternization policy at Winslow Designs. Any relationship between Sebastian and myself would need to remain strictly business."

"At the office, of course. But after hours?"

"All the time," Kathleen added. This was madness. Even if he wanted to spend more time with her, the way he'd said, they'd be putting their jobs at risk. She needed her paycheck. He wouldn't give up his promotion for Kathleen.

"You ready to go?" Aria asked.

No point changing her clothes. Who was she trying to impress, anyway? "Let's go."

They walked out and Kathleen locked her door. A town car waited in the gravel lot outside.

"Why do you care about Sebastian's personal life?" Kathleen asked.

Aria laughed. "I may have mentioned how ramrod straight his back has always been. Never a word or gesture that might be interpreted as unprofessional. Until now. I like him, and I like you. Blame the movie star in me for looking for that happily ever after ending."

The driver opened the back doors for them.

"Did I mention I also have an intense dislike of Renee Quinn?" Aria said once they were closed inside. "Now *there* is an unpleasant woman. She's a social climber if ever I saw one, and she clearly has her sights on Sebastian. If Sebastian's grandmother is Chicago royalty, Renee sees him as a rung on a ladder."

"You can't possibly know that," Kathleen said, even though she laughed as she spoke.

"I know the type. I'll tell you something else. I'll bet money she's hired press to be at that party tonight. That way they make the society page, with my picture to prove how important she thinks she is." Aria glanced over her shoulder as they drove away from Kathleen's apartment. "You know, if you need a place to live, I'm rarely at my house in Lake Forest. I suppose you'd want to pay rent, but I'd feel better if someone was there when I'm not, and I have a feeling you and I would be great friends. It would be fun to have a friend around when I'm home."

Like a coveted pet? "I like my apartment," Kathleen told her. "And I have great neighbors, at least for now. I do plan to buy my own place. Soon." One that required a job to fund. "Besides, I'm close to my family here."

"There are days I wish my life was simpler, and yet I wouldn't trade what I've been given for anything." Aria raised her chin. "The houses? Yeah, they might be more than I need, but another downside of celebrity is the crazies. I sometimes have to have a security detail, and that means a place for them to stay when I'm in residence." She shrugged. "In my position I can do good I might not otherwise be able to." Aria rubbed her hands together. "Like fixing you up with Sebastian."

Kathleen laughed again. "Stop. Whatever happens with me and Sebastian, it'll develop on its own." She shook a finger. "Without anyone's interference."

"See, you're holding out on me. Humor me. I don't get to have much normal conversation, girl talk, that kind of thing. We've got to be close to the same age, aren't we? Twenty-six? I need more real friends. The problem is I'm working so much, I don't get the time to do all those normal things, like hanging out and talking on the phone for hours."

"Hours?" Kathleen asked.

Aria shrugged. "Yeah. Now it's more like text messages or Snapchat in between takes." She smiled sheepishly.

The car turned into a circular driveway. Lights poured through a panel of windows separating the first floor from the second, showcasing a double staircase inside. Cars lined the edge of the driveway and the street. The driver stopped by a grand staircase that led to a double front door.

This was where Sebastian had grown up? The breath rushed from Kathleen's lungs and her knees went weak. She was so far out of her league.

A man who'd been leaning on one side of the staircase straightened and raised a camera.

"Paparazzi. Told you," Aria whispered. She smiled for the photographer and led Kathleen up the steps.

Another man wearing a tuxedo opened the front door.

"Why do I feel underdressed?" Kathleen said, struggling to breathe properly.

"The guy in the tux? Hired help. Renee did say business casual." She stopped to look Kathleen over once more. "Be prepared for Renee to be overdressed. She wants to make sure she's the most important person here, even if it is Sebastian's birthday. Mark my words."

"I shouldn't be here," Kathleen said.

"You absolutely should be here, but we can keep this brief. A couple of drinks and then we can leave."

Kathleen nodded.

The house opened to a gallery that led to the back of the house, but the party was in the spacious living room to her left. Or it might be considered a ballroom based on its size. The guests looked to be wearing clothes with designer labels. Kathleen checked her Clark sandals and working class skirt a second time.

A couple of drinks, she'd wish Sebastian happy birthday, and then they could leave.

⸻ ◦ ⸻

Renee, thankfully, had affixed herself to Sebastian's father, meeting and greeting while Sebastian disappeared into a corner to watch from a distance. She wore a red dress with a deep cut down the front, held together with flesh colored mesh. Heaven forbid she should have a wardrobe malfunction. She appeared to have a semblance of cleavage, although he'd bet most of it was attributable to a push-up bra or strategically placed body tape. He was pretty sure her bust looked better in the dress than out. Sebastian tilted his head, wondering again if he'd ever actually seen Renee's tits. Maybe back in college, but not in recent years.

Huh.

"She's working the room, preparing everyone for a big announcement," his mother said, standing behind him.

Sebastian turned to face her. "I can't imagine what that might be."

His mother scowled. "Don't play coy with me, Buddy."

"Try not to get to that, will you? An announcement?"

"Sebastian, what's going on?"

He drew a deep breath. "I have to plead idiocy. Until recently, I hadn't realized what she was up to, the carefully worded hints, the suggestions it might work to our advantage to join forces, as it were. She's not the woman I want to marry, and I plan to make that clear to her tonight. After the party."

"Then why bring her at all?"

"I'd already invited her as a plus-one. I couldn't un-invite her, now could I?" Sebastian took a sip of his Manhattan, watching Renee work the crowd. "Tell me again why Dad wanted to throw a party?"

"It's your birthday." She took hold of his arm, leaned in and kissed him. "Happy Birthday, Sebastian."

"Thanks, Mom."

She sighed. "I suppose your father wanted an excuse to have a party."

"And open The Showplace so everyone can see what a brilliant architect he is."

Renee pulled her cell phone from the bag she had looped around her wrist, looked at it and then scanned the room until she located Sebastian.

"Don't make a scene," his mother whispered.

"I wouldn't think of it," he replied as Renee cruised toward him wearing her Botox smile—yes, that had to be what it was. Was she even old enough to need Botox?

Renee looped her arm through his. "Aria's arrived," she said. "And her little pet."

"If you're referring to Kathleen, I expect you to be more gracious. Kathleen is an excellent architect."

"She's a brown noser and a parvenu."

Sebastian faced Renee. "A what?"

"Darling, it's the most flattering term I could think of for her blatant attempts to get ahead, no matter the cost."

He spared a glance at the safety net in the vee of Renee's dress. Nope, nothing to see there. "You will be polite to Kathleen, no matter what you think of her. It was rude of you to invite Aria in front of her."

"You're not defending that woman, are you?"

"Do I need to?"

Renee's fragile smile turned into a glower. "Let's greet our guests, shall we?"

"You do mean my guests, don't you? I thought this was my birthday party."

She tugged him toward the front door. "What has gotten into you this evening?"

"Have I said something wrong?" he asked.

Her smile reappeared as Aria and Kathleen walked through the door. "Aria, I'm so glad you could make it."

Sebastian made a half-bow to each of them. "I'm honored. Kathleen, thank you for coming."

Renee squeezed his arm tighter. "Don't you look cute," she said to Kathleen.

It was the same outfit she'd worn to dinner with her sister in New Orleans. Summery. The sleeveless shell brought out the blue in her print skirt—and her eyes, eyes that were filled with doubt.

Aria touched Renee's shoulder, staring at the safety net. "You know, most of the people I know who wear these dresses don't have…" she touched the top of the insert, "this."

Renee blinked several times, her mouth drawn into a thin line as she tugged at the hem of her dress.

Aria moved to the other side of Sebastian and leaned in for a hug.

When Renee recovered her smile, it was more fragile than usual. She was clearly pissed off, but Aria was a celebrity. Aria would be able to get away with a host of sins where Renee was concerned.

"I'd love to get a picture with all of us." Renee directed Sebastian and Aria away from Kathleen.

Sebastian stalled and turned to Kathleen. "Won't you join us?"

Another squeeze to his arm.

Kathleen cocked an eyebrow, lighting that blue spark he was accustomed to seeing. "If you insist."

"We should get a picture of the two of us," Renee amended. "For the newspapers, you know, and the announcement."

"What announcement?" Sebastian asked.

"Well naturally, I assumed, when Kathleen said you'd mentioned our relationship to her, she did make it sound as if you were planning to…" She forced another smile. "Oh, where are my manners. I thought you might like a picture of the two of us. It wouldn't be the first time we made the society page."

This wasn't going to end well, but he'd promised his mother he wouldn't make a scene. "My guests need a drink. Ladies?" He bowed again and led them into the formal living room where the bar was set up. An entourage followed them, people lining up to be introduced to Aria Walton.

Renee took over as hostess, introducing Aria as her best friend. "…And I told her she just had to come," he overheard her telling people.

"I shouldn't be here," Kathleen whispered beside him.

He looped an arm around her waist, unable to keep from touching her. "I want you here. I would have corrected Renee already, except I promised my mother I wouldn't make a scene. Speaking of whom—" Sebastian guided her to his mother.

"My mother, Marjorie Brooks. Mother, may I present Kathleen McCormick, my associate at Winslow Designs? She's been working with me on Aria Walton's house in New Orleans."

Kathleen took his mother's hand and smiled. "Pleased to meet you, and thank you for allowing me to join the festivities. I feel rather like a party crasher with such a last minute invitation."

"Nonsense." His mother covered Kathleen's hand and smiled brightly, with a glance to Sebastian indicating approval.

Until right now, he hadn't realized he'd wanted his mother to like Kathleen. He exhaled a sigh of relief.

"I see where Sebastian gets his eyes," Kathleen said. "Such an unusual shade of hazel."

"Yes, I imagine that's all he got from me. His coloring comes from his father."

Sebastian hadn't mentioned he came from a mixed-race marriage, but certainly Kathleen would have guessed. Would that bother her?

"Might as well get it over with," his mother said softly, as if she could read his mind. "He's going to want to present you eventually."

Kathleen's brow furrowed.

"Let me introduce you to my father," Sebastian said, taking his mother's cue. "Be forewarned, he'll probably offer you a job and tell you how much better you'd have it with his firm than at Winslow."

"There he is," his father boomed as they approached. The gray at his father's temples seemed to be spreading through his short curls. His moustache was losing color, too, making his bronze skin, a shade darker than Sebastian's, appear that much darker.

"My father, Gerald Brooks. Father, may I present Miss Kathleen McCormick? She's an associate of mine at Winslow."

"Miss McCormick," his father said, covering her hand in both of his. "A pleasure. So glad you could join us."

"Thank you for having me," she said, a smile on her face.

"But what have you done with Renee?" he asked, scanning the room.

"She's making the rounds with Ms. Walton," Sebastian told him.

"Of course. She'll make a fine hostess. Always knows exactly what to do." With another smile, his father turned away to continue another conversation.

Dismissed. Just as well.

"Sorry," Sebastian said to Kathleen.

"Don't be. He doesn't know me, and we interrupted him. Didn't we?" She smiled. "But please tell me I don't have to be presented to your queen of a grandmother. I already feel terribly out of place."

He turned to face her. "Does it bother you? My grandmother's social status?"

Kathleen winced. "It does reinforce that I don't belong here."

"Join the club." He glanced to the vaulted ceiling, at the guests, most of whom hadn't even offered a courtesy birthday wish. "I've never fit in with my father's crowd. He still feels the need to prove himself, and me, by proxy." He raised his glass to her. "You look beautiful, by the way. I loved that outfit when you wore it in New Orleans."

"This old thing?" She did a curtsey. "My go-to, doncha know. I forgot my cocktail dress at home."

"Renee told you business casual." He waved a hand at his own khakis and oxford shirt. "She's the one who's overdressed." He leaned closer. "Since you're here, want to see my bedroom? I'd bet no one will miss us."

Her cheeks flushed as she grinned. "Aria will. I'm her new best friend."

A proprietary hand was back on his arm. Sebastian straightened and forced a smile for Renee.

"I asked your father to announce our engagement in a few minutes. I hope you don't mind," Renee said, flashing a false smile to Kathleen as she spoke to him.

"What engagement would that be?" he asked.

Renee's hands went to her hips. "You're being very rude to me tonight."

He cocked his head. "How so?"

"For starters, I've hardly seen you since I got here."

"That's because you've been networking with my father."

"And now you're whispering with your little associate. It doesn't look good, Sebastian."

He straightened and gave her a patient smile. "Doesn't look good for whom?"

"I've been very patient up 'til now," Renee said evenly.

"I'm not sure what engagement you expect to announce, Renee."

She tugged him into the kitchen, where caterers were lining trays with hors d'oeuvres. "If you intend to play with your little associate, you're going to lose your promotion and your job."

"Funny you would be jealous of Kathleen, and not Aria."

Renee shrugged. "Aria Walton is a movie star."

"And your point?"

"I'm not jealous, I'm merely concerned about appearances." She blinked. Too many times. Her hands went to her hips. "Something's different about you, Sebastian. I haven't seen you act so irresponsibly since we were in college."

"I don't suppose you have, although I don't know that irresponsible is the word you want."

"Explain yourself."

He rubbed his chin. "Have you considered this is one of the most personal conversations we've ever had? Don't you find that odd?"

Her chest heaved with an exaggerated sigh. "What I find odd is that you seem to be dragging your feet on proposing. Do you or do you not intend to marry me?"

"I do not."

Her spine straightened. "But your admin told me you'd been preparing a prenup, and your associate said…"

He turned to face her, angry she'd made Margot one more person he'd have to fire. "Kathleen didn't *say* anything. And why would you be discussing my personal life with my admin?"

She was blinking again. "We understand each other, you and I. It isn't as if we haven't discussed the benefits, particularly to our careers."

"So you want a marriage of convenience? Sterile? No unnecessary attachments? Ten minutes once a month?" He was losing patience.

"Your parents seem perfectly happy with their marriage, and didn't they get married to make a statement at a time when mixed marriages weren't *au courant*?"

Renee had no idea. Sebastian had promised his mother he wouldn't make a scene. "My parents' marriage is not your concern."

"But your father said…"

"His father would never have suggested I marry him as a political statement," his mother said, stepping into the kitchen. "How dare you imply to know anything about my marriage."

Two pink spots appeared in Renee's cheeks, barely visible beneath her makeup.

"I didn't mean…" Renee said.

"Oh, I think you did," his mother said. "Sebastian, I'm afraid I cannot support this engagement. Do what you will, but this woman is not welcome in my home."

"Mrs. Brooks," Renee said, "my deepest apologies, but Mr. Brooks implied…"

"I don't care what you thought Mr. Brooks implied," his mother said.

Renee turned to Sebastian. "I think it's time you took me home."

"And leave my own birthday party?" he asked.

Renee stared at him a moment, lips pursed, nostrils flaring. "You did say we should have a discussion after the party, did you not?"

"And I think we've just had it," he told her. "I know you've been campaigning for a proposal, and I meant to set you straight. We've been friends a long time, Renee, but I have no intention of taking this any further."

"How dare you!"

"I think you've got that backward," his mother said.

"Don't expect to call me the next time you need a plus-one," she muttered.

"I wouldn't think of it," Sebastian replied.

She turned, stumbled in her heels, and walked out the back door.

"I'm sorry, Mother. I didn't mean to involve you."

"I can't say I'm sorry." She smiled at Sebastian and he hugged her.

With one arm across her shoulders, he guided his mother out of the kitchen.

"There he is," his father said.

This couldn't be good.

"Everyone, my son has an announcement he'd like to make." His father raised his glass.

Sebastian scanned the room and found Kathleen, laughing with Aria. As if she could feel his eyes on her, she turned and smiled at him, raising her glass in a toast.

"Thank you all for coming to my birthday party," Sebastian said. All those people he didn't know mumbled birthday wishes.

"Get on with it, boy," his father said. "I've been told you have something more to tell us."

Damn Renee. Sebastian glanced around the roomful of people he hardly knew.

"Don't keep us waiting any longer," his father said, his voice low and threatening. Clearly Renee had told him Sebastian was dragging his feet.

Sebastian dug his hands into his pants pockets and closed around the ring box.

No. Not here. Not now. His heart beat like a ticking time bomb.

"I'm not sure what you're referring to," Sebastian said as evenly as he could manage.

"I was told there was a proposal in the offing. Where is Renee?"

Sebastian surveyed the room. "I believe she's gone home."

His father set his drink on a table. "What did you say to her?"

"I'm not sure what you mean," Sebastian replied.

"Renee told me you meant to propose to her."

"Shouldn't your son be the one to give you that kind of information?" his mother asked.

God bless his mother.

His father held out a hand. "Something's not right here. What did you do to offend the woman you're supposed to marry? Sebastian, explain yourself."

Sebastian reined in his temper, determined to keep his promise to his mother that he wouldn't make a scene, although his father apparently hadn't gotten that memo. "I'm not sure what you need me to explain, Father. I had no plans to make any announcements tonight."

"Renee said…"

"Renee said what?" Sebastian asked sharply.

His father narrowed his eyes and drew a deep breath. "You're thirty years old and you still haven't got a brain in your head."

Kathleen crossed the room, eyes flashing, and stopped beside Sebastian. "He's a brilliant architect and highly respected—by everyone except you, it would seem."

Sebastian held out an arm to hold her back. "You don't have to defend me."

"And who are you again?" his father bellowed. "I suppose your case of hero worship for your boss has turned his head. Is that it? A pretty little tramp turns your head and you offend the woman you're supposed to marry?"

Sebastian lowered his voice. "You owe Kathleen an apology."

His father laughed and his mother stepped between them.

"Stop this nonsense. I won't have you insulting our guests and spoiling Sebastian's birthday party," she said.

His father flapped his lips.

Kathleen turned to Sebastian. "I'm sorry, I shouldn't have said anything. I think it's time to go. Do you mind if I ask Aria to take me home?"

"I'll take you home." Sebastian took her hand.

"Now wait just a minute," his father said.

Sebastian cast a glance at his father. "Thanks for the birthday party."

Aria turned to Sebastian's father. "I think I've worn out my welcome as well." She hugged Sebastian's mother. "Thank you for allowing me to help Sebastian celebrate his birthday."

Chapter 20

When negotiating, state your position clearly.

Sebastian kissed Kathleen goodnight and all her good sense deserted her. They made out in the car like a couple of teenagers, and then their hands got involved, at which point she'd invited him inside.

An hour later, Sebastian was sound asleep in her bed. Kathleen eased out and crept to the big front porch of the Victorian house. She sat on one of the chairs with her knees to her chest. Her temper had gotten the best of her once again, but what kind of a father called his intelligent, successful son an idiot? Sebastian was on the short list to become a partner in Winslow Designs. Most parents would be proud of his accomplishments, especially at such a young age.

His parents must hate her. She and Sebastian hardly knew each other, and after what she'd seen, she was pretty sure they orbited in different solar systems.

What was she doing? This relationship would cost them their jobs.

A soft voice called from the window of the other first-floor apartment. "Hey girlfriend, watcha doing out there? Didn't you bring a man home?" Her neighbor Jennifer peeked out.

"What are you doing up in the middle of the night?" Kathleen whispered.

"Wondering why, when you've been banging the headboard, you'd retreat to the porch. Seems like you'd have better places to be, better things to do. Unless you're trying to ditch him."

Kathleen chuckled. "No. Just needed a minute to think."

"Wanna talk about it? Or I could go in there and kick him out for you."

"No, and no." She hugged her knees tighter. "This has been one hell of a month."

The front door opened and Sebastian stood there, in his shorts and nothing else, looking sexy as sin. "Kathleen?"

"Hey."

Jennifer stepped away from the window, but it remained open.

"Everything okay?" he asked.

"I needed air." She let her legs drop to the porch and pushed to her feet. As much as she loved her neighbors, they didn't need to hear her drama. She wasn't even sure *she* wanted to know what was really going on. "Did I remember to wish you a happy birthday?" she asked, struggling for something to say.

"Technically, that was yesterday, but thank you, anyway." He rubbed his arms. "The night air is chilly. Come back inside?"

As she took a step toward him, something scraped across the porch deck. Sebastian reached for her and yelled, "Look out!"

Her foot hooked on the leg of the small patio table, enough to overturn it and send her arms windmilling to catch her balance. Sebastian caught hold of her hand before she went tumbling down the stairs.

"Kathleen!" Jennifer ran out the front door. She turned on Sebastian. "What happened?"

"Did you see that?" Sebastian said, looking from one to the other of them.

Kathleen clung to him. "See what?"

"That woman. The same one I saw in New Orleans." He glanced around the porch, holding her tight. "You could have been hurt."

"What woman?" Jennifer asked.

"She moved the table," Sebastian said.

"I didn't see nobody," Jennifer said. "It's dark. Maybe you saw a shadow or something."

"The table moved," Kathleen said.

"Then I'd be worried about him," Jennifer said. "He's the only other one out here."

"I didn't…" Sebastian started. "Can we go inside?"

Kathleen nodded and squeezed Jennifer's arm. "I'll talk to you in the morning?"

"You okay?" Jennifer asked, sending a murderous look at Sebastian.

"Yes."

Kathleen led Sebastian to the sofa in her living room. "What did you see?" she asked.

He bent over his knees, forearms on his legs. "Your neighbor's right. It was probably a shadow."

She touched his shoulder, allowing herself a gentle squeeze but refraining from trailing her hand down the broad planes of his chest. "What did you see?"

"In New Orleans, I was drunk." He shook his head. "There was no woman."

"When?"

"It's crazy."

"No crazier than the ghost in our hotel room." She had a bad feeling.

"There was no ghost."

"Talk to me," she said.

"I imagined a woman in a long dress. A costume." He wound a finger around the top of his head. "Her hair was in braids like a crown on her head. I could have sworn I saw her push you toward the street in New Orleans, but then she disappeared. Like sun spots. One minute you see them, the next you don't."

"And you saw the same woman tonight?"

"It's dark out there."

"Sebastian, you have to tell me."

"Why? So you can tell Barrett Winslow I'm the crazy one?"

"I don't think you're crazy.

He met her gaze, his jaw pulsing. "The table moved. By itself."

"Not by itself," she said.

He squirmed. "I thought I saw the same woman, the one I saw in New Orleans, put it in your way." He scowled. "I must be more tired than I thought."

Helene. "But why?" she wondered out loud.

"I'm sure it was my imagination."

"I'm not."

"You're not going to start with the ghost thing again, are you? And I thought your ghost was a man."

Kathleen hadn't been afraid of Victor. If Sebastian was right, why was Helene trying to hurt her?

Sebastian put an arm across Kathleen's shoulders and pulled her close. "Let's go back to bed. No more nocturnal wanderings, okay? It's too easy to lose your footing in the dark." He rested his chin on the top of her head. "I don't want you to get hurt."

"That makes two of us." Even if tripping— twice—hadn't been accidental, her feelings for Sebastian were as much a threat to her wellbeing as an angry ghost.

She should let Jared know about the ghost. She'd send a text to Siobhan to let them know what Sebastian had seen. If Helene was haunting her, Jared would know what to do. As for Sebastian, she'd have to figure that out on her own.

———◆———

Kathleen had slipped silently out of bed and into the bathroom. After last night, Sebastian was aware of every movement she made.

The shower turned on and Sebastian reached for his phone. As expected, a barrage of texts waited for him. Three from his father and two from Renee. He expected the ones from his father, but the ones from Renee caught him off-guard. He wouldn't have been surprised if she'd cursed him to hell and back, or if she'd frosted him over with precisely worded logic.

Her texts apologized for putting him on the spot and she wanted to discuss what happened.

Did she actually care about Sebastian?

Sebastian glanced at the closed bathroom door. He felt obligated to hear Renee out, knowing it wouldn't change anything. Kathleen's genuine nature highlighted the manipulating Renee had done. Renee had called Kathleen a parvenu, a social climber. A classic case of pot/kettle.

No, Kathleen wasn't a social climber.

Kathleen had defended him to his father. He grinned at the way she'd clapped back at his father's insults, at the memory of his father's face, suffused with rage.

He wanted to blame Renee for setting him up, his father for goading him on, but the truth of the matter was Sebastian had been off balance from the moment he'd met Kathleen. She'd shown him what a real life looked like. He wanted that so badly. Yes, he'd bought a ring for Kathleen, but he'd considered proposing to Renee, too. He needed to think this through and not make a rash decision.

What if Kathleen represented an ideal? Lust for life, forbidden desires, broken rules—what if that had translated into lust for Kathleen? She deserved better than that, and he hated he wasn't sure he could tell the difference.

"Hey," Kathleen called from the bathroom door, wrapped in a towel the same way she had been in New Orleans.

"Hey," he replied.

"You look so serious."

"I should do damage control," he said lamely.

"Renee?"

Again, he considered how amazing Kathleen was. She could have been screeching at him about Renee. Could have railed about how rude his father was. Should be running away from Sebastian after his lunatic ramblings about a disappearing woman every time Kathleen stumbled.

"I was thinking about my father, but yes. I should follow up with Renee, too."

"Do you want me to come with you?" she asked.

As if he needed a shield. His heart warmed with her offer. "No. You'd only give him the audience he craves."

She nodded.

Sebastian stared at her, struck by how gorgeous she was in nothing more than a towel. He'd taken advantage of the way she'd opened herself to him, but his conscience demanded he evaluate his motives. Renee, as detached as she seemed, was clearly upset. He didn't want to make the same mistake with Kathleen.

"I can make you breakfast," she offered. "Let me get dressed first."

"You don't need to go to all that trouble."

She smiled. "Okay, then let me get dressed and we can talk some more."

Sebastian nodded, then moved to the living room where he sent a text to Renee.

Are you available for a meeting today?

She'd obviously been waiting to hear from him. Her response came within moments.

No. Can I meet you in your office in the morning?

He sent an okay and tucked his phone into his pocket.

"We could go out for breakfast, if you'd prefer," Kathleen said, buttoning her shirt as she walked out of the bedroom.

"I should probably…" He turned away, afraid if he didn't leave now, he wouldn't be able to. He wanted to hug her, to reassure her everything was going to work out, but in the bright light of morning, the events of the night before weighed heavily. He should have spoken to Renee sooner. No, Kathleen deserved better than what he'd given her thus far. "I should head over to my folks."

She licked her lips, her expressive blue eyes clouded. "Okay."

He hugged her and leaned in for a kiss. "You okay?"

She smiled. "Why wouldn't I be?"

He hugged her again. "I'll call you later."

"Okay."

She wasn't smiling, and her eyes were missing their sparkle. She didn't look okay. Sebastian squeezed her hand before he let go. "Bye."

Kathleen folded her arms as he trotted out to his car, waved as he pulled out of the lot in front of the Victorian house.

If he stopped by his parents' house this morning, his father would be on the golf course. He'd talk through his plans with his mother first and see what she had to say.

When he walked up the front steps half an hour later, his mother met him at the door. The expression on her face said she was worried about him, but that was nothing new. She hugged him and he gave her a kiss on the cheek. "Hi, Mom." She stepped aside so he could walk into the house, through the gallery to the kitchen. "Dad golfing?"

"Yes," she said.

He helped himself to a cup of coffee and sat at the table in the breakfast nook.

"Thanks for sticking up for me last night," he said, sipping his coffee.

"That's what mothers do." She sat across from him and put a hand over his. "Although I noticed a certain young lady also rushed to your defense."

He bowed his head. Talking to his mom wasn't as hard as listening to his dad tell him what a screw-up he was.

The silence stretched. He wasn't sure what he wanted to say.

His mother spoke first. "Why did Renee think you were going to propose to her?"

"Renee and I have been friends and business associates since college. Helping each other out. In hindsight, she's been hinting at a proposal for a long time, but I was too stupid to realize. I was looking at rings when I went to New Orleans, considering marriage as a business proposition." He raised his eyes, but couldn't hold his mother's gaze.

His mother sat silently, listening. Waiting.

"When I met Kathleen, she said some things that resonated with me. I realized Renee had been trying to manipulate me, and I nearly let her." He did meet his mother's gaze then. "I realized what I'd been missing."

She smiled. "Kathleen seems like a lovely girl." She released his hand, her smile fading. "Are you in love with her?"

"Winslow has a strict non-fraternization policy. One or both of us could lose our jobs."

"But?" she prompted.

"The more I think about it, the more it makes sense for me to leave Winslow Designs."

She pushed away from the table. "That's rather drastic. What about your promotion? Are you considering going to work with your father? After all this time?"

"No." He shook his head. "I don't care about the damn promotion anymore. I'll give Winslow a month's notice in order to transition my clients. I've been targeting firms that deal with restorations."

His mother's lips curled into a smile. "And that's what you want to do?"

Sebastian took another sip of his coffee. "I got caught up in trying to prove myself. Stepped on someone else's treadmill and couldn't get off."

"I've been telling you that for years."

He shrugged. "It might have gotten lost in Dad's noise."

"And Kathleen?" she asked.

God, he felt like a heel. "She's a colleague, and a very talented one. My resignation will give her the chance to advance in her career."

"Are you sure that's what she wants?"

"I don't want to say anything to her until after I've tendered my resignation. She doesn't want to lose her job. I need to get off the hamster wheel before I consider anything more." He tugged on his ear. "Dad's going to expect me to sign on with him when he finds out."

"You haven't let that get in your way before," his mother said with a quirk of the eyebrow. "But it might not be such a bad idea in case it takes time to land a new job."

"No. That's not an option." He heaved a sigh. "I'm not sure why it took me so long to make the move."

"I'd give the credit to a certain young redhead."

"Not going to argue." Sebastian smiled.

"Buddy," his mother said gently, "you've been too focused. Maybe this girl is a good thing if she's helping you think of things other than your ambition. The things you want from life should include more than your job."

Images of Kathleen flitted through his mind. Doing the as-built when she dabbed the drop of perspiration between her breasts, standing in her hotel room wearing nothing but a towel, curled up beside him in bed. "And if you can't have the things you want?" he asked.

"If it's what you want, it's worth putting in the extra effort," she said. "You certainly know how to do that."

Sebastian had spent the last five years cultivating control and precision. Buried in work, he didn't have time to feel or to think. He dealt in accurate measurements and planned outcomes, his life predictable and structured. No surprises meant things were going well.

It was also boring as hell.

Forbidden fruit always tasted better. Was that why he wanted Kathleen McCormick?

"I don't know what I want."

"Then you damn well better figure it out," his father said. He walked in from the garage wearing his golf attire—plaid pants and a yellow polo. He closed the door behind him. "To what do we owe this honor?"

"I'll leave you two to talk." His mother excused herself to wash the breakfast dishes.

Sebastian immediately straightened his back, preparing for the inevitable confrontation. "I'm leaving Winslow Designs."

His father raised his chin, effectually looking down his nose at Sebastian. "Ready to join the family business then?"

"No. Ready to use the degree I earned doing what I want to do."

"So they fired you?"

"No, I plan to resign."

His father folded his arms and narrowed his eyes. "Because…?"

"I think I just told you why."

"Ah. Didn't get that promotion. I told you not to be too disappointed, boy. Not like you to quit, though. Do the smart thing. Work for me."

Sebastian shook his head. "Not going to happen, Dad. Not unless you have room for a restoration architect."

His father shook his head and walked off, mumbling as he went. "Idiot son. He's your boy, Marjorie. Always was. Not a brain in his head."

Sebastian rose to his feet. "Did you mean to insult my mother? You owe her an apology."

His father stopped halfway down the hall, turned slowly and glared at Sebastian. "Pretty sure you were the one I was insulting."

"My mistake. Then you owe me an apology."

His father shook a finger at Sebastian. "When you wise up and do the right thing, then maybe I'll give you an apology."

"And what's the right thing? What *you* think I should do?"

"Sebastian," his mother scolded him. "He's still your father."

"And he did insult you, Mom. Why do you put up with it?"

She ran from the kitchen, leaving Sebastian and his father glaring at each other.

"And now you've made her cry," his father said.

"I think you share part of that blame."

"You don't know what you're talking about."

"I take responsibility for my actions," Sebastian said. "You want me to respect what you say to me? You need to do the same."

"Same smart-mouthed kid you always were."

"Not a kid anymore. And I don't have to put up with this shit." Sebastian stalked down the hall and walked out. He'd done what he came to do, told them both what he'd come to tell them. It was time to go.

His mother met him by the door and lay a hand on his arm. "I'll talk to him, make him apologize. We could all go to lunch and he could apologize to Kathleen, too."

Sebastian scoffed. "He'll never apologize."

She wrapped her arms around him and he returned the hug.

"Fine," he conceded. "I'll see if she's willing to break bread with him."

Chapter 21

"Life isn't about finding yourself. Life is about creating yourself." – George Bernard Shaw

Kathleen pressed the call button several times—where was an elevator when you needed one?—and when it arrived, she stepped inside, punched the button for twelve and folded her arms. Monday mornings were daunting in the best of circumstances, and she had a pile of work waiting on her desk. As the doors started to close, a hand came in to hold them open.

Sebastian shouldered in, alongside the half dozen other Winslow Designs employees.

"Good morning, Miss McCormick," he said with a lazy smile.

And there went her heart getting all fluttery again. "Mr. Brooks."

"You're saving me a phone call. Can you stop by my office to discuss the New Orleans project this morning?"

They were never going to be able to pull this off. Even Aria Walton had commented that she could see the sparks flying between them. Kathleen was determined not to violate the non-fraternization policy at Winslow Designs. At least not in public.

She needed a job if she ever wanted to buy a house.

"Is it urgent? Or do you mind if I stop at my desk first?"

"It'll only take a few moments, if you don't mind riding up with me," he said.

"Very well."

The elevator made intermittent stops until, at the nineteenth floor, the last of the other riders had gotten off.

Sebastian was so close she could smell him, that clean cola scent, his breath hot on her neck.

Twenty.

"We're running out of floors," he whispered in her ear, sending shivers across her skin.

Twenty-one.

"I need to kiss you."

Twenty-two.

She faced him, saw the fire in his eyes, the passion he hid so carefully. The passion she'd unleashed. She grabbed the back of his head and kissed him until she was breathless.

Twenty-four.

The elevator dinged ahead of its arrival and they broke apart. She put her hands to her face, aware of the heat that undoubtedly flushed her skin.

The elevator doors opened.

Barrett Winslow stood there, waiting. He glanced from one to the other of them.

Sebastian lifted his chin. "Good morning."

"Sebastian." Mr. Winslow turned to Kathleen. "Kathleen."

"Mr. Winslow."

Sebastian cleared his throat. "If you'll come with me, we can clear up the latest modification Aria sent," he said to Kathleen.

She bowed her head and followed him to his office.

Kathleen took a seat while Sebastian closed the door. He perched on the corner of his desk.

"You think he saw us?" she whispered.

Sebastian smiled. "I have a solution for the non-fraternization issue. If you're free after work, I can fill you in. Too many ears here."

Her skin tingled with the nearness of him. She folded her hands in her lap. "Yes, I'd be interested to hear what you have in mind. I trust your meeting went well yesterday?"

"I'd say so." He leaned forward. "My mother suggested we get together for lunch one day soon, the four of us, so that my father can apologize to you."

Kathleen's mouth went dry. "I'm not sure…"

"And I'd like to meet your family, unless you have an objection."

"We have dinner together every Friday. You're welcome to join us." Dinner with the family. The weight of her words hit her. She'd never invited a man to dinner with her family.

Her mother's house was light years from the house Sebastian's parents lived in. What would Sebastian think of her mother's home?

Sebastian's eyes focused outside his office. He straightened. "I have another appointment this morning, and I see she's arrived. Dinner. Tonight. I'll meet you in the lobby at six?"

Kathleen turned to look over her shoulder. Renee was visible in the sidelight beside his office door, wearing a perfectly tailored black suit, arms folded. Kathleen rose to her feet, her pulse kicking up. She shouldn't be surprised, Renee was doing the interior design for Aria, after all.

"Talk to you later," Kathleen said, reaching for the door handle.

"Miss McCormick," Renee said icily.

Miss McCormick? Kathleen wasn't going to get drawn into the formalities with this woman. "Good morning, Renee."

Renee walked past her, into Sebastian's office. Kathleen headed toward the elevators, with one last glance over her shoulder. She rolled her fists closed, wishing she could be a fly on his wall.

<hr>

"Thank you for agreeing to meet with me this morning," Renee said. "I acted badly, and I want to apologize. I'm sorry if I ruined your birthday." She shot a glance at the door. "I still think that girl is trouble."

Sebastian bowed his head. He wasn't going to get into an argument about Kathleen. "I apologize if I've taken advantage of our friendship," he said. "It was never my intention to mislead you."

She arched a perfectly manicured eyebrow. "Mislead?"

"Renee, I don't think either one of us wants a marriage of convenience, a business arrangement." She started to protest, but he held up a hand. "I know we'd discussed the benefits several times, but you couldn't seriously consider that. You deserve more."

Her expression was unreadable. Carefully cultivated. "Certainly it would have been more than a business arrangement. We do have affection for each other. Respect."

"I do respect you," he said.

"Is it that woman? That associate? Is that what made you change your mind?" she asked.

He'd obviously underestimated Renee's feelings. He took her hands. "You remember when we were in college? When we used to laugh and have fun?" Except even in college, she'd never wanted to spend the night together, and neither had he. He hadn't thought twice about spending the night with Kathleen.

"We've grown up since then," she said. "What is this about, Sebastian?"

"Ten minutes," he said.

"What on earth does that mean?"

"And children," he continued.

"Who has time for that muss and fuss?"

"And I definitely want more than ten minutes—ten minutes that I have to schedule."

"Is this a negotiation?" she asked. "This is about the sex? You know you never last longer than ten minutes, but if you think you can…"

"And children?"

She stared at him, her expression still tight and unreadable.

Margot knocked and stuck her head in the door. "Mr. Winslow asked to see you…"

"Can't you see Mr. Brooks is in a meeting?" Renee snapped.

Margot raised her eyebrows, backed away and closed the door again.

"We're two of a kind," Renee said, her voice hushed. "Where is this coming from? We've always appreciated that we're both goal-oriented, ambitious, career-driven people. That's what I most admire about you. I never worried you'd want more from me than I had to offer, and vice-versa. You want children?" She scoffed. "I won't do that to my body, but I might consider adopting a third-world brat and hiring a nanny if that's what you wanted."

Sebastian shook his head. "I'm not asking you to."

She straightened her suit jacket, picked at an imaginary piece of lint. "You're right. We've been friends a long time, Sebastian, but I'm afraid you've abused that friendship." She gave him her iciest smile. "As I told you Saturday night, there can be no more friends with benefits. No more plus-one events. Our relationship from here on will be strictly professional."

"I understand."

She stared at him a moment before she continued. "I never pegged you for a dreamer. Not since you've been with Winslow. I thought you'd grown out of your idealistic college days." She offered him her hand, princess fashion.

Sebastian took her hand between both of his, raised it to his lips and kissed it. "I am sorry this didn't work out the way you'd hoped. I apologize for the inconvenience."

Tears welled in her eyes, the first sign of real emotion he'd seen from her. Her voice was choked. "I've been waiting for you to propose for years. This is more than an inconvenience, Sebastian." She turned and walked out.

Renee had never given him any indication of her feelings. He felt like the ass Kathleen had accused him of being.

He escorted Renee to the elevator and waited for the doors to close before retracing his steps.

"Margot. My office," he called as he passed her desk.

While she followed him in, he sat at his desk. "Close the door."

She did as he asked, eyeing him warily. He knew he should invite her to sit, but until he found out what she'd told Renee, he meant to keep Margot on her toes.

"I'm sure you know Ms. Quinn," he began.

"Of course."

He folded his hands and leaned on his desk. "She said something that distresses me. Is there any reason you might have told her I was drawing up a prenuptial agreement?"

Margot's face screwed into a mask of confusion. No one could be that good of an actress. "I've never spoken to her other than on business-related matters." Her eyes grew large and her lips thinned into a straight line. "She said I...? Sebastian, I would never..."

He held up a hand to stop her. More of Renee's manipulations?

"Oh..." Margot said, dropping into a seat across his desk. Her face paled. "Oh, Sebastian."

"Then you did say something?"

She shook her head. "No, but I did make a note. You were in a meeting with Mr. Winslow when your lawyer called you back. He said he'd left you a voicemail, but wanted to see what your availability was for a meeting about your prenup. Ms. Quinn was standing by my desk." Margot frowned. "She must have read my note. Sebastian, I'm sorry."

Margot was a good admin, and at this point, he was more willing to believe her story than Renee's. Considering he had his letter of resignation prepared, the truth didn't matter. "Thank you for clearing that up. That's all."

She rose from the seat, clearly expecting the worst. Head hanging, she opened his door. "Don't forget Mr. Winslow wants to see you."

Promotion day. Was he calling Sebastian in to give him the news? Sebastian stepped into Barrett's office, shook his hand and they both sat. "You wanted to talk to me?"

"This new project seems to agree with you," Barrett said. "That, or you've finally popped the question? How is Renee?"

The perfect opening, but Sebastian didn't step into it.

Barrett folded his hands in the center of his desk and made direct eye contact. "I promise you, you'll be my first pick next year."

Next year? "Excuse me?" Sebastian said.

"I couldn't swing a promotion for you this year. The partners voted to hold you back one more year."

One more year. When he'd be thirty-one. A year later than his father had achieved his perception of success.

Don't be too disappointed when it doesn't happen.

Barrett steepled his hands. "In addition, I know you'd mentioned Kathleen McCormick seemed unpolished, rough around the edges. She's worked with Lauren Ferguson on numerous projects, and Lauren agreed that although Kathleen's work is exceptional, she seems to be lacking in the area of interpersonal skills."

"She can be fiery," Sebastian said. "But she handled herself well when we met with Aria Walton. I think she understands the need to be diplomatic when the situation calls for it, and her work *is* exceptional."

"It sounds as if she's won you over," Barrett said.

"I will admit to some hesitation when you assigned her to me, but she proved herself."

"By submitting her designs to the client instead of yours?"

"An honest mistake, one that worked in our favor." Sebastian's skin tingled. He didn't like the direction this conversation was headed. The only other person who knew about Kathleen's mistake other than Aria was Renee.

"Renee expressed concern after meeting Kathleen," Barrett continued. "She felt Kathleen was disrespectful toward her. Do you know anything about that?"

"I don't think they became fast friends, no, but I wouldn't put all the blame on Kathleen."

Barrett straightened. "Renee suggested Kathleen might have a crush on you, and while she knows you would never act inappropriately, she didn't trust the young woman who'd insulted her. You are aware of the non-fraternization policy?" Barrett continued.

"Of course." Had Barrett seen the kiss in the elevator?

"Do you have anything to add to Renee's observation?"

"I'm surprised you would indulge in gossip," Sebastian said.

Barrett cocked his head. "It's of no consequence, but based on Kathleen's behavior and the error she made in New Orleans when she sent the wrong designs, I thought it best to terminate her employment. I'm sure she and Renee would have butted heads on the Aria Walton contract."

Sebastian's heart did a dead-stop. Was he next? "You might have reassigned Kathleen."

"And then there's the subject of the gossip you brought up," Barrett said.

Here it comes.

"I'll ask you again if there's anything you'd like to add."

Sebastian's hands tightened in his lap. "As much as I've viewed you as a father and I've appreciated your mentorship, you are not my father. If you have a question to ask, I'd rather you were forthright rather than fishing for an answer you may or may not already have."

Barrett considered his response a moment and must have decided not to pursue it. "You know I think very highly of you. You're right, I shouldn't concern myself with gossip."

Except Sebastian already felt he was being punished for the mistake Shep Collier had made, a mistake the associate had tried to deflect to Sebastian. "Can I ask you to be frank?" he asked. "Why didn't I get the promotion this year?"

Barrett sat back and folded his arms. "I told you. The board didn't feel you were quite ready. You're still young. You'll get it next year."

Except he didn't believe that. He'd outperformed all the other candidates for promotion. "And what will be the excuse next year?"

Barrett narrowed his eyes. "Perhaps assigning Kathleen to you was a mistake. It seems her truculence has rubbed off on you. This isn't what I expect from you, Sebastian."

It would have been nice to leave with the promotion, an extra star on his resume, but he'd made his decision. Promotion or not, Sebastian was done bringing prestige to a firm that didn't recognize his efforts. Done compromising his goals to fit someone else's ambitions.

"Since I'm here, I'd like to tender my resignation. I've prepared a letter and I can have it on your desk in five minutes."

Barrett rose to his feet. "You're being hasty. This isn't like you at all, Sebastian. Do I need to worry about what went on between you and Kathleen McCormick? Is the gossip true?"

"Still looking for a way to discredit me?" Sebastian fired back. "I've given you everything you've demanded of me and more. There are other projects I want to pursue, projects that don't line up with Winslow Designs' vision."

"Now, look. I don't know what's going on between you and Kathleen McCormick…"

"Draw whatever conclusions you see fit," Sebastian interrupted him. "My letter is already prepared. If you'll excuse me, I'll get it to you right away." He rose from his chair and walked out of Barrett's office, his heart pounding.

"Sebastian, you should reconsider," Barrett said, standing in Sebastian's doorway a moment later. "You've been working hard. Your work ethic is commendable, but every man has his breaking point. Maybe you need time off to recharge."

"You're right. Every man has his breaking point," Sebastian echoed. "And I've reached mine."

"If it's about the girl, you might be grateful. By letting her go, I've cleared the way for you to pursue her."

Sebastian shook his head. "No, you let a talented associate go. You passed me by for a promotion I deserved based on the testimony of a disgruntled employee, Shep Collier—or am I wrong? Or is your prejudice based on gossip?"

When Barrett didn't respond, Sebastian nodded.

"Blame it on the girl if it makes you feel better," Sebastian said. "It's time for me to pursue the projects I went to school for."

Chapter 22

"I didn't say it was your fault. I said I was going to blame you."

Kathleen slammed her car door and stomped up the steps of the Victorian house. Not only did she have to put house hunting on hold, she didn't know how much longer she could afford to rent her apartment.

On the bright side, she didn't have to worry about missing a mortgage payment.

She could always take Aria Walton up on her offer to live in Lake Forest.

Inside the foyer, her hands shook as she struggled to slot the key into her apartment door.

"Dammit," she said, tears clouding her vision.

She dropped to sit on the first step of the ornate staircase that led to the two apartments upstairs and held her head, taking deep breaths to calm down.

Jennifer peered through her open door across the foyer. "Kathleen?"

Kathleen wiped her eyes and jumped to her feet. "Sorry. I didn't know you were home."

Jennifer glanced at the front door. "Um, my car's in the lot out front." She opened her door wider. "I don't have a flight until this afternoon. You want a cup of coffee? You don't look so good."

"I got fired," Kathleen sobbed.

Jennifer stepped out of her apartment and hugged Kathleen. "What happened?"

"He said he had a solution to get around the non-fraternization policy," Kathleen said. "I certainly hope firing me to clear the way for his promotion wasn't that solution. Have I been deluding myself that his inner jerk might have changed his ways? Then again, why bother to take a female architect seriously? None of the guys I went to school with did."

Jennifer steered Kathleen into her apartment. "Are we talking about the guy who stayed over Saturday night? The one who tried to push you down the stairs?"

"He didn't push me down the stairs. He kept me from falling." Her cell phone rang. Sebastian.

"Is that him?" Jennifer asked.

"Yes. I can't talk to him. Not right now."

"Not right now, and not ever if he's responsible for getting you fired. What kind of a jerk would do that?"

Kathleen winced. He wouldn't have done that to her, would he? "He let me take the lead on an important project. Let me do the presentation, even after we got back." She held out her arms. "But that stupid promotion was pretty important to him. Why am I surprised?"

"Block him. Delete his number. You don't need someone like that trying to ruin your career. What reason did he give for firing you?"

"He didn't. HR called me down. Illinois is an at-will state. They don't have to give me a reason." Kathleen took a calming breath. "But they could have. Winslow has a non-fraternization policy, which we clearly violated, even if no one else knows. Maybe the CEO saw us making out in the elevator. Maybe Sebastian got fired, too." She replayed the moment the elevator doors opened in her head. "No, he couldn't have seen us, but my damn complexion gives me away every time. I'm sure I was flushed."

"I can see where making out in the elevator might have been a bad idea." Jennifer chuckled.

Kathleen's phone chimed with a text. "Damn," she said, reading it. "He's coming over. I can't talk to him. Not yet. I'm going over to my ma's."

"Want me to give him a message?"

"No. Don't tell him anything. You haven't seen me, in case he asks."

"I'd tell you to stop over when you come home, but I have an overnight hop. Flying to California. I'll be back tomorrow, though. Want me to knock when I get home?"

"I'll be okay. I better get out of here." Kathleen gave Jennifer one more hug and crossed the hall to her apartment.

Sebastian would need at least forty-five minutes to get to her place from the city. She had time to change and let her mother know she was coming.

A man who thought he was doing Kathleen a favor by firing her was definitely a jerk. Or maybe he thought he was doing 'them' a favor. Tigers don't change their stripes. Leopards don't change their spots. How many other trite analogies could she think of to remind herself Sebastian Brooks was a jerk? She'd known it then, but she'd pushed aside good judgment once again.

She slipped out of her skirt and tugged on a pair of jeans, tucked her feet into a pair of sandals, grabbed her purse and called her mother while she ran out of the apartment.

No answer. Kathleen paused when she sat in her car. It was mid-morning. Ma might be in the yard gardening, or she might still be in bed with her new husband, Duncan. She shuddered. Kathleen definitely didn't want to barge in on that.

Duncan was a hospital administrator. Certainly he'd be at work by now. The home she'd grown up in wasn't home anymore, and now she couldn't afford to buy her own house. Not until she got another job.

Where would she get a job making what she earned at Winslow? She'd have to start from scratch, prove herself yet again.

Kathleen navigated across town and pulled into Ma's driveway. Liam's car was parked to one side. That reduced the chances of Kathleen interrupting something she didn't want to see. She got out of the car and walked in through the back door. Ma was at the sink washing dishes.

"Hey, Ma." Kathleen hugged her mother. *Be it ever so humble*. Ma was 'home.' The music from Liam's favorite video game played in the living room.

"Hello, baby brother," she called out.

"Hey, Kath," Liam called back.

"Let me do that for you." Kathleen pushed her mother aside.

Ma set her hands on her hips. "Out with it."

"Out with what?" she said, thrusting her hands into the dishwater.

"Something's ailing you. And why are you home in the middle of the day?"

As small as her Ma was, she was still a force to be reckoned with.

Kathleen leaned against the counter and snuck a glance toward the living room. "I got fired," she whispered.

"Whatever for?"

The tears started again. She'd cried after she'd left, in Winslow's parking garage, but then she'd bucked up. Until she'd reached her apartment. Apparently she wasn't done yet. "I don't know. The client—Aria Walton, Ma! —Aria Walton liked my designs. He said he couldn't fire me once she asked to meet me, and he still fired me."

"Who is this he?"

"The project manager. Sebastian Brooks."

"Did he not give you a reason?" Ma asked gently. "This Sebastian Brooks fellow?"

"Technically, he didn't fire me. HR did."

"Which is it then?"

"I don't know. Both of them." Kathleen wiped her eyes. "I did a good job. Aria Walton liked my work."

"Then maybe it's Aria Walton you need to talk to."

Kathleen smirked. "I'm a lowly junior associate. Winslow owns my designs. There's no reason for her to intervene."

Ma pulled out a kitchen chair and tugged Kathleen toward the table until she sat. "What happened?"

Kathleen shook her head. "I don't know. I mean, I do, but he said he had a solution. He couldn't be responsible, could he?"

"What on earth are you talking about?"

How much could she tell her mother? Kathleen wiped her eyes. "I sort of dated my boss, and there's a non-fraternization policy at work."

"Oh, Kathleen. When will ya use the good sense God gave ya?"

The tears fell again. "Maybe I didn't get any good sense. I've made so many foolish mistakes…"

Ma raised her eyebrows.

It was supposed to have been one night to break out of her drought. She'd slaked her thirst, and then some. How had Sebastian lodged himself in her heart so quickly?

The kitchen door opened and her older brother Kevin walked in.

"What's all this?" Kevin asked.

Kathleen rose from her seat and threw her arms around him.

"She's lost her job," Ma said, leaving out the rest of the story. She took Kathleen's hand. "And this man, his name is Sebastian? Isn't he the one you asked to invite for dinner on Friday?"

Kathleen nodded.

"New boyfriend?" Kevin asked.

"Not anymore," Kathleen told him.

"At least she invited this one," Kevin said.

"And what does that mean?" Kathleen asked.

Kevin rubbed his jaw. "That you can't keep secrets from family?" he said. "You didn't really think we wouldn't know about Russ, did you?"

Kathleen started to protest until a cold breeze stirred her hair. She wrapped her arms around herself.

"There's someone else here," Kevin said.

"Liam's in the next room," Ma said.

"That's not who I was referring to."

Kathleen felt a presence, too. Victor's appearances had been unannounced for the most part. One minute he was there, the next he was gone. Whatever entity they were dealing with now wanted to make itself known. Victor's wife, Helene? "Can you see her?" Kathleen asked.

"See who?" Ma asked, her voice shaky.

"We encountered a ghost in New Orleans," Kathleen told her. "I called Jared to help him move on—that's what the ghost wanted, but I think there's another one. His wife. She seems to be angry. I think she wants to hurt me." She turned to Kevin. "You've seen a ghost. And Amy. What do I do?"

"I'm no expert," Kevin said.

The globes hanging from the kitchen light fixture swayed with the wind that swept through the room. Ma crossed herself.

"What do I do?" Kathleen asked again.

"Have you called Jared?" he asked.

She nodded.

"And?"

She rolled her eyes. "I haven't heard back from him."

Kevin pulled up a chair at the table. "And this ghost's wife. Why does she want to hurt you?"

"I don't know."

"What's all the hullabaloo?" Liam asked from the kitchen doorway, wearing a brace on his leg and leaning into crutches.

"What happened to you?" Kathleen asked.

"Ugly collision on the soccer field," he said.

Kathleen drew a deep breath, checking the corners of the kitchen for any ghosts who might be lingering. "How serious?"

He shrugged. "Out for the rest of the season."

The kitchen lights creaked as they swayed overhead and lurched against the cap that held the fixture to the ceiling.

"Kath, look out!" Kevin herded them all into the living room.

Liam tripped and fell to the floor. "Ow!" he groaned, curling into a ball, his injured leg sticking out straight.

The light crashed to the table, sending shards of glass from the globes across the floor.

"Oh, my babies." Ma shook a fist in the air. "I'll not have spirits harming my family nor tearing up my home. Begone with ya."

"I think we'd better try Jared again," Kevin said.

Sebastian pulled into the driveway in front of the Victorian house. He hadn't taken a good look the last time he'd been here. It was well-kept, considering it had been divided into apartments. He could understand the charm that attracted Kathleen.

He got out of his car, checking his phone once more. No return text, no return call. Did she think he was the reason she'd been fired? If he was honest with himself, he probably was. Either for kissing her in the elevator moments before Barrett Winslow discovered them together, or because Renee had voiced her dislike for Kathleen to Barrett.

Inside the foyer, Sebastian glanced up the staircase. A stained glass window cast a rainbow of colors on the carpeting, another of the niceties you wouldn't expect to find in a rental house. He knocked on Kathleen's door, the apartment on the right. No answer. He opened the outside door once more to check the small lot. Two cars were there aside from his own. He didn't know what kind of car Kathleen drove. Another reason he shouldn't be acting so impulsively. What did he really know about Kathleen?

Enough that he wanted to discover more.

He went back to her door and knocked again. "Kathleen?"

The door across the hall opened. A woman with smooth brown skin and wearing a flight attendant uniform looked back at him. "She's not home."

"Do you know where she went?" he asked.

She shrugged. "Couldn't say, but her car's not in the lot."

How well did Kathleen know her neighbor? In a house like this, with only four apartments, the chances were better than a regular apartment building. "I wanted to make sure she was okay," he said.

"Kathleen's always okay," she said, an edge to her voice.

She started to close her door, but Sebastian held out a hand. "Wait."

The woman put her hands on her hips as she assessed him. "You're the one who was here Saturday night?" she asked.

"Yes."

She gave him a tight smile. "I can see why she brought you home." She put a hand on the door to close it again. "I have to get to the airport. Good luck tracking her down."

Where was Kathleen?

He returned to the front porch, surveying the area, trying to decide what to do.

Kathleen's neighbor bustled past him with a wheeled suitcase. "You have a good day, now," she said with a mysterious smile. She got into her car, gave him a wave, and drove off.

"Yeah. You, too," he said absently. He sat on the porch steps and rested his arms on his knees. How long should he wait? Should he wait? Clearly, Kathleen was upset with him or she would have answered his texts.

He reached into his pocket for the ring he'd bought Friday night. Yes, he knew Kathleen was 'the one,' but what if she didn't see it that way? When they were in New Orleans, he'd overheard her talking with her sister about a long-term relationship, one where she didn't "feel the same way." What made him think he might be any different than the last guy?

If that was the case, he wanted to hear it from her. No, he wouldn't make a fool of himself and propose.

Sebastian wiped a hand over his face and reached for his ear. He'd give her half an hour, and then he'd have to go home. Or back to work.

When was the last time he took time off from work? He'd given Winslow a month's notice, and he surely had that much in accrued vacation time, not that he'd get it. Too many projects on the line, including Aria's.

He watched the street for cars that might slow and turn into the gravel parking lot that filled half of the front yard. A wave of color caught his eye in the lot. Indistinct and yet noticeable, the wave of color took the shape of the woman he'd seen first in New Orleans and then right here, on this front porch. Sebastian rose to his feet.

A chill touched his spine. One he couldn't ignore. Two times might be imagination, but three times? Bad things tended to happen when he saw the apparition. "Who are you?" he whispered.

The phantom turned toward him, her features indistinct aside from the old-fashioned dress and the braids on her head.

Gravel crunched beneath car tires. Kathleen? The car accelerated slightly as it aimed for an empty spot, and then the driver let out a shriek as the ghost—or whatever it was—floated directly in front of the car. The driver turned the wheels and slammed into a tree with the sounds of crunching metal and breaking glass.

Sebastian ran down the steps. Steam hissed from the radiator. He pulled open the driver's side door, where red hair draped over the steering wheel.

"Kathleen!"

Chapter 23

Invest in people who invest in you.

"What the hell?" Kathleen whispered. She glanced around, searching out the woman who'd been standing in front of her car a moment ago, and ended up looking at Sebastian.

Why hadn't the airbag deployed? Her head hurt. She reached up to massage it and her skin was slick with moisture. When she checked her hand, it was wet with blood.

Sebastian's voice pierced through the fog of confusion. "I need an ambulance."

"Did I hit her?" Kathleen asked, pushing out of the car.

Sebastian's jaw pulsed as he pulled her into him, holding her tight with one arm while he relayed information through his phone. His eyes went to her forehead, smoothing back her hair. "Are you okay?" he asked Kathleen. He shrugged out of his shirt. "No, she's conscious," he told the person on the phone. "But she's bleeding." He pressed his shirt to her forehead.

Kathleen held the material against her head. Where was the woman who'd been standing in the driveway? "What happened?"

A police cruiser arrived, lights flashing. The strobing made Kathleen look away and squeeze her eyes shut. She turned into Sebastian, and then cringed when she recognized the policeman's voice a moment later.

"Kathleen?"

She bowed her head and pushed against Sebastian's chest to turn toward the officer. "Hi, Russ."

His mouth twitched. This might be the first time she'd used his given name on purpose, instead of calling him Brutus.

"What happened?" he asked.

"I saw…. I lost control…" She took a deep breath. "I hit the tree."

The ambulance arrived and pulled up beside Kathleen's car.

"Were you in the car with her?" Russ asked Sebastian.

The two men faced each other like bucks in rutting season, or maybe Kathleen imagined it that way.

Sebastian's arm tightened around her shoulders. "No, I was sitting on the front porch."

"So you saw what happened?" Russ's hand rested on his utility belt.

Sebastian narrowed his eyes, hesitated, and then said, "There was a reflection of light as she turned in. She overcorrected and hit the tree."

"Kathleen?" Russ asked.

"I thought I saw someone standing in front of my car." She turned out of Sebastian's embrace and walked to the front of her car. No woman. No body on the ground.

"Trick of the light," Sebastian said, sending her a message with his eyes.

He'd mentioned seeing a woman before, when she'd sworn someone pushed her toward St. Charles Street in New Orleans, and again when she'd tripped on the front porch. And then there was the light fixture in Ma's kitchen. What did Helene want with her?

A paramedic took Kathleen's arm and directed her away from the car. "Do you know your name?" he asked.

"Kathleen McCormick," she told him.

A second paramedic rolled a cot up behind her. "Have a seat on the cot so we can take a look," he said, easing her down.

The first paramedic waved a penlight in front of her eyes. "How many fingers?" he asked, holding up his hand.

"Three," she answered.

The second paramedic unwrapped Sebastian's shirt from her forehead. "Do you know how you got the cut over your eye?" He turned to Sebastian, offering him the shirt. "Yours?"

Sebastian nodded and wadded his shirt into a ball.

"Pretty sure my head hit the steering wheel. Shouldn't the airbag have deployed?" She locked eyes with Russ. Of all the policemen to answer the call…

"Depends on the impact. You need stitches," the paramedic told her. "We're going to run you to the hospital."

Tears threatened. What else could go wrong?

The paramedic continued to ask her questions as he cleaned her forehead and taped her up with butterfly bandages.

"I don't think you have a concussion, but we'll let the doctor decide once we get you to the hospital. Does anything else hurt?"

"No." Yeah. She hadn't expected to feel as bad as she did when she saw Russ. And Sebastian. Why was he here?

"Ready to go?" the paramedic asked her.

"I guess."

"I can drive you," Sebastian said. "That way you won't have to pay for the ambulance."

She frowned. Thoughtful, considering he was likely the reason she was no longer collecting a paycheck.

Russ adjusted his hand to his gun. "I can drive you to the hospital."

"You're working," Kathleen pointed out to Russ. "And you probably should be," she said to Sebastian.

"Not until we've had a chance to talk," Sebastian said.

Russ smirked. "Good luck with that."

Yet another shortcoming in Russ's eyes. Whenever he'd tried to have a serious conversation, she'd tried to make light of it. She'd never wanted to "get serious" with Russ. Looking between the two of them, she wondered if Sebastian wasn't a rebound man, if he was the next, nearest man to slake her drought.

Except she wasn't afraid of those serious conversations with Sebastian.

The paramedics glanced between Russ and Sebastian, waiting for Kathleen's decision.

"Let's go," she said to Sebastian, and then she turned to the paramedics. "Thank you for your help."

Russ shot Sebastian a menacing glare. "Call me if you need me."

Kathleen nodded. She signed off the forms for the paramedics and climbed into Sebastian's car. Eyes closed, she leaned into the headrest.

"You okay?" he asked.

"Yes."

"Then you'll need to tell me how to get to the hospital."

She opened her eyes and smirked. "Looks like this car has a nav system."

Sebastian stared at her, clearly not as amused as she was. She leaned forward and started programming the GPS.

"I can do that," he said.

"Too late." The canned voice was already telling him to drive the highlighted route.

When they arrived at the hospital, Sebastian helped her out of the car and walked her into the ER. She left him in the waiting room when a triage nurse escorted her into a cubicle, where a handful of people bustled around her, asking questions, filling out forms.

One by one, they dispersed, until the last nurse closed her chart and told her they'd be in to do her stitches shortly.

The weight of her day crushed her. No job, and now her car was out of commission. The only thing left to lose was her apartment. Yes, she could move back home, but seeing Ma with her new husband was awkward.

If she had her own house… a dream that was back on hold.

Kathleen's collarbones ached, likely from being jarred. The cut on her head pulsed. She felt a pity party coming on, and started humming *Don't Worry, Be Happy*, instead.

A head peeked around the curtain. Russ. "Aren't women supposed to be able to carry a tune?" he teased. He'd told her the same thing a dozen times while they'd been dating.

"I'm so sorry, Russ. About everything. I should have invited you over to Friday night at Ma's," she babbled. "It isn't as if they didn't know about you."

"No thanks to you," he said with a sly smile. He stepped around the curtain into her cubicle. "And I know you're delirious if you aren't calling me Brutus."

"And I'm sorry about that, too."

He smiled. "You can stop apologizing. I'm over it. Time marches on, and all of that."

He was over it. Over her. Fresh tears fell.

"Hey," he said, sitting on the edge of her bed. "What's this about? You aren't one to cry."

She shook her head. "Bad day. Ignore me."

"Anything I can do?"

"No. Sweet of you to ask, but I don't want you pissed off at me all over again."

"Kathleen?" Sebastian called from the other side of the curtain.

"Yeah."

Russ took a step back, hands on his utility belt.

Sebastian parted the curtain, took a look at Russ and then at Kathleen. "Is it okay to come in?"

Kathleen nodded and the pulse over her eye amped up. She put a hand to the gauze covering the butterfly bandages. "Russ, meet my boss, Sebastian. Sebastian, Russ."

They shook hands, stiffly assessing each other.

"At least he was my boss until today," she grumbled.

Russ raised an eyebrow. "I just wanted to make sure you're okay." He turned to leave, bowed his head, and stopped. "And to make sure you know you can call me, huh?"

"Thanks."

Sebastian took a step toward Kathleen as Russ left through the narrow opening in the curtain.

"He's the guy you were telling your sister about in New Orleans?" he asked.

Kathleen swallowed hard. "Yes."

"He still loves you," he said.

"He's a good guy. He deserves more than I can give him."

Sebastian's jaw pulsed and he tugged on his ear, scrutinizing her.

"You saw her? The woman I almost hit?" she asked.

"Yes. Third time's the charm. I'm starting to believe in your ghosts, but didn't you say the ghost in our hotel suite was a man?"

"My brother-in-law came to help him move on. I only saw her for a moment, but I think this ghost is his wife."

Sebastian took her hands. "Why is she trying to hurt you?"

"I have no idea. Why are you here, Sebastian?" The tears fell again.

"Because I need to talk to you." He reached into his pocket, lowered his eyes and looked away.

A doctor walked into the cubicle, looked from one to the other of them and smiled. "How are we doing today?"

"My car has a crunch in it, my head has a hole in it and I got fired today," Kathleen told him.

"Well, I can fix the hole in the head, but I think you're on your own with the other problems." He turned to Sebastian. "Maybe you'd like to wait outside?"

"I'd rather stay, if you don't mind." He met Kathleen's gaze.

"Kathleen?" the doctor asked.

"Yeah, he can stay." The hole in her head must be bigger than she thought.

Chapter 24

Twenty years from now you will be more disappointed by the things that you didn't do than by the ones you did do.

"I can take you to dinner," Sebastian suggested as Kathleen signed the last of her discharge papers.

"That's not necessary," she said.

Which translated to she was still mad at him.

"You might as well let me have it," he said. "I can see you're angry with me, but I've got a few questions of my own."

"I lost my job," she said angrily. "Tell me you're not responsible for that."

Her eyes flashed with the lightning he admired, but he had to proceed carefully. "Not directly, no."

"What does that mean, exactly?"

He looked away. "I didn't know they were going to fire you. You might recall I wanted to meet you after work. I'd already made up my mind to tender my resignation so there wouldn't be a fraternization issue. Did they give you a reason?"

She crossed her arms. "No, and now you don't have to resign. How convenient."

"I did anyway. When Barrett told me they'd let you go, I told him he'd made a mistake by firing a talented architect." He reached for her hand, but her arms were still folded. "Come on. I'm taking you home."

"I don't want to go home."

"Where do you want to go?"

Her forehead creased with questions, and he watched as his words registered. "You resigned anyway?"

"I did."

"Why?"

He glanced through the emergency room ward, not wanting to have this discussion in public. "We've both missed dinner. How about we stop and get something to eat and we can talk about everything else then, including why this ghost is trying to hurt you."

She dropped her arms and surveyed the room. "Okay."

He waited for her to walk past him, but she motioned him forward. "Ladies first," he told her.

Kathleen pursed her lips and walked out. In the parking lot, she stopped. "Where did you park?"

Sebastian placed a hand in the middle of her back and guided her to his car.

"A Beamer?" she asked when he clicked his key fob to unlock the doors.

"You don't like BMWs?"

She assessed him a moment. "I guess it suits you."

He wasn't sure why that pissed him off, but it did. He helped her into the car before he slid behind the wheel and started the engine. "Where do you want to go?" he asked again. "We're in your 'hood, so you know the way."

She sat back, folded her arms again. "We should go somewhere we can talk, where people won't overhear our conversation."

He was on board with that.

She turned in the seat to face him. "I want to see where you live."

"Food," he reminded her.

"You don't have food in the house?"

What was she playing at? "I don't spend much time there."

"Why not?"

He rolled his eyes. "Because I practically live in the office, a habit I intend to remedy."

"Then you should stock up on food. Where do you live?"

He was running short on patience. "A condo in the city. Look, Kathleen, before we go anywhere, I need to know about this ghost of yours. Why is she trying to hurt you?"

"I don't know." She folded her hands in her lap and bowed her head.

Shit.

He threw the gearshift into drive and started out. The ghost knew where she lived. Kathleen wasn't safe there. If she wanted to see his damn condo, he'd take her there.

How did the ghost know where she lived?

"You're going to have to educate me, because until today, I didn't believe in any of this," he said curtly.

"Yeah, well, until we went to New Orleans, I didn't have any experience with ghosts either."

"And didn't you say the ghost in New Orleans was a man? Why do I keep seeing a woman?"

"I assume it's Victor's wife. He said he wanted to move on, insisted I get Jared there to help, and now I appear to be enemy number one in the spirit world. Last time I try to do a favor for a ghost."

Sebastian shook his head. He laughed.

"I'm glad you're amused," she said.

"Not exactly the type of conversation I'm used to."

"No, I'm sure of that," she said sarcastically.

His temper flared again. "Why are you so mad at me? I already told you I didn't get you fired."

"Except something tells me I wouldn't have gotten fired if I'd never met you," she said. "And we would never have 'fraternized.'"

"I'm the one who said we should stop, if you'll recall."

"So *now* you're sorry?" she asked.

Sebastian stopped to take a breath. "Not even a little." He chuckled. No, he wouldn't trade their time together in New Orleans for anything, or any of the moments they'd shared since.

She sighed softly. "What are we doing?"

"Apparently, we're going to my condo where we can hopefully find something to eat. Or order out."

Kathleen slouched in the seat. "What do you want from me? You have your world, I have mine. It isn't like we even know each other."

"We know more about each other than you think. What happened in New Orleans…" he tugged his ear to pull away his nerves.

"Didn't translate well to Chicago," she finished for him.

"It might." Maybe she didn't want him. Hadn't she let the cop go?

"All right," she said, crossing her arms. "If you know so much about me, let's hear it. Because I don't know anything about you."

"I know you had a tough childhood, that your father was an alcoholic."

She didn't say anything. Did she think he was an alcoholic?

"I'm not a drunk. That day in New Orleans when I was doing interviews I was distracted. I didn't stop to think when the cocktail waitress asked what I wanted to drink." He huffed. "You twist my head so many ways."

"Right back atcha, buddy." She slapped a hand over her mouth, as if she'd realized she'd called him buddy again.

This time he recognized the generic name for what it was.

She shifted in her seat.

He turned up his palm and curled his fingers. "Ask me. What do you want to know?"

"Tell me about Buddy."

"It's a nickname my mother uses. My father wanted to name me something classical, and one of his friends jokingly suggested Johann Sebastian Brooks. My mother put her foot down at Johann, but lost the fight on Sebastian. She thinks it's too pretentious, so she calls me Buddy, mostly in private, to poke my father. My father has visions of grandeur where I'm concerned."

"Didn't sound like that the night I met him," she said quietly. "And where did you learn to gavotte?"

He wasn't about to discuss his father—not yet— and few people knew he could dance. "I could ask you the same thing."

She lowered her eyes. "You wouldn't believe me."

Sebastian scowled, considering all the things he'd hidden from the rest of the world about his formative years. If he wanted to get information from her, he had to give some. "Since my father saddled me with such a ridiculous name, I figured it might annoy him if I took ballroom dancing. All part of the classical thing. I can waltz, polka, tango, and by coincidence, gavotte."

They rode in silence for a couple of miles.

Kathleen lowered her arms. "You resigned because of me?" she asked.

"Partly. You made me see things I'd forgotten. I wanted to pursue my own dreams, not the dreams someone else designed for me." He tightened his grip on the wheel. "And I wanted to be with you. Winslow would have made that difficult."

She went quiet again, and her silence preyed on him. "Talk to me."

She scowled "I don't fit in your space."

"I want you in my space," he said. "Unless you meant it when you told your sister you only wanted an outlet. Is that all I was? The nearest man for you to use?"

"No!" She blurted out and then huffed. "I'm too impulsive. My little sister was only sixteen when she died. Her death made me realize how short life is, and I vowed to make sure I didn't miss a moment. You? You're very structured. You aren't the type to take a chance on anything."

"I took a chance on you," he told her. "On us. I'm taking one hell of a chance right now, a chance I'm not the only one who feels this thing between us. If you don't want me, I'll walk away, but Kathleen, I hope you'll give me a chance." He reached for her hand.

They fell into silence again, until she swiveled in her seat once more. "What kind of music do you like?"

First date questions? "Depends. I enjoy classical music when I need something to relax, when I'm working and I need to concentrate. I like hard, driving rock and roll when the situation warrants. Not a big fan of country music."

Her eyes welled with tears. "No."

Sebastian's heart thudded. Was this where she told him to turn around and take her home? "No?"

"No, you weren't just an outlet. Or maybe you were, but that's not where it ended." She locked eyes with him. "Tell me about Renee?"

"What about Renee?"

"You were going to propose to her. She must mean something to you."

He shook his head. "I was clutching at the only thing I knew to do to get that promotion. I think I mentioned to you at the time it was a business proposal. I truly believed that. Poor judgment on my part."

"You didn't count on her wanting more?"

He looked up, and Kathleen's lips quirked into a half-smile.

"No. Not really," he said.

Kathleen scoffed. "Then you must be clueless, because her claws were definitely out when I met her."

No, he wasn't clueless. "It might be more accurate to say she and I didn't want the same thing."

"What do you want, Sebastian?"

He steered into the parking garage beneath the high rise that housed his condo and drove to his assigned parking space. Sebastian turned off the car, bowed his head, and reached into his pocket. The ring was still there. Her ring. Would she accept it?

Kathleen sat sideways, looking at him. Waiting.

"I want you," he told her.

Chapter 25

*Behind every setback is an opportunity. Don't let a hard
lesson harden your heart.*

Sebastian sat there long enough that Kathleen grew
uncomfortable. He seemed caught in indecision.
Certainly after a man made a statement like that he
should kiss her. Or say something more. Or invite
her into his bedroom.

Instead he stared at her, in the car, one hand in
his pocket.

"This is where you live?" she asked, grasping for
something to say.

He pulled his hand out of his pocket and opened
the door. "Let's go see what's in the fridge."

"It's a beautiful night. You want to dance?" she
teased as they walked through the garage.

"I'm not very good," he said. "The lessons
accomplished what I needed them to, but I never won
any competitions."

"He said that's why he made me dance that
night," she said. "To remind you of something you'd left
behind. Victor, that is."

"And Victor is…?"

She smiled. "The ghost."

"Oh, yeah." They stepped into the elevator and
Sebastian pressed a button. "Stay with me tonight?"

"Said one bum to the other," she joked. "We're both unemployed. Unless there's something you haven't told me."

"No, I don't have a new job yet, but we'll figure it out. We could start our own business, huh?" He guided her down the corridor, stopped before a door and slotted his key. "Want to buy a condo?"

"No," she said, walking past him, into his place. "I want to buy a house."

"I might be able to help you with that. I have some designs you might be interested in."

He flipped on the light and her heart stopped. The place was stark. Soulless. Like the man she'd met at Winslow. The carpet was gray. The leather sofa was a darker shade of gray. The coffee table was glass and chrome. The curtains were gray with black stripes.

"You live here?" she whispered.

"In a manner of speaking."

"No wonder you spend so much time at the office."

"You don't like it?" he asked.

Was that a trick question? She forced a smile. "I wouldn't say that…"

"Renee designed it."

That explained a lot.

"About that house," he said. "I'd love your input on the one I'd like to build. I drew up the designs, but I can't seem to get them right, and I'm always worried I'll leave something important out. Like a kitchen."

She laughed, afraid if she said anything, it would be rude or unkind, but her curiosity got the better of her. What kind of house would this man design? "Okay."

"But first, food," he said. "I'm starving." He walked into the kitchen and opened the stainless steel refrigerator. "Milk. Eggs. I could whip us up an omelet?"

"Maybe we should have gone out," she said quietly.

"I did warn you."

She laughed. "Yes, you did."

He closed the refrigerator and put his arms around her waist. "You feeling okay? I could heat up the soup."

"As long as it isn't cream of blah," she said, and then put her hand over her mouth. His apartment was depressing.

He checked the refrigerator once more and retrieved a bowl. "Chicken tortilla?"

She nodded.

"I bought rolls to eat with it, but apparently that was a while ago." He held up a plastic bag of rolls covered in green fuzz.

"Yeah, I think I'll pass on those."

He laughed, dropped them into the garbage and popped the bowl into the microwave.

"Come with me." He took Kathleen's hand and drew her into the dining room, pulling out a seat at the white laminate table. "While dinner's cooking, you can look over my designs and tell me what you think." He set his laptop on the table and booted it up.

If his designs were as awful as this condo, how was she going to be diplomatic? Then again, he'd grown up in a mansion in Lake Forest. Kathleen swallowed her trepidation, once again feeling as if she didn't belong in his world.

Sebastian turned the computer toward her and reached over her shoulders to open his drafting program.

"I'm counting on you to tell me if you hate it," he said. "Or at least to suggest improvements, like you did with Aria's house."

Aria's house. She'd give anything to be back in Aria's house right now, even if the walls were being demolished.

"Sebastian, I'm not sure…"

He silenced her with a kiss. "We still have a lot to talk about. After dinner. Then you can tell me what you're not sure about. In the meantime, why don't you have a look?"

The microwave called him to the kitchen.

Kathleen didn't dare look at the computer screen until he disappeared.

The floor plan looked like a hundred other floor plans, except something about it seemed familiar. She switched to the exterior view and her adrenalin kicked in.

A Craftsman-style house. Low-pitched roof, overhanging eaves supported by brackets, front porch tucked beneath the main roof. Stone fascia halfway up the front. He'd even included landscaping. Foliage along the curving sidewalk to the front door, bushes, flowerbeds.

Kathleen's mouth hung open. Sebastian's rendering might have been one of the pictures in her screensaver.

"You like it?" he asked, carrying two bowls from the kitchen.

She struggled to find the words, and instead gave him a "mmm-hmm."

He went back to the kitchen and returned a moment later with glasses. "Didn't figure you'd want a beer, so I brought you a glass of water. Is that okay?"

"Mmm-hmm." She couldn't seem to say anything. She dragged the image around, a 360-degree view. If she were to design her own house… "It's beautiful. You designed this for yourself?"

He hesitated. Tugged on his ear. "Yes."

"But you live in a condo in the city. Or an estate in Lake Forest. Why would the great Sebastian Brooks draw a Craftsman house?"

He stood beside his chair, one hand resting on the back. "You don't like it?"

"What's not to like?" she blurted. "Let's start with this. You would actually live in a house like that? A Craftsman house?"

"Is that so hard to believe?" He pulled out his chair and sat. "I've been looking for the land to build on."

"The man with the condo in the city?" She waved a hand in the air. "This condo?"

He leaned over the table. "There's no color here. No life. Everything is perfectly ordered, nothing out of place. I hate it.

"You, on the other hand, represent a 3D color rendering of a complete life and not the flat, black and white sketch I live in," he said. "It's a little overwhelming. Have I mentioned you scare the hell out of me?" He cocked his head toward the computer. "Tell me what I overlooked."

Was this what Victor had meant when he'd told her Sebastian's imagination lay in the plans he'd drawn for himself? Her hand shook as she picked up the spoon. "I should eat something first."

⁂

Sebastian missed color.

Okay, so he hadn't gotten that promotion, but he had set aside enough money to buy a piece of land, build the home he'd always wanted. Not a showplace like his father had created. Not an office away from the office. A home. Cozy. Comfortable. He was going to build that damn house, reclaim the life he wanted and stop trying to live up to everyone else's expectations.

Except Kathleen's opinion mattered. She'd said it was beautiful, but something was off, and he couldn't figure out what. Maybe it was the stress of the day. Or the cut to her head, although the doctor had said she didn't have a concussion.

"I've modified the designs a dozen times," he said. "Eliminated as much of the negative space as I could. Checked each of the rooms, added stained glass touches a la Frank Lloyd Wright." The perfectionist in him wasn't satisfied, but the realist in him told him everything was probably fine.

The emotions roiling through him told him Kathleen was the missing piece. Still she didn't say anything.

"You did the renovations at the Frank Lloyd Wright house in Highland Park," he went on, filling the quiet with reasons why her opinion was important. "I've added several similar touches." He was babbling. Sebastian Brooks never babbled.

Kathleen stared into her bowl of soup. "Look, I think it's great. The house." She smiled. "I'm a sucker for a Craftsman style house myself, but is that what *you* want? And how can you afford it without a job?" Her spoon shook so much the soup splashed into the bowl. She set the spoon down and clasped her hands in her lap.

"I've never shown anyone those designs before," he told her.

"You really want to live in such a conventional house?" she asked.

Why was she stalling? Sebastian reached across and closed his computer. "Forget it. I thought you might have something to add, the way you did to Aria's plans."

"Oh. That's it. You're still mad at me because she liked my designs better than yours. So this is a test? How can I possibly know what I'm talking about? I'm only a junior associate." Her voice caught. "Scratch that. I'm an unemployed architect."

"You're a damn fine architect," he said, throwing her words back at her. "I wouldn't have asked your opinion otherwise. What's going on here?"

"I'll tell you what's going on. Where do I fit in this picture? I don't know what you want from me. How could you know…?" She thrust a hand in the direction of his computer, then rested her palm to her chest. "I don't know what to think."

Sebastian rose to his feet, shoved his hand into his pocket and closed it around the ring. No. Not now. Not like this. He placed his hands on the table, staring at her.

And then her phone rang.

Kathleen pushed away from the table and retrieved her phone from her purse. With a glare at Sebastian, she answered. "I have been trying to reach you."

The tinny voice—a voice that sounded like one of the Pierce brothers—boomed loud enough for Sebastian to overhear.

"I know," the voice said. "Kevin told me what happened at your mother's."

"And the ghost tripped me on the steps at my apartment, and tonight I had a car accident. She ran in front of me and I had to swerve to avoid her."

"Clever," the tinny voice said. "You can't run over a ghost, you know."

"You think I don't know that?" she shouted. "You have to make her stop." She tightened a fist in her hair, closed her eyes and drew a deep breath.

"I've been talking to my daddy," the man on the phone said. "I told you there were too many souls in that hotel, and now it seems we've added one more. Baby, I'd love to come up there to help you, but I can't get away, and it seems as if Victor's wife might have attached herself to you. Any chance you can come back to New Orleans? I'm not even sure I can help you, but my daddy can."

"I can't afford another vacation." Kathleen speared Sebastian with a glare. "I got fired."

"Then you can come right away," the voice said. "Before Helene does any more harm. We'll pick you up at the airport. You can stay… No, that's probably not a good idea. I don't want to invite a malevolent spirit into my home, but I can find you a place."

"I'll figure something out, and I'll let you know when I've made the arrangements," she told him.

"Have a care, Kathleen."

She disconnected the call and dropped her phone into her purse. Then rounded on Sebastian. "I got fired," she said. "Tell me again why?"

Sebastian didn't know for sure, and there wasn't an easy way to tell her. "Barrett said he'd had reports that you were difficult to work with and, unfortunately, Renee seems to have added her two cents into the mix."

"Renee," she spat out. "And did you tell him I was difficult to work with, too?"

He pushed away from the table, his temper sparking. "I think I already told you what I said to him.

Were you difficult to work with?" He nodded. "Yes. You unleashed every single one of my emotions. I don't know how any of this works, but I love you, Kathleen McCormick, and that's not something I've ever said to anyone else in my lifetime. And *that* scares the hell out of me, too."

Sebastian straightened, stunned by the words he'd said. This wasn't how it was supposed to go. Kathleen deserved hearts and flowers, not having 'I love you' hurled at her as a point in an argument.

Tears streamed down her face. "I love you, too," she whispered.

Relief swept over him and he took her into his arms. "Stay with me."

"I have to go to New Orleans."

"Then I'm going with you."

"You still have a job. At least for the next month," she reminded him.

"And I have a client in New Orleans. I can justify my trip."

"Sebastian?"

He cupped her cheek and met her gaze.

"I hate this condo." She giggled.

He laughed. "You and me both." He kissed her. "Let's finish the soup and we can find somewhere else to go."

She nodded.

Chapter 26

*Bad things happen every day to everyone. The difference is
how we deal with them.*

First order of business on Tuesday was scheduling
another trip to New Orleans, but Sebastian spent
most of the morning replying to a dozen other
emails that diverted his attention.

While he typed a reply on a set of contractor
drawings, he reached absently for his ringing phone.
"Brooks."

"Sebastian, what is this I hear someone else is
taking over my renovation?" Aria asked him.

He straightened. "I'm leaving Winslow Designs.
Your project is in good hands and I'm sure they'll do an
excellent job for you, but I did request another trip to
check the progress on-site. In fact, I'd like to leave
tomorrow, with your permission."

"Will Kathleen be taking over for you?"

He gazed out the window. The overcast sky
turned Lake Michigan a dreary shade of green. "Barrett let
Kathleen go."

"What's going on there? Tell me what firm you're
going to. I'll cancel my contract and re-sign with your
new firm."

What could he say? The truth. "Thank you, Aria,
but I'm legally prohibited from soliciting my clients."

"You're not soliciting me, I'm soliciting you," she
pointed out. "My contract is contingent on no changes in

the design team, and Winslow is making two major changes to my team. You are not in violation of your contract, Sebastian. Winslow is."

He smiled, pleased to know she thought that much of his architectural skills. "I've done the hard part. The permits on your house in the Garden District will be submitted soon, and Lauren Ferguson is an excellent project manager. It's mostly keeping the contractors on task from here on out."

"Why are you leaving?" she asked.

"Winslow's business model doesn't fit my career goals."

"I'm not good with change, "Aria said. "When I find someone I like working with, I prefer to keep working with them and avoid the hassle of getting comfortable with someone new."

"I'll send you my contact information from my personal email account," he told her. "How many more houses do you plan to buy?"

She laughed. "Listen to you, making a joke. You didn't used to do that, you know. I think your trip to New Orleans did you more good than you know."

"I think you're right."

"Can I assume as ex-employees, you and Kathleen are free to fraternize?"

"That's fairly personal, Ms. Walton. I prefer to keep my business life separate from my private life," he said with a touch of irony.

She laughed again. "I'd like to think we're more than business associates, Sebastian. I did go to your birthday party, after all."

"Yes, you did."

"And I like Kathleen. I asked her to be my friend. Did she tell you?"

He grinned. "She might have said something."

"Aha! I knew it. Will Kathleen be joining you in New Orleans?"

Sebastian rolled his eyes. "Yes."

"Charge her ticket to my account. And Sebastian…"

When she paused, he waited for the conditions he expected her to attach to his request.

"I'll expect an invitation to the wedding," she finished.

His grin grew. "You got it."

"I'll expect a full report from your trip, and we'll be in touch, Mr. Brooks."

He closed his hand around the ever-present box in his pocket. He'd come close to proposing last night, but he and Kathleen were both off balance, both needed a moment to regroup.

He'd never connected with anyone as quickly as he had with Kathleen. He could try to rationalize his feelings for her all night, but the truth of the matter was she'd discovered a place in his heart no one else had found.

He phoned Margot to make the arrangements for the trip—two tickets—and checked with the project manager in charge of Aria's construction drawings. His last call was to the finish contractor in New Orleans.

While he straightened his desk, Margot called him back.

"No rooms available at the Folies," she told him. "In fact I had a hard time finding you a room. I'm sending you a link to an inn I found in the French Quarter. I went ahead and booked it, but if you'd rather I keep looking, I can cancel the reservation."

Sebastian checked his email while she talked, found the link and clicked. Not a five-star hotel, no on-site restaurant, but it looked serviceable. "This looks fine, thank you," he told her. "If I need to change it, I'll let you know after I've arrived."

"Mr. Brooks?" she went on somewhat tentatively.

"Yes?"

"I just wanted to say… well, first, you're welcome, and whatever changed… what I mean to say… You didn't used to thank me for anything…" She sighed. "If you need an admin wherever you're going…"

He smiled. Yeah, he knew he'd been difficult to work with. "I'll keep you in mind, Margot," he told her. "In the meantime, you've got a few more weeks to put up with me here."

"Yes, sir. Thanks."

He disconnected the call and shut down his computer. With the trip booked, he had to run home, pack, and pick up Kathleen from her brother's house, where she'd apparently been told she would be safe from the ghost with the vendetta.

When he stepped into the elevator and pressed the button for the lobby, he shoved his hand into his pocket one more time and made up his mind. He'd propose to Kathleen in New Orleans. That's where she'd opened his eyes, showed him all the dreams he'd let slip away.

He wasn't going to let her slip away. She was one dream he still wanted to chase.

Chapter 27

Look beyond imperfections. Seek out the good in others and celebrate it.

They weren't traveling first class. They weren't staying in an upscale hotel. Sebastian was pretty sure he had *not* made a good impression on Kathleen's family.

And he was on another damn airplane.

At least if he was going down in flames, he had Kathleen beside him.

He squeezed her hand and smiled at her.

"You gonna be okay, boss?" she asked.

"Fantastic," he replied sarcastically.

"What's the agenda," she said. "If nothing else, it'll take your mind off the landing."

"You told your sister we don't need a ride from the airport?" he asked.

"Yep. Told her Aria Walton's picking up the tab. You ordered a limo?"

"I did." He brought her hand to his lips and kissed it. "So I'm thinking we go to the inn, get settled, then head over to Aria's house to justify the business expense. I promised her I'd leave her in good shape before Lauren takes over the project."

Kathleen shook her head. "I think I'd rather stay at the inn until Jared and his father show up. Wouldn't want to tempt Helene to shove me into traffic again."

"I can wait with you until after your brother-in-law shows up."

Again she shook her head. "I'm sure I'll be fine. Can't get into too much trouble in a hotel room."

He glanced out the window. As the ground rose to meet them, he screwed his eyes shut and braced for impact. Kathleen squeezed his hand, and a moment later, the wheels touched down. Not so bad. He'd experienced bumpier landings.

He leaned into his seat until they'd slowed enough to taxi toward the gate.

Sebastian cleared his throat. "Did Jared tell you what time they expected to arrive?"

"He figured sometime around five," she said. "After he finishes work, picks up his dad, and then the drive over."

He breathed a sigh of relief as the plane came to a stop. "We should stay together, and we'll be back by then. Don't you want to go to Aria's? See how the house is progressing?"

"Maybe after. I'd rather keep a low profile."

"Assuming they can dispatch your ghost, we can take them to dinner after. Unless you think Troy will be joining them," Sebastian said.

She laughed. "No. From what I've been told, Troy missed out on the ghost genes. I don't expect he'll be with them."

One less obstacle to deal with.

And then after dinner, they could take a walk along the river, and as long as the mood was right, he'd propose to her under a moonlit sky.

"What are you grinning about?" she asked.

"Am I?" he asked innocently. He took a strand of her beautiful red hair between his fingers. "I suppose I was remembering our last trip here. Dancing with you in the parlor."

Her cheeks flushed as she cocked an eyebrow. "And by dancing, are you referring to the gavotte?"

He shook his head and she laughed again.

Armed with their carry-ons, they joined the herd of people exiting the plane and, without luggage to claim, they headed for the pick-up lanes to meet the limo.

The inn was sandwiched between souvenir stores, a nondescript doorway. They walked into the narrow lobby, checked in, and a bellman led them through a courtyard which served as the inn's lounge, dotted with metal lattice tables and chairs, connecting the four buildings that made up the inn.

A fountain bubbled against one of the courtyard walls beside a brick-arched carriageway that led to a rickety elevator.

When they arrived at their room, the bellman unlocked it and handed Sebastian the keys.

"Not as big as our room at the Folies, but it will work, don't you think?" Sebastian said as he tipped the bellman.

"I think it's charming," Kathleen replied. "My main criteria for a hotel room is a comfortable bed." She ran a hand over the brick wall and headed toward French doors that opened to the balcony.

He slipped his arms around her waist. "Do me a favor and stay off the balcony. I know we're only two stories up, but I don't want anything to happen to you." He kissed the tip of her nose.

Caught between his responsibility to Aria and wanting to keep Kathleen safe, Sebastian weighed his options. He'd only be gone an hour, and Jared wasn't due for another two hours. "I should really pop over to Aria's house. I just thought if I get this out of the way, and if there are any issues with the renovation, identifying them now would give me time to resolve them while we're in town. You sure you don't want to come?"

"No, I'll hang around here. I can sit in the courtyard and be sociable."

Still he hesitated, worried about what the angry ghost might do. "I could wait. Go to Aria's tomorrow."

Kathleen gave him a push toward the door. "I'll be fine. I promise not to sit on the balcony. Hurry back?"

He hugged her tight. "I hope these guys know what they're doing, Jared and his father."

"You and me both."

———◆———

The room didn't have much in the way of extra space. Kathleen sat on the bed and turned on the television, flipping through the channels before she decided she'd rather sit outside in the sun.

She slipped her room key and her phone into her pocket, picked up her tablet, took one look at the shaky elevator and took the staircase instead. She sat at one of the tables in the courtyard and opened a browser on her tablet to move her job search forward.

Her phone rumbled in her pocket and she checked the display. Jared.

"Hey, baby, where y'at?" he said.

"We arrived at the inn about half an hour ago. Do you know where that is?" she replied.

He chuckled. "I meant to ask how you're doing. I forget you all aren't familiar with our ways of talking down here. Any more incidents?"

She wrapped one arm around her middle and sat back. "So far, so good, but if all the hotels in New

Orleans are haunted, the way they say, what's to say another ghost won't pop up while you're trying to send Helene away?"

"There's always that possibility," he said. "I put my daddy onto finding out more about who we're dealing with. He has some interesting theories to share, and once again, it makes me look bad for trying to send your Victor on his way without doing my homework. I should have asked more questions. Found out more background."

"To be fair, Victor was a very impatient ghost."

"No signs of him?" Jared asked.

"No, he seems to have moved on. At least we got that part right."

"Listen, I'm picking up my daddy now. We'll be there in about an hour. You tell that man of yours to hold onto you until we get there."

Kathleen smiled. "He's out taking care of business, but he said he'd be back by the time you get here."

"Then you be careful, y'heard?"

"I'll be careful."

"See you soon."

She disconnected the call and tucked her phone into her pocket. Her tablet chimed with an incoming email. A request for an interview? She opened the mail app and shielded the screen against the glare of the sun. She struggled to see and she was getting hot. Time to reassess her decision to come outside.

An alcove across the courtyard housed vending machines. Kathleen closed her tablet and walked over to get a lemonade. She'd continue her job search in their room, where it was cool.

She drained her can of lemonade and started up the staircase. A muffled sound pricked her ears. Crying? She paused, uncertain where it was coming from.

"Someone please help me?" a muffled female voice asked.

"Hello?" Kathleen called out. She took a tentative step up. The crying continued, but the woman didn't reply.

Should Kathleen call the bellman? Go to the front desk? She hesitated again.

Was it a trick?

"Please?" the muffled voice said between sobs.

Kathleen continued up the stairs, cell phone at the ready to call for help should she need it. She passed the door to the second floor and her room.

"Are you hurt?" Kathleen called out.

The crying grew louder as she passed the door to the rooms on the third floor. The stairs ended at a door one more flight up. The fourth floor? A room? A suite? She considered turning back and going to the front desk, but if the woman was in distress, navigating the maze of buildings would take too long. Instead, she stopped to look up the inn's number and called.

"This is Kathleen McCormick. Someone's calling for help in my building. Can you send someone over?"

The clerk repeated her room number as a question, and Kathleen confirmed.

"The bellman stepped outside a moment," the clerk told her. "but I'll send him over as soon as he returns."

"The cries seem to be coming from the fourth floor," Kathleen told her.

"That's the attic," the clerk said. "There shouldn't be anyone up there."

"I could be mistaken," Kathleen said, "but she must be somewhere near here."

"I'll send the bellman as soon as he gets back."

Kathleen disconnected the call and started down the staircase.

A baby shrieked, followed by the frantic voice again. "Please. Help me!"

Okay, she'd considered that it might have been Helene trying to trap her, but could a ghost mimic both a woman calling for help and a baby crying? Kathleen approached the door and knocked, but no one answered. She tried the door, and it opened to a short, wooden staircase leading into the attic. With one hand on the bannister, Kathleen took tentative steps up. "Hello?"

Dust covered the bare wood floors. Spider webs hung from the beams that supported the hipped roof. Dormer windows overlooked the street below. Furniture hid under dust covers beneath the rafters, along with pictures and other décor, but no woman in distress.

Time to go. Kathleen hurried down the stairs as a cold wind swept by her and slammed the attic door shut. She twisted the knob, but the door wouldn't open. Cell phone in hand, she pressed the wake-up button. Dead. While she pressed the power button to restart it, she glanced up the stairs. The dust covers looked more like sheet-wearing ghosts, or maybe that was her imagination.

Her phone lit up, showing her battery at zero percent before it shut off again. How could that be? The battery had been three-quarters full when she'd talked to Jared. She tried her iPad, with the same results. Dead battery.

The attic was at least ten degrees hotter than it had been outside, without the benefit of a breeze. Kathleen mounted the steps once more to open one of the dormer windows until the bellman arrived, but the windows were nailed shut, with iron safety bars mounted on the outside.

Perspiration beaded her brow. She blew a strand of hair from her face and set her hands on her hips.

"Okay, Helene. I know it's you. What's your complaint with me?"

A shimmer of light caught her eye.

Chapter 28

There is no elevator to success. You have to take the stairs.

Kathleen wasn't answering her phone. And she wasn't answering the phone in their room.

Sebastian got out of the cab and took long strides into the lobby of the inn. Two men rose from their seats and approached him. One of them was the second Pierce brother, and the other was older. Their father?

"She's not here?" Sebastian asked.

"Doesn't appear so," Jared replied. "I talked to her an hour ago, called to let her know we were on our way."

Sebastian took in Jared's father. "I'm Sebastian Brooks."

"Amos Pierce," Jared's father replied.

Sebastian led them through the courtyard, to their room. No sign of Kathleen. Or her cell phone. Or her tablet. "I don't like this."

"I'd suggest we go back to the courtyard," the elder Pierce suggested. "There should be less interference outside."

"Interference?" Sebastian asked.

"Of the ghostly variety," Jared replied.

"Right." That's why they were here, after all, but that didn't mean Sebastian liked it. If he hadn't seen the ghostly woman with his own eyes, and he still questioned if what he'd seen might have been his imagination, he'd have written the Pierces off as kooks.

They walked down the staircase, through the carriageway and sat at one of the wrought iron tables.

"What do you know about Victor Mercier?" Amos asked Sebastian.

"That's Kathleen's ghost from the Folies?" Jared nodded.

"Not a thing, other than she mentioned he was a prankster."

"The information I got was from the concierge at the hotel," Jared told his father. He turned to Sebastian. "I assume you don't know anything about his wife, Helene, then?"

"She's the one I've been seeing?" Sebastian asked. "Long dress, hair braided around the top of her head?"

"Sounds right." Jared faced his father. "And that's where I apparently made my mistake, in not checking into the whole story first."

Amos raised an eyebrow.

"And what difference does that make?" Sebastian asked.

Jared scratched his jaw. "Kathleen told me the ghost was anxious to move on, and I've been somewhat preoccupied with work lately. When she asked if I could pop over and see what I could do, I didn't ask enough questions."

"It helps to know the ghost's history," Amos said. "In this case, from what we've learned, Helene Mercier murdered her husband and escaped to France to avoid prosecution."

"Okay," Sebastian said, waiting for the rest of the story.

Jared leaned forward in his chair. "When a ghost needs help moving on, we generally call another family member who's already passed to help them on their way. Someone they love and trust." He turned to his father. "That was another of the issues. The Folies is filled with ghosts looking for attention. I had a hard time filtering them out."

"Are you sure it was his wife that came through?" His father asked.

"Couldn't say for certain, but I'd bet on it."

Sebastian tugged his ear, waiting for them to get on with it. All this talk wasn't helping to find Kathleen, and if she was in trouble…

"The portal opened," Jared went on. "Victor went through, but not before his wife shouted for him not to go."

"Why wouldn't she want him to go through?" Sebastian asked.

Amos and Jared exchanged glances. Jared held out an arm, inviting his father to explain.

"It has been my experience, and merely a theory on my part since we don't know the true facts, that when a murdered ghost lingers, so does their murderer. When the victim moves on, he more or less condemns the murderer to their eternal fate, which isn't always a happy one."

"Clearly, she hasn't moved on," Sebastian said.

"But now, instead of lingering quietly in the background, she's been separated from the spirit that held her to the 'in-between' state. Some refer to this state as purgatory," Amos told him. "Now she has to face her crime and make restitution."

"She's damned to hell?" Sebastian asked.

"Those answers are beyond our knowledge," Amos said. "Religions and beliefs vary on this topic, from a benevolent and forgiving God who takes a whole life into account, the life of each individual soul, to the devil who comes to collect his due."

Sebastian shook his head. "So… what?"

"Our job isn't to judge," Jared said. "It's to help the spirits move on."

"And this spirit is angry that she's being held accountable. Is that it? She has to face judgment for her crimes during her life?"

"Essentially," Jared said.

Sebastian shook his head. "And she's angry with Kathleen for bringing that about."

"It would seem so."

Sebastian's skin crawled. "That doesn't help us to find Kathleen. She could already be hurt." He should have stayed with her instead of going to Aria's. Should have proposed when he had the chance instead of waiting for the right moment. "How do we find her?"

Again Jared and Amos exchanged glances.

"I'd suggest you start calling the police and the hospitals, like you'd normally do if you were concerned she might be hurt or in trouble," Amos told Sebastian. He turned to Jared. "And you and me ought to find out what Helene will tell us. From what we know, she's hostile, so we'll have to be cautious."

<hr>

Kathleen pounded on the door once more. "Hello, is anyone out there?" She tried the knob again with the same results. It was either locked or jammed, and the attic was getting hotter and stuffier.

Where was that bellman?

"So this is the way it's going to be?" she called out to the dusty air around her. "You're going to keep me locked up? Why? Because I danced with Victor? Because I helped him move on? Or did he move on?" She searched the rafters, checked the dark corners. "Victor?"

A female laugh echoed through the attic.

"Well, I'm glad you're amused," Kathleen muttered. "Me? I'm pissed off."

The brick walls would mute her calls for help. Her best chance was that someone would hear her through the door. Or she could bang on the furnace chimney, assuming it was galvanized metal and not masonry—she surveyed the attic to locate it. Yes, it was metal, but she didn't have anything to strike it with, unless she used her iPad or her phone—neither of which was a good option. And she was in New Orleans. The guests at the inn might think a strange noise was a ghost and not investigate, but she had to try.

Sweat trickled down her face. Her shirt stuck to her skin.

The dormer windows might be nailed shut, but if she broke one she could call for help. The bars on the windows would make that difficult, and she was four stories up. Would the people on the street hear her?

Kathleen tugged at dustcovers, looking for something that might be hiding underneath to break the glass.

As if on cue, a calliope began to play *When the Saints Go Marching In*. Kathleen peered through the dirty window to the boat docked on the Mississippi River. A woman stood on the roof of the boat, playing the steam organ. A pre-sail concert? No one would hear Kathleen over that noise. What time did the boat sail?

She had no way of knowing what time it was. Her phone was dead. Her iPad was dead.

Helene was dead.

The calliope tooted out *Merrily We Roll Along,* the Looney Tunes theme song. Kathleen definitely felt looney-tunes.

Had Jared and his father arrived at the inn? Certainly they'd be looking for her, or would they wait until they knew where she was before they tried to send Helene away? And if they sent Helene away, would the attic door suddenly become unjammed? Or would Kathleen be locked up here to expire in the heat?

She needed to find something to break a window. The calliope concert wouldn't go on forever.

Kathleen checked her pockets. She had the plastic keycard to her room. She could bang on the furnace chimney, that would have to do for now. She crossed the attic toward the chimney, raised her hand and…

…Brushed against a spider web. A spider landed on her arm and she brushed it off. Another dropped to her other arm, and then a third. She brushed frantically. A bump rose on her skin where the first spider had been, two tiny holes where the spider had bitten her. Her lungs seemed to squeeze tight and Kathleen bent over to catch her breath.

What the…?

Another black spider hung upside down on a string of silk in front of her face, a spider with a red hourglass. Kathleen reached out to swipe the web away, but it was stronger than what she'd expected, more like fishing line.

And then the spider crawled toward her.

Chapter 29

"Do or do not. There is no try." – Yoda

Sebastian paced the courtyard while he called the police. Amos and Jared continued their conversation, their voices low.

"Not a good idea," Amos said, raising his voice.

Jared said something in response that was too quiet to hear. Sebastian strained to listen while also trying to explain to the dispatcher he knew it was too soon to file a missing person's report, but he wanted to make sure they knew to keep an eye out for Kathleen in the meantime. The call was an exercise in frustration. He disconnected and sat beside Jared.

"What's not a good idea?" he asked.

"Helene, or so we assume that's who she is, first came through at the Folies," Amos said, "so we were considering going over there, but Jared mentioned the other spirits lingering, and since we're not one hundred percent for sure we're looking for Helene, that might not be the best option. It does appear this spirit has attached itself to Kathleen, so the 'where' might not be the most important factor."

"Addressing the spirit would be easiest if we knew where Kathleen was," Jared added. "And since that seems to be the question of the moment, we're trying to decide our next course of action."

Sebastian glanced at the building that housed the lobby. "Maybe the desk clerk saw her leave." He charged into the main building.

"Excuse me, have you seen my…" What was she? He didn't have time to play around with words. "My girlfriend?"

"The pretty redhead?" the clerk asked.

"Yes, that's the one."

"No, I'm sorry I haven't." She gave him a smile, and then a shadow crossed her face. "Wait. She called down a while ago. Said she heard someone calling for help, but when I sent the bellman over, he couldn't find anything."

"When was that?"

"Maybe half an hour?" the clerk said.

"So she was here half an hour ago."

"Oh, he didn't see her. She said she heard something coming from the fourth floor of your building. He checked the door and it was locked. It normally is, it's the attic. He didn't hear anything unusual, so he came back to the lobby."

Sebastian checked the bell stand by the door. "Where is the bellman now?"

"Oh, he's gone to dinner. Just left, so he'll likely be gone an hour."

Sebastian huffed and stormed back to the courtyard. He relayed what the clerk had told him.

Jared slung a backpack over his shoulder. "I've got a hunch. It might seem cliché, but what do you think about the attic?"

"Can't hurt to check," Amos said.

"You might want to wait here," Jared told Sebastian.

"Like hell."

They headed for the staircase with Amos in the lead and stopped at the door on the fourth floor.

"It's locked," Amos said.

"That's what the desk clerk said. Kathleen wouldn't be in there if it was locked, would she?" Sebastian reached for the doorknob. It didn't budge. He knocked. "Kathleen?"

A squeak sounded from the other side of the door, barely noticeable, but definitely there.

Jared unzipped the backpack and retrieved a bowl and a baggie containing weeds.

"Is that legal here?" Sebastian asked.

"Sage," Jared said. "To clear the negative energy." He handed it to his father and reached in again. This time he brought out an atomizer.

Chills crept down Sebastian's spine. "How does perfume help?" he asked sarcastically.

Jared zipped his pack again and faced the door. "Palo Santo. As effective as a key if it's the spirit holding the door closed." He spritzed the lockset, a musky aroma that smelled something like furniture polish, while Amos muttered something barely audible.

Jared took a step back.

"Open," Amos said in a commanding voice.

And damned if the door didn't open.

Sebastian dashed through, up a short staircase into the attic. Silvery threads shimmered in the dim light. Kathleen knelt on the floor, bent over.

Chapter 30

You can remain in the box. Or you can break out of it. Every moment of the day it's your choice.

Footsteps!

Kathleen heard footsteps on the short staircase that led to the attic, but she couldn't turn her head to look. She closed her eyes and *felt* Sebastian in the room behind her.

And then he spoke. "Kathleen."

Her arms were slick with perspiration and she was doubled over with stomach cramps. Kathleen swallowed, tried to speak, but couldn't catch her breath. Either she was scared stiff, or the damn spider bite had something to do with it, or Helene… could ghosts control the living?

"Helene Mercier," another voice boomed. He sounded like Jared, but it wasn't quite the same. Mr. Pierce?

The shimmering figure in the corner moved forward, growing more opaque. In the dim light, her long dress took on a forest green hue, the material something similar to velvet. Dark braids circled the top of her head. Angry whispers echoed in the attic, the woman speaking what Kathleen assumed was rapid French.

Aromatic smoke tickled Kathleen's nostrils, a clean, soothing scent.

Mr. Pierce's voice slowed to a hypnotic chant, his words foreign to Kathleen, again, most likely French.

Jared's voice pitched low. "Call an ambulance, y'heard?"

"I can't leave her," Sebastian replied.

"I need to be here, and she needs help," Jared said.

Kathleen heard a scuffle, a hesitation, and then retreating footsteps.

"I will not go," the ghostly woman shouted, rattling the windows.

Well that was clear enough. Kathleen winced at the force of the words. Her skin crawled with the sensation of millions of tiny feet all over her body, but she couldn't move to swipe the sensation away, real or imagined.

"Spider." The word was little more than a breath of air, but she'd been able to speak it.

Mr. Pierce appeared in Kathleen's peripheral vision, waving a stick that trailed wisps of smoke in Helene's general direction as he continued to chant. He moved forward as the ghost retreated.

Kathleen closed her eyes against a blinding light that beamed in through one of the attic windows, and a moment later a hand brushed her arm. She opened her eyes. Jared.

"We have to hurry," Jared told her.

The pain had spread to her back and she still couldn't catch her breath. "Can't," she managed.

Jared bent, slid one arm behind her back and the other behind her knees. He lifted her, adjusted his balance and carried her to the staircase.

Sebastian waited on the other side of the attic door, held out his arms to receive her, and then the door slammed shut between them.

Jared turned slowly, Kathleen still in his arms. A dozen bugs skittered across the attic floor, eye level from where they stood on the staircase.

"Daddy?" Jared called out.

"The spirit wouldn't go through," his father replied.

"Mind the spiders," Jared said.

"I see 'em."

"You okay?"

"Gonna take the both of us," his father replied. "Would have been nice if we could have left Kathleen out of this."

Jared met Kathleen's gaze. "Don't you fret. We'll take care of you."

More dots swung from the rafters, attached by silvery threads.

Mr. Pierce appeared from one of the dark corners, the stick in his hand still smoldering. He stopped beside one of the dangling spiders and extended the burning end. "We mean you no harm. We ask safe passage to leave." He held out his arms and raised his face to the roof, then waved the stick in a circle.

The spider beside him skittered upward on its strand. Kathleen glanced around. All the black spots that had been there a moment earlier seemed to have disappeared.

Jared set her on the floor, her back against a support beam.

Mr. Pierce took Kathleen's hand and wrapped it around the burning bundle. "Can you hold this?" he asked.

"Think…" she managed to say, grimacing with the pain of making a fist.

He nodded to her and then to Jared. "Helene fears her fate," he said. "Will her husband help her move on?"

"Yes," Kathleen said for Jared. "Yes."

Jared smiled. "I believe he will, yes."

<hr>

Sebastian leaned his forehead against the closed door, one fist against the wood over his head.

He should have stayed with Kathleen. Aria's house was progressing normally, which he should have known. He could have waited until after Jared and his father had arrived.

Hindsight.

What was happening in the attic?

He straightened, then slid his back down the door until he sat on the floor. The ghost apparently wasn't done with Kathleen, but what could ghosts do to humans? Possession? Would Kathleen be a different person when this was over?

Would this be over?

He cradled his head in his hands, waiting for the paramedics to arrive.

And then Sebastian nearly fell backward into the attic. The door opened slowly. The same way it had when he and Kathleen had stayed at the Folies.

"Victor?" Sebastian rose to his feet. He didn't care if there were ghosts in the attic. The hairs on the back of his neck rose with the sound of footfalls on the steps, but nobody was there.

The footsteps stopped, shuffled. Sebastian took hold of the railing and followed the sound.

As the attic came into view, a ray of light streaked through one of the dormer windows. Sebastian shielded his eyes with his forearm. He could barely make out the shape of a man in vintage clothing, the same man he'd caught glimpses of in their room at the Folies.

Kathleen was propped against one of the support beams, holding a bundle of sage like the one Amos had been carrying.

Whispers chased around the corners, barely audible.

Jared held up a hand to halt Sebastian. He desperately wanted to go to Kathleen, but he trusted Jared enough to wait.

Dust motes illuminated the woman, the ghost he'd seen push Kathleen toward the street in New Orleans, the one who'd appeared in front of her car at home. Sebastian took a step forward and then stopped again when he saw the man-ghost point into the beam of light.

Amos recited something that wasn't English in a cadence that made his words sound like a prayer, or a ritual. Glowing arms reached from the light for the woman-ghost. She reached for the man-ghost, but the glowing arms pulled her in. The man-ghost disappeared and the light faded away, leaving the attic in relative darkness.

"Kathleen, you all right?" Jared asked.

"Pain," she replied.

Sebastian crossed to where she was sitting and took her in his arms. "I shouldn't have left you."

She opened her mouth, but no sound came out.

Footsteps thundered in the stairwell and two firemen appeared.

"I believe the lady's been bitten by a black widow spider," Jared told them.

Chapter 31

Plant some seeds today. Be the light that helps others see.

"You sure you weren't bitten by a vampire?" the ER doctor joked.

Kathleen scowled, but after they'd given her the antivenin, the pain had decreased. "I believe the paramedic brought you the body," she replied lethargically.

"He did indeed, but you know those fang marks…" He gave her a wink. "The hydromorphone we gave you before we tried the antivenin is going to make you sleepy for a while. How's your pain level?"

"Better." She licked dry lips, afraid to move anything else.

"It might be a few days before the pain subsides completely," the doctor went on. "You have a waiting room full of people who are anxious to see you."

She managed a smile. "I'm sure. My sister?"

"From what I understand, along with other extended family?"

She nodded, and winced with a lingering streak of pain.

"I'll send them in."

Kathleen closed her eyes when he left the cubicle, reveling in her lethargy.

"Honey, are you okay?"

Siobhan's voice called to her from far away. Kathleen fought to open her eyes and smiled. "I'm fine."

"I was so worried when Jared told me you couldn't speak or move or …"

"Between the spiders and the ghost…" Jared wiped a hand across his face. "And I gotta tell you, that ghost was no joke."

"Gee, sorry I missed it," Siobhan quipped, reaching behind to slap at her husband.

Mr. Pierce sat in the bedside chair, and Sebastian hung back near the door, his hands thrust into his pockets.

"The doctor thinks I'll be fine," Kathleen told whoever cared to know. She focused on Jared. "One thing that's bothering me. Why did Victor look so real at the hotel? I thought he was alive, but I could hardly see Helene when she showed up."

"Victor lingered a long time," Jared told her. "He wanted to be seen."

"How did you know I was in the attic? The bellman never showed up. Or did he, and I didn't hear him?"

"According to the desk clerk, he tried the door and it was locked, like it was supposed to be, so he didn't investigate any further," Mr. Pierce said.

"You didn't let loose any new ghosts this time, did you?" she asked with a tired smile.

"They kept their distance," Jared said. "That part of the city was a haven for pirates and riff-raff back in the day, and the ghosts who linger don't want to move on, probably for the same reasons Helene didn't want to move on—fear of facing judgment."

Kathleen turned her head and whimpered. "I don't want to see any more ghosts."

"Helene's moved on," Jared reassured her.

"And with the other spirits at the inn shying away from us, I feel confident they won't be bothering you," Mr. Pierce added.

"I have to tell you, the property manager wasn't too pleased with having ghost chasers on-site without his approval," Jared said.

Sebastian hadn't moved from his spot beside the door, but his eyes were fixed on her. He'd certainly had his belief in ghosts tested in the past several weeks. She lifted her chin, waiting for him to tell her he'd had enough of this nonsense, waiting for the return of the old, skeptical Sebastian.

"Everything okay at Aria's?" she asked.

"Yes," he answered simply. "No." He huffed. "I felt obligated to check, you know, since she's the one footing the bill. At least make a show of doing my job." He stepped forward and took her hand, and she winced with the gentle pressure. "It could have waited. I could have skipped going over there altogether and she wouldn't have cared. If I'd been with you… how did you end up in the attic?"

Kathleen shrugged. "I heard someone call for help. I wasn't going to go in, worried it might be Helene, so I called to the front desk to let them know. Then I heard the baby crying. I figured I had my cell phone with me so I could dial 911 if I needed to, except when I tried, my battery was dead. And my iPad." She looked at Jared. "I had battery life before I went into the attic."

"Spirits use energy. Helene likely tapped into your batteries," he replied.

"I should have stayed with you," Sebastian whispered.

"Not sure that would have made a difference," she told him.

"Would have given us a chance to get to Helene first," Jared said. "Before she got you alone. Might have saved you a spider bite."

"Or the bed would have been crawling with spiders," Mr. Pierce added.

Kathleen shivered, the sensation of a thousand little legs on her skin. "Thanks for that."

Siobhan nudged Sebastian. "Something you wanted to say to her?"

Sebastian smiled at Kathleen and reached into his pocket. He pulled out a box, turned it in his hands. A jewelry box.

She was wide awake now.

———◆———

When Sebastian retrieved the ever-present ring box, Kathleen recoiled. Not the body language he would have hoped for, but he pressed forward. Too late to turn back now.

"With everything that has happened in the last couple of weeks, one thing has remained clear to me. I bought this ring because I knew I wanted to marry you, Kathleen, but my head was crowded with all the other garbage—the idiocy with Renee, the non-fraternization rules. One thing I know for sure. I want a future with you. I don't want to lose you. Marry me, Kathleen. You said something that resonates with me. We may not be guaranteed to live another day. As long as I'm drawing breath, I want you beside me for whatever days I have left." He took the ring out of the box and held it out to her.

"And how did you know what he wanted to say?" Kathleen asked Siobhan.

"He asked permission," Siobhan said. "He probably would have preferred a more romantic setting with less of an audience, but I couldn't wait."

"Nothing like turning the screws," she muttered. "You don't have to do this," she told Sebastian.

He chuckled. "I know I don't have to. Maybe instead of yelling at your sister, you'll give me an answer. I've been carrying this around since the first time we got home from New Orleans, waiting for the right time to give it to you. Say yes and we can have the wedding here. Arrange for a parade through the streets. Unless you want something more traditional. Oh, and Aria said she wants an invitation."

"Aria?" Kathleen shook her head. "Since you've obviously lost your mind, how are we supposed to live? Neither of us has a job."

"Will you quit finding reasons not to marry me? I'm going to think you don't want to." He cupped the ring in his fist. Had he moved too fast? Scared her off? "You don't want to?" he asked.

"Let me see it." She reached for his hand and uncurled his fingers, taking the ring. "Rose gold."

"That's going to make the difference? What the ring looks like?" he asked.

"Yes, if you bought me something like you were thinking of buying for Renee."

"I bought the one you said you wanted."

She glanced at him, her eyes shining with unshed tears. "You remembered."

"Of course I remembered."

She squeezed her eyes closed and tilted her head. A side effect of the spider bite?

"You sure she's okay?" Sebastian asked the nurse who hovered by the door.

The nurse smiled.

"You really want to spend the rest of your life with me?" Kathleen asked.

He nodded. "And we're going to build that house. The one we both want."

She smiled then and his heart unclenched.

"You did say you loved me," he reminded her.

"And he's still waiting for an answer," Siobhan pointed out.

Kathleen slipped the ring on her finger. "Ghosts and all?" she asked.

"They might be easier to get rid of than my father."

She swiped at her eyes and laughed. "He's never going to accept me, you know."

"He doesn't have to. Hell, he doesn't accept me half the time."

"Can you just say yes, for the record?" Jared said.

Kathleen's smile broadened. "Yes."

Dear Reader:

Thanks so much for reading this book. If you enjoyed the story, I hope you will encourage others by "liking" my books on Goodreads.com and everywhere the option is offered, and by posting an honest review to the site where you bought this book and/or at other book blogs/reading sites so you can help other readers decide whether it's worth their time. Authors like and need to get feedback to make each new book as good as it can be.

—Karla Brandenburg